THE AGENT

ALSO BY NANCY HERKNESS

The Consultants series

The Money Man

The Hacker

Second Glances series

Second to None: A Novella

Second Time Around

Second Act

Wager of Hearts series

The CEO Buys In

The All-Star Antes Up

The VIP Doubles Down

The Irishman's Christmas Gamble: A Novella

Whisper Horse novels

Take Me Home

Country Roads

The Place I Belong

A Down-Home Country Christmas: A Novella

Stand-Alone novels

A Bridge to Love

Shower of Stars

Music of the Night

THE AGENT

NANCY HERKNESS

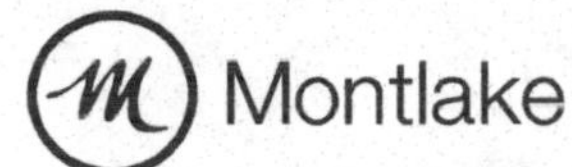

This is a work of fiction. Names, characters, organizations, places, events, and incidents are either products of the author's imagination or are used fictitiously.

Published by Montlake, Seattle

www.apub.com

ISBN-13: 9781542018616
ISBN-10: 1542018617

Cover design by Eileen Carey

Printed in the United States of America

To Mary McElroy, with gratitude
for sharing her extraordinary wisdom
and warm empathy
throughout our many years of friendship.

Chapter 1

Natalie Hart took a sip of champagne and ignored the bride's attempts at matchmaking from across the wedding party's table. Alice had seated Natalie next to the best man, Tully Gibson, and kept flicking hopeful glances between them. Since Alice was one of Natalie's best friends, she knew that Natalie had no intention of ever marrying again. Natalie had also told her friend that Tully wasn't her type. But she and Tully were the only two singles in the wedding party, and romantic Alice believed love conquered all. So she'd done her best to throw them together during all the wedding festivities.

The bandleader spoke into the microphone. "Let's get the best man up here for a toast!"

"That's my cue." Tully pushed his chair back and rose to his considerable height.

Natalie watched him make his way across the dance floor, his short brown hair and vast shoulders outlined by the golden light of the crystal chandeliers, his custom-tailored tux enlivened by his signature cowboy boots—this pair, a subdued polished black.

He was too big, too confident, and too physical for her. Which was why she did her best to quell the thrill that ran through her body every damn time he put his hand on the small of her back to politely guide her through a doorway. Or when she'd tucked her arm through the crook of his elbow to walk down the aisle and could feel the steel of his muscle against her palm.

Those were nothing more than simple physical reactions.

Tully took the microphone with the practiced ease of a man used to giving business presentations to CEOs, since he was one of the three founding partners of KRG, a multinational consulting firm. The groom, Derek Killion, was the firm's financial wizard. Leland Rockwell, KRG's computer genius and the co–best man, sat across from Natalie, looking relieved that he didn't have to make a toast.

Tully's area of expertise was corporate and personal security for their clients. Which was why, at the rehearsal dinner, she had almost asked him about the strange, creepy emails she'd been getting. However, she had decided not to impose on him professionally at a celebratory social occasion.

Tully's voice boomed out in the measured cadence that reminded her of a cowboy. "It's a great honor to toast the joining of my good friend and partner, Derek, with the beautiful and brilliant Alice. I'm proud to say that they found each other because of a program Derek himself started at KRG, the Small Business Initiative, which offers free assistance to small business owners. How fitting is it that because my partner wanted to give back, he himself received a gift in return? The gift of Alice's love."

The audience sighed.

"You know the joke about the accountant with insomnia? When the doctor suggests counting sheep, the accountant says, 'That's the problem—I make a mistake and then spend three hours trying to find it.'" Laughter from the audience made him pause a moment. "Well, Alice and Derek are numbers people, so they had to find *other*"—Tully waggled his eyebrows—"ways to fall asleep."

More laughter rippled through the room as he turned to look toward the newlyweds. Alice was blushing right down to the low square neckline of her Regency-inspired wedding gown. Natalie noted with pride that the cascading curls she'd created for Alice at her hair salon that morning still draped gracefully over the bride's shoulders.

"Who knew that a passion for numbers could generate another kind of passion?" Tully continued. "A passion that blossomed into the profound love surrounding these two with a slightly nauseating but radiant glow." More laughter as Tully pivoted back to speak to the room at large. "For Derek's bachelor party, Leland and I dragged him on a white-water rafting trip. We encountered death-defying rapids, majestic bald eagles, and scenery that took our breath away. But the sight that really socked me in the gut was when we paddled up to the riverbank for our last night on the river. As a surprise, I flew Alice out to meet us. The look on Derek's face—and hers—when they saw each other got me all choked up."

Another sigh ran through the crowd. Natalie wouldn't have expected the tough ex–FBI agent to get choked up about anything, but his sentiment sounded genuine. It even made her feel a little teary eyed.

"So let's raise our glasses to the best partner and friend a guy could ask for and the woman who makes him even better." Tully lifted his champagne flute. "To Derek and Alice!"

Applause filled the large ballroom.

"That was a very Tully toast. Down to earth but heartfelt," Leland said before he turned to smile at his fiancée, Dawn, the light flashing off his tortoiseshell glasses. "However, yours was equally eloquent."

"They were both terrific," Natalie agreed, as relieved as Leland that she had avoided having to speak in front of the assembled guests, since they included quite a few prominent and intimidating clients of KRG.

Natalie glanced around to see that Tully had been buttonholed by an older silver-haired man in a well-cut suit. He stood with his head tilted down attentively as the gentleman talked.

Tully puzzled her. She'd pegged him as a player because he made no secret of the fact that he had no intention of getting married and settling down. Yet so far she'd seen him skillfully shake off at least two women who had clearly shown their interest in him. She'd also discovered that he was an enthusiastic and conscientious Big Brother to an eleven-year-old kid in New York City. When he talked about the boy, his gunmetal-gray eyes lit up with genuine affection. Not quite the playboy she'd expected.

Alice had gotten up from her seat across the table and plunked down beside Natalie in Tully's empty chair, her silk skirt floating around her. "Is my mascara smeared? Because the toasts made me get all weepy."

Natalie examined her friend's face. "You look perfect. And glowing with happiness, as Tully said."

Alice chuckled. "You forgot the 'nauseating' part."

"I was being tactful."

Alice's gaze sought her new husband, who had gotten up to chat with the guests at another table now that the toasts were over. Her face softened while her radiance grew even brighter. "I still can't believe we're married. I mean, look at him!"

Derek did, indeed, have the looks of a movie star, a fact that caused him more annoyance than pleasure. He glanced up and smiled at his bride, making his already-perfect face almost blindingly handsome.

"He's a married man, so I'm not allowed to stare at him anymore," Natalie said.

"As long as you don't touch, it's fine." Alice grinned, then turned serious. "Are you having a good time? I want everyone to have a wonderful time at my wedding."

"Honestly, it's the most amazing wedding I've ever been to," Natalie said, looking around at the champagne fountain, the towering flower arrangements, and the twenty-piece band.

Alice followed her gaze. "I don't mean all that stuff. The wedding planner did that. I mean is it *fun*?"

"It's not only fun, it's full of love and that makes it special," Natalie assured her friend.

Nowadays Natalie looked at weddings with double vision because her marriage had ended in terrible failure. She hoped and even believed that Alice and Derek would be blissful and in love for the rest of their lives. But she had believed the same thing on her own wedding day. It had never occurred to her then—or even for the next ten years of her marriage—that she would find herself fleeing from her husband with nothing more than a hastily packed suitcase and fifty dollars.

She banished that ugliness from her mind. Tonight was for celebrating, so she polished off the rest of her champagne and prepared to enjoy herself.

A couple of hours later, she ran into Tully leaning against a column on the edge of the dance floor while he sipped a beer and watched the dancers gyrate in a kaleidoscope of swirling skirts, glittering sequins, and flashing light-up party favors. "Taking a break from the social whirl?" she asked, surprised to find him alone.

"Replacing my electrolytes," he said, holding up the half-empty glass. "That reminds me that I haven't had the pleasure of a dance with you since that first stuffy waltz."

Probably because she'd been avoiding that just like she'd avoided the bouquet that had been tossed straight at her. Why give Alice any more ideas?

Just then the high-energy pop number ended, and the band segued into a twangy country tune.

"Now we're talkin'." Tully tilted back his head and finished his beer in one long swallow. Plunking the glass down on a nearby table, he held out his hand. "They're playing our song."

"I don't know how to dance to this kind of music," she said, even as she automatically put her hand in his big, enveloping grip. It would have been rude to do anything else.

"But I do, so just follow my lead." He tugged her onto the dance floor and then spun her into his arms. "It's a two-step. Quick, quick, slow, slow." He adjusted her left hand so it rested on his shoulder while his right hand rested on her shoulder blade, allowing him to support the entire length of her arm. "Here we go. Right foot behind you first."

She felt his weight shift a second before he pressed her backward while he stepped forward. She moved her right foot as though it was the natural thing to do. Because that was how it felt when he was leading. The first time around the dance floor, she concentrated on the steps and finding the rhythm of the music.

The second time she began to notice things she didn't want to. How warm Tully's hand was as it wrapped around hers. The coiled energy that radiated from him as he moved in perfect time with the music. The way his arm provided a rock-solid support for her so she never stumbled.

"Tully! My man! Show us how it's done!" someone called out.

And suddenly the center of the dance floor cleared, leaving the two of them alone on the expanse of parquet while the other dancers stood in a wide circle, clapping to the beat.

"Let's give 'em a show." Tully's grin flashed in the low light of the dimmed chandeliers.

"I don't—"

But he was already spinning her away from him so the pale pink chiffon of her skirt swirled around her ankles. Then he reeled her back in and started the two-step rhythm again. Except he began to twirl her as they moved, his left hand holding hers high over her head, his right hand guiding her shoulder in the direction he wanted her to turn. Then he somehow wove their arms together so they danced shoulder to shoulder before spinning her into their face-to-face position again. Another shift in position and they were whirling side by side with their hands still joined.

Exhilaration fizzed through her as she gave herself over to the man and the music in a way she hadn't in years. When she faced him again, she smiled straight up into his eyes, wanting to share the delight she was feeling. He missed the beat of the next step by a fraction of a second and his easy grin disappeared, replaced by something intense and focused. Something that sent a shiver of awareness through her. He kept her facing him for longer than usual, the two of them locked in each other's gaze.

She lowered her chin to stare at the onyx-and-gold studs of his tux shirt. And then he was spinning her again, so she had no time to think about the heat sizzling between them.

Until the song reached its final bars, when he pulled her in against him from knee to chest—his body like a hot, living wall—before he lunged to the side, taking her with him in a dramatic dip.

Their faces were a mere inch apart for a long moment as the guests whistled, stomped, and applauded. She could feel the feathering of his warm breath on her cheek and see the sheen of perspiration on his forehead. A waft of some clean, sharp, woodsy scent drifted past her.

And then she was lifted upright in a whoosh before he draped his arm casually around her waist while he bowed in mocking acknowledgment of the applause. She followed his lead and gave a quick curtsy.

As they left the dance floor, Dawn and Leland approached them. "I didn't know you could dance like that," Dawn said.

"I didn't either." Natalie slanted a smile up at Tully. "My partner gets all the credit."

"He wasn't the one spinning like a top without falling over," Leland said in his slow Georgia drawl.

"Natalie here is too modest," Tully said. "She took to two-stepping like a duck to water. I wouldn't have tried some of the more complicated moves if she hadn't been so graceful and perfectly balanced." He winked at Natalie. "I'm thinking another beer after all that hard work."

"Natalie only drinks Manhattans," Dawn said.

"Time for her to broaden her horizons and replace her electrolytes." Tully strode off toward the bar, leaving Natalie still trying to catch her breath—whether from the exercise or the man, she wasn't sure.

"Did *you* know Tully could dance like that?" Natalie asked Leland.

"Tully is a man of many surprises," Leland said. "You never know what he'll be able to do."

~

Tully leaned his hip against the carved-stone baluster of the mansion's terrace, where the three partners had retreated together before he pinned Derek with a glare. "If you even *think* about working while you're on your honeymoon, Leland is going to put a block on your computer."

"Oh, I already have," Leland said, the flickering torchlight reflecting on his lenses. "He'll have to go old school and use a pencil and a calculator if he needs a spreadsheet fix."

Derek gave a snort, but there was an amused glint in his eyes. "I've got far better things to do on my honeymoon than work."

"Like stay in bed as much as possible." Tully grinned.

"I meant sightseeing," Derek said with a bland look. "For all the places I've traveled, I've barely seen more than the inside of office buildings and hotels."

"You've earned the right to do whatever you want to . . . as long as it's not related to your job," Leland said. "But Alice might have some opinions too."

Derek smiled in a secret inward way that meant he was thinking about his bride. Sadness twinged in Tully's chest. Alice was one great lady, and Derek deserved the happiness he had found with her. But his marriage meant a change in the dynamic between the three of them.

Tully loved Derek and Leland like brothers. No, *more* than his shithead of a brother, because he had gotten to choose them. For all the years between their first meeting in business school through the challenges of founding and growing KRG until today, it had been just the three of them always having one another's backs.

Now there was Alice in the mix. Not to mention Leland's fiancée, Dawn, another terrific woman.

For a moment, loneliness wrapped a dark shroud around Tully, but he shook it off. He'd made his life choices for good reasons.

Tully clapped his hand on Derek's shoulder. "You and Alice are real good together, partner. You're going to be one of those couples who celebrates their fiftieth anniversary with the same stars in your eyes you have today."

Alice flopped onto a blue velvet chaise longue in the bride's room, her feet in their embroidered-satin french heels flexed in front of her. "I don't really have to go to the bathroom," she said. "I just wanted us three to have a little time alone." She gave Natalie a sideways look. "And to say that you and Tully made a great couple on the dance floor."

Natalie wasn't going to argue with the bride. "He's a good dancer," she said as she perched on a gilded faux-bamboo chair.

Alice looked dissatisfied, but she didn't push the subject any further. "I can't believe we're traveling for three whole weeks for our honeymoon."

Dawn pulled up a velvet-covered stool, her rose-colored skirt pooling on the floor around it. "I don't think you and Derek have ever taken off that much time combined."

"I know." Alice's lips curved into a dreamy smile. "I'll have him all to myself for the entire trip."

"You mean when you're drinking the nasty spring water in Bath? And seeing all the skulls in the catacombs of Paris?" Natalie asked.

Alice had chosen some of the destinations because they appeared in her favorite books.

"Yeah, that's just creepy," Dawn said. "But safer than that place in France where you drown if you're walking out to it when the tide comes in."

"Mont-Saint-Michel, and it has a bridge now," Alice said. "You make my honeymoon sound like a nightmare. Besides, you're forgetting the glass bathtub in our villa in the Maldives. I mean, Derek, naked, against a turquoise sea."

There was a moment of awed silence before they cracked up. "We will never, ever tell him that we were all picturing that," Natalie said.

"You are the best girlfriends ever," Alice said, her laughter turning misty eyed.

"Because we're drooling over your new husband?" Natalie said with a teasing smile. "You have a strange idea of what girlfriends should do."

Alice sat up and swung her legs off the chaise longue. "Because you're happy that I have an incredibly handsome new husband, and you don't think it's weird that he loves me."

Alice's mother had made her daughter believe she was unattractive all her life, so Alice still felt unworthy of the stunningly attractive Derek.

Dawn threw a glance of exasperation at the ceiling. "Did you look at yourself in the mirror today? You're just as gorgeous as he is."

"Today doesn't count. Natalie and my dress designer made me look amazing." Alice reached out to clasp each of their hands in hers. "Thank you for getting me to this day. I wouldn't be here without your support and belief in me."

"Sweetie, you would have gotten here without us," Natalie said, her heart swelling. "But we wouldn't have had the pleasure of sharing your joy, so thank you."

"Group hug," Dawn commanded.

Amid the perfumed billows of satin, lace, and chiffon, Natalie took comfort in the strength of these two amazing women and wished for them all the happiness she had been unable to find.

Chapter 2

When the bride and groom finally departed in a glossy stretch limousine, showered by torrents of birdseed, Natalie joined the crowd of guests meandering back to the ballroom in order to retrieve her purse and wrap. She dropped into her chair at the dinner table to pour herself a glass of water from the cut-crystal pitcher set out in the middle. Leaning back, she admired the arrangement of exotic lavender and white blossoms that cascaded down from a six-foot-high crystal pedestal in the center of the table and thought how wonderful it would feel to take off her high-heeled silver sandals.

She sat up straight when Tully settled himself in the chair next to her. "That looks like a good idea," he said, grabbing a glass and filling it. He lifted his water goblet to touch hers with a clink. "Helluva wedding!"

"It was a beautiful ceremony," she said.

"It got me like a mule kick to the chest." His voice sounded as though he was holding back his emotions.

She nearly laughed at his vivid image. "They're going to be very happy together."

"As long as they stay out of trouble." He shook his head and she knew he was remembering how close Alice and Derek had come to being shot by a crazy computer hacker.

She took a sip of her water but watched him over the rim. His black silk bow tie was untied but still draped around his neck, allowing his collar to stand open down to the first stud in his pleated shirt. He'd shed his tux jacket and rolled up his sleeves to his elbows. She couldn't help noticing the shift of muscles in his neck as he drank or the dusting of brown hair over the tanned skin of his forearm where it rested on the white linen tablecloth. She had a powerful urge to touch his skin in both places to test its textures.

She choked on her water.

"You okay?" He leaned forward in concern.

"Fine," she sputtered. "Just went down the wrong way."

He drained his glass. "Can I offer you a ride home?"

She studied him, trying to decide if he was asking her because he'd felt the flare of attraction between them or if he was just being polite. Alice and Derek had put a limousine at her disposal for the entire day, so she had a ride. Maybe it wasn't a good idea to accept after that unexpectedly heated dance.

Then she thought of the creepy anonymous emails and walking into her empty house late at night while the darkness pressed around it. The prospect of having Tully's big, powerful presence nearby when she got home was appealing.

Irritation flashed through her. She hated the anonymous creep who was making her afraid to go home alone. It stirred up feelings she'd worked hard to push into her past.

"A ride home would be appreciated, thank you." She hoped that made it clear that the ride was all she was accepting.

Should she ask him about the emails on the drive back to her house? No, she didn't want to mar the joyful afterglow of their friends' wedding with such unpleasantness.

He nodded before he pulled out his phone and tapped at it. "My car will be out front in five minutes." After shrugging into his jacket, he pulled out her chair and offered his arm. "Shall we?"

"We're not walking down the aisle any longer." Natalie picked up her purse and the fine wool wrap that matched her dress before she slipped her hand through his proffered elbow. She might as well enjoy the chance to feel the muscles in his arm again.

"That wedding planner made us rehearse so often, it's a habit now," he said with a grin.

He would have made the same gesture regardless because he exhibited an old-fashioned gallantry toward women. It must be a cowboy thing. Living in New Jersey, Natalie hadn't met many cowboys. She found it hard to reconcile Tully's down-to-earth speech with the high-powered consultant in custom-tailored suits. Yet he wore the suits with the same ease and confidence he did his ornately stitched boots.

They chatted about the success of the wedding as he swept her across the rented mansion's marble-floored hallway and through the front door. Idling at the foot of the front portico's stone steps was a sleek black Maserati that seemed to be going a hundred miles per hour even though it was standing still.

"Nice car, sir," the young valet murmured reverently as Natalie and Tully came down the steps.

"Thanks, son," Tully said. "You didn't take it joyriding, did you?"

"Oh, no, sir, I would never—" He caught the humorous glint in Tully's eyes and smiled. "I was tempted."

"I'd be disappointed if you weren't," Tully said, handing the young man a folded bill.

The valet glanced down at it and his eyes went wide. "*Thank* you, sir!"

Tully opened the passenger door for Natalie, his grip on her hand firm but gentle. She pulled the yards of her chiffon skirt inside the car and nodded that it was safe to close the door.

"You missed some." Tully bent to tuck the last fold of chiffon inside the car. "Don't want the hem of that pretty dress getting dragged through the mud." When his fingers brushed the bare skin of her ankle, a flicker of delicious sensation danced over her skin.

So maybe he *was* her type in some primitive way. But she was old enough and wise enough to control her less intelligent impulses.

~

"Nice place," Tully said as the Maserati growled to a stop in the driveway of Natalie's Craftsman bungalow–style home. "You've got a lot of land for suburban New Jersey."

"The woods in back are part of a Green Acres space that's preserved for wildlife and hiking," Natalie explained.

The windows of her house glowed with welcome, thanks to the lights she'd set on timers. She usually loved the three deep, asymmetrical roofs, the rustic stone foundation of the columned porch, and the embrace of trees around her backyard. Tonight, though, she felt a reluctance to leave the security of the powerful vehicle and the formidable man who drove it.

But Tully had already swung his door open and unfolded his big body out of the low-slung sports car. She was still gathering up her skirt when her own door opened. He held out his big square hand and she found her fingers once again enveloped by warmth and support. An echo of the awareness she'd felt on the dance floor shimmered through her, leaving a trail of sparks in its wake.

As she stood, she felt the urge to sway closer to him to get a last whiff of his distinctive scent, which she had caught again in the closed space of the car.

"I'll walk you to the door." He held out his arm and she took it without hesitation this time.

"I appreciate that," she said as they stepped onto the flagstone walkway. "Coming home so late to an empty house makes me a little nervous."

There, she'd admitted it.

"You should get a big dog. You've got the room for it to run."

"I work too many hours to have a dog. I make do with a security system."

He grimaced. "Tell me it's not one of those with a recording of a dog barking."

"No barking, just an ear-splitting siren and a call to the monitoring station." As she lifted her skirt to navigate the steps, he glanced around with a disapproving frown. "What is it?" she asked.

"That siren better be real loud."

"I know. My house is somewhat isolated by the green space." Her porch floor was made of solid wood but she felt a slight sag when Tully stepped onto it. Something about that broke down the courage she'd been holding on to. "May I ask a favor?"

Surprise flickered over the craggy angles of his face. "I'm at your service."

"Would you mind just, you know"—she waved a vague hand, finding it harder to frame her request than she expected—"checking through the house before you leave? I feel silly but it would make me less . . . tense." She took a deep breath to calm the flutter of anxiety in her rib cage.

His gaze scanned her face like a laser. In return she gave him a straight look with no undercurrents. He finally said, "Be happy to."

When she opened the front door and disarmed the alarm, his expression sharpened into alert watchfulness. "Lock the door," he said.

She turned the dead bolt and stood with her back to the door, watching him prowl through the open plan of her first floor like a hunting cat—in his black tux, maybe a panther. He didn't take just a cursory glance around the living room. He walked behind the sectional sofa, inspected the interior of the coat closet, and checked the window latches.

When he reached the dining area, he frowned at the big sliding doors that opened out onto the patio. An odd thrill ran through her when he pushed aside the sheer curtains and ran his fingers over the locking mechanism. "This would take about ten seconds to pick," he said. "You need to put security bars on these sliders." He scanned the opposite wall with an expert gaze. "Although at least you have glass-break sensors."

"The alarm company was supposed to install the bars but they got busy and never finished the job," Natalie said. "I forgot about it until now."

She'd never felt the need for them before. She had always loved the way light poured in through the big doors, but now the darkness seemed to loom against them like a menacing shadow instead.

He continued his survey, striding into the kitchen to circle the marble-topped island. She followed him so that she could watch the coiled power of his body as he checked the pantry, his posture tense and poised as though he expected someone to spring out at him. She couldn't decide if the seriousness of his inspection made her feel more secure or more frightened.

He toured her small office, the powder room, and the attached garage, where he even knelt to check under her car.

She felt more than a little foolish by now. "You don't have to be that thorough," she said. "I don't really think anyone would wedge themselves under my car."

He straightened to his substantial height. "You looked worried. I take that seriously."

"That's kind of you, but now I feel like I overreacted."

He came around the car to where she stood in the doorway, her chiffon skirt swirling around her ankles in the cooler air wafting in from the garage. Even in her heels and standing on the raised threshold, she had to tilt her head back to see him smile in a way that was meant to be reassuring but had a hint of steel underlying it. "It's always better to take precautions. Let's check upstairs."

She nodded and pivoted to head for the stairs. She could almost feel his presence grazing the skin exposed by the low back of her gown. When they reached the foot of the staircase, he stopped her by clasping her nearly bare shoulder so that the heat of his palm seemed to leave an imprint on her skin, reminding her of his strong guiding touch while they had danced.

"I know it's not gentlemanly but let me go first," he said, lifting his hand away almost immediately.

She was amazed at how swiftly and silently he climbed her stairs. A man of his proportions should have sounded like an elephant on the uncarpeted oak treads. Maybe he really was part panther. By the time she got to the top step, he was already entering the guest room. She heard the closet and en suite bathroom doors open and close, and then he was back out in the hallway.

As he walked toward the door to her bedroom, she tried to remember if she'd left anything too personal out in plain sight. Since she'd done the wedding party's hair and makeup at her hair salon, the Mane Attraction, she hadn't left a scatter of cosmetics on her dresser or bathroom vanity. In general, she was tidy, partly by preference and partly because she hadn't wanted to give her ex-husband fodder for his constant criticism.

Tully disappeared into her room while she stopped on the threshold again. Seeing his muscular, confident body moving around her most intimate space made something fiery coil low in her belly. He knelt to check under the bed, his hand braced on the pale blue quilt for balance. Seeing his masculine fingers splayed across the velvet she slept under fanned the heat into a flame.

She must have had more to drink at the reception than she realized.

When Tully opened her closet door, she closed her eyes to avoid seeing him touch her clothing. Still, she could hear the rustle of fabric and slide of hangers as he pushed them aside to check the depths behind them.

She retreated to the hallway before he went into her bathroom. She didn't want her brain remembering the vision of this man in his well-fitted tux outlined against the delicate cream tile.

Natalie was examining the abstract landscape she'd bought from a local artist when Tully came out of her room.

"There must be another room up here," he said, looking down the hallway. "The guest room doesn't take up enough space in the floor plan."

She was impressed, but she reminded herself that he was an expert at his job. "There's a storage room down here." She led him toward the back of the house, opening a low door and flipping on the light switch. Boxes of Christmas decorations stood against one wall beside a couple of trunks. A few miscellaneous pieces of furniture were lined up along another wall.

"You travel light," he said with a note of approval in his voice as he surveyed the nearly empty room.

"I've only lived here about eighteen months," she said. "There hasn't been time to accumulate much junk." And she'd brought virtually nothing from her married life with her.

"I know folks who would have filled this up the day they moved in," he said, following her out of the room and toward the stairs. "Your interior is clear. I'll take a look around outside before I leave."

She turned. "That's above and beyond. You really don't have to tromp around outdoors in your tuxedo."

"Hey, I've got my boots on." He grinned. "That's one good thing about refusing to wear prissy patent leather loafers."

She laughed. "I won't tell Derek what you said about his shoes."

"Oh, I told him myself," Tully said.

"That I believe." Holding on to the bannister tightly to counteract whatever alcohol seemed to be overwhelming her better judgment, Natalie descended the stairs. Tully made somewhat more noise behind her this time. She supposed he was no longer trying to sneak up on an intruder.

When they reached the front entranceway, Tully moved in front of her, his penetrating gray eyes softened by concern. "You don't strike me as someone who gets spooked easily. You want to tell me what this is about?"

For a moment she was tempted to tell him about the creepy emails coming from a different address every time. He was a pro at this sort of thing, so it would be a relief to just drop it on his broad shoulders. But she stopped herself. They weren't exactly threatening, just unsettling.

"One of my customers at the salon had her house broken into last week. She lives only about a mile away," she lied with a rueful smile. "It made me feel a little anxious about coming home to an empty house. You've been so generous to indulge my case of nerves. I feel completely safe now."

He searched her face again before he nodded. "Glad I could help. I'll text you that everything's clear outside before I leave."

"You really don't have to—"

He held up his hand to halt her words. She could see by his expression that he was going to inspect the outer perimeter of her house no matter what she said.

"Thank you for the ride home and the security inspection. I appreciate them both."

"The pleasure was all mine." Before she could puzzle out how to say goodbye, he leaned down and brushed a feather of a kiss over her cheekbone. She had to stop herself from leaning in to feel more of those warm, firm lips against her skin. "Good night."

He was out the door but turned to look over his shoulder, the porch light finding golden highlights in his brown hair. "Set the alarm behind me."

She watched him tread lightly down the stone steps and disappear into the darkness beyond. After closing the door and sliding the dead bolt home, she stood for a moment, feeling a wrenching sense of loss.

An unwelcome question danced its way into her mind.

If she'd asked him, would Tully have stayed?

Chapter 3

When Natalie opened her eyes on Sunday morning, she was shocked to see that it was after ten o'clock and the sun glowed brightly around the edges of her window shades. Most days she could barely sleep until eight.

Something about Tully's thorough inspection of her house had made her feel safe and secure enough to rest.

She threw back the sheets and stood up, stretching and yawning. When she padded into the bathroom, she thought she caught a whiff of Tully's woodsy soap still lingering, so she inhaled more deeply. A tiny shiver rippled through her.

"Stop it!" she said to her reflection as she finger-combed her angled blonde bob into some semblance of order. She'd cut off her long curls about a year before on her fortieth birthday and it was amazing how liberating that had been. She had realized she'd only been keeping it long because her ex liked it that way.

Craving coffee, she threw on jeans and a white T-shirt and headed down the stairs to the kitchen, barefoot and braless. Once the coffee maker was up and running, she started to open her email app but stopped before touching the envelope icon on her cell phone screen. Looking out at the soft spring light slanting through the pale green leaves of the woods behind her house, she decided not to risk ruining her peace quite yet. Instead, she fixed herself a cheese-and-veggie omelet, which she ate at her sun-dappled dining table while she tried not to remember how it felt to be so perfectly in sync with Tully on the dance floor. Or the flare of heat in his eyes as she lay across the solid bar of his thigh in the final dip.

She took a long swallow of orange juice and pushed her plate away. Might as well face the realities of today. Bracing herself, she tapped the email icon. She skimmed down the list but saw no unfamiliar email addresses. The knot of tension in her neck eased.

She was scrolling through the wedding photos friends had shared on social media when the doorbell shrilled through the silence, making her nearly drop her phone.

She walked to the door and checked the video monitor that the alarm guy had recommended she install.

"Oh my God!" Her hands flew to her hair to smooth it when she saw Tully standing on her front porch, holding a corrugated cardboard box and staring straight at the video camera. She realized how ridiculous she was being since she had on no makeup, no shoes, and—oh, hell!—no bra.

Disarming the alarm, she pulled the door open. As a cowgirl might say, Tully looked like one long, cool drink of water in a black T-shirt, faded jeans, and well-used brown cowboy boots. She wanted to drink him in to slake the heat sizzling through her veins.

"Mornin'," he said. "I brought security bars for your sliders." He held up the box as his gaze skimmed over her casual attire, making her nipples tighten under the thin cotton of her shirt. "I should have called. My apologies. I was worried about you."

"No need for apologies. It's nice of you to be concerned." She stepped back to let him in, and there was that faint hint of the woods again as he moved close to her. It stroked over her nerve endings like a touch, and his sheer size made her feel fragile and feminine. "I was being lazy after all the excitement yesterday."

"Weddings are harder on the ladies than the gentlemen," he said with a twinkle in his eyes. "Let me just install these bars and you can get back to your lazing."

"Can I offer you breakfast? Or maybe that would be brunch by now." She followed him into the dining area, enjoying the way the worn denim hugged his tight butt and muscular thighs. A girl could look, after all.

"Thanks, but I ate earlier." He flipped open the end of the box and pulled out the hardware. "I'd take a cup of that coffee I can smell, if you have extra."

"How do you like it?"

He knelt in front of the sliders. "Straight-up black."

That didn't surprise her. He was a straight-up kind of man. She filled a mug and carried it over to the dining table behind him. As he worked on attaching the hinged bar to the door frame, the muscles of his back bunched and released in a display that made her want to lay her palms against them.

"Your coffee is on the table behind you," she said, forcing herself to back away from the unsettling view. She perched on the sectional sofa so the table was between her and Tully.

"Thank you kindly," he said with that faint cowboy drawl of his.

"Where are you from originally?" she asked.

"Western Pennsylvania," he said, still working. "Why?"

"Because you sound like you're from Wyoming or something. And you wear cowboy boots."

He chuckled. "I worked on a cattle farm after school, so I got in the habit of wearing boots back then. Maybe I picked up some of Farmer Hollinger's speech patterns since I spent a lot of time with him. He was a real live cattleman." His tone was nostalgic and admiring.

"I've noticed that FBI agents and pilots often sound a bit like they're from the West."

"My boss at the FBI sometimes called me a cowboy but he didn't mean it as a compliment." His tone was dry.

"I see." Her curiosity got the better of her. "Is that why you decided to start your own consulting firm?"

She heard a metallic click and a small grunt of satisfaction. "No, that decision came after I spent a summer working for a large international security firm between my first and second year at business school. Starting at the bottom again was not to my taste."

"I can't see you sucking up to the boss, I have to admit."

"Oh, it was way worse than not sucking up. Of course, now I have to deal with two partners who have no hesitation about expressing their opinions." Another click and he straightened, the span of his shoulders and the length of his legs outlined against the bright window. "Luckily, I can express mine right back and they can't fire me."

She laughed, picturing Tully, Derek, and Leland squaring off in a huge office at the top of a Manhattan skyscraper. "I'd love to be a fly on the wall at one of your partners' meetings."

"When they get too rowdy, I just pull out my six-shooter and fire a couple of shots at the ceiling. That quiets 'em down." He dusted off his hands and took a swallow of coffee. "Ah, that's good stuff. Your bars are installed. You just flip them up to open the doors and back down to brace them." He fixed her with a serious look. "Remember to flip them down as soon as you come in through the doors. People get careless about that."

"I promise. What do I owe you for the bars? I know I can't afford to pay the hourly rate for your time." She gave him a teasing smile.

He leaned his hip against the table so his thigh muscles flexed underneath the jeans and took another swig of coffee. "This was my idea, so it's on me."

"Seriously, buying security bars was on my to-do list for the day. Please let me reimburse you for those." Gifts always came with strings attached, no matter how hard it was to see them. Although she was grateful to Tully for making her home safer.

"This fine cup of coffee is all the payment I need." His tone said the discussion was over. She wondered how often his partners heard that tone and whether it shut down whatever they were arguing about.

"You're very nice to do this for me."

A shadow darkened his gaze for a moment. "'Nice' is not a word I hear very often." He took another gulp and pushed away from the table. "I'll just wash this and let you get on with your day."

She leaped up from the sofa to step between him and the kitchen. "Please just leave it on the table. I don't expect my guests to wash their dishes. Especially when the guest has been so helpful."

She tried to think of a reason to prolong his visit. His presence unsettled her because it stirred longings that she didn't want to feel. Yet at the same time, he made her feel protected. The combination was potent, so maybe it was better that he left now.

He put the mug down on the table. "I'll sleep better knowing you have the bars, so they benefit both of us."

It was just a figure of speech but she had a vision of him tangled in bedsheets—his chest and shoulders bare—thinking about her in the dark. Which sent a streak of arousal down into her belly. She swallowed a gasp at her unexpected response while her eyes flew to his. He must have seen something of her reaction in them because his gaze turned hot.

Just like that moment on the dance floor, they remained suspended, staring at each other before she dragged her attention away from the blaze in his eyes. She scooped up his mug and held it in both hands as though it could shield her from the attraction flashing between them.

His eyes were still locked on her when she glanced up again. With slow deliberation he reached out and brushed a strand of her hair away from her face, sending delicious tingles flickering through her.

She caught her breath and stepped back. "You've been great. I don't want to keep you any longer. It's your day off."

He gave a tiny shake of his head before he lowered his hand. "And yours. Have a good one." He spun on one boot heel and strode toward the door. "Make sure you arm the alarm system after me."

"I will. Thank you again!" She made it to the door as he was jogging down the steps. He lifted a hand in farewell without looking back.

She felt like an idiot. Even worse, a sexually frustrated idiot.

Tully settled into the Maserati's leather seat but sat with his hands on the wheel. His body was coiled tight with physical tension. He was tempted to blow off work—it was Sunday, after all—and drive the extra thirty minutes west to the barn where he boarded his horse. The thought of flying across a field at a full gallop battled with the pile of projects that waited for him at the office. With a huff of frustration, he punched the ignition button and said "KRG" to his voice-activated GPS.

But his overactive conscience couldn't stop him from thinking about Natalie as he drove.

He shouldn't have surprised her on a Sunday morning but he'd been concerned. She didn't seem like the kind of woman who was scared to walk into an empty house after dark. In fact, until last night, he had thought her elegant poise was impossible to ruffle. Whatever story Natalie's customer had told her must have been bad because it had really spooked her.

So he'd barged in on her relaxed Sunday morning like a bull in a china shop. If she had been out, he'd planned to leave the security bars on her front porch so she could install them herself. The ones he had brought were a hell of a lot stronger than what she would have gotten at the local hardware store.

What he hadn't planned on was Natalie looking like she'd just gotten out of bed, with sleepy bedroom eyes, rumpled hair, and breasts clearly outlined by her thin T-shirt. Even her slender bare feet with their pale pink polish had made his cock twitch. When she'd turned to lead him into the house, all he could think of was filling his hands with the tempting curves of her nicely rounded butt.

He had to admit that since the wedding activities had forced them to be a pseudo-couple, he might have had a few fantasies about seeing if he could get past that cool, controlled exterior to see what smoldered beneath. He thought he'd made progress after that dance, when their bodies had moved together so perfectly, almost like making love. Except that at the end, his cock still ached.

Last night, when she'd asked him to inspect her house, his cock had been hopeful again.

And this morning, when he'd seen her nipples harden so they pushed at the fabric of her shirt, he couldn't stop himself. He'd given in to the impulse to touch her silky hair and brush his fingertips over the soft skin of her cheek. Her blue eyes were lit with the same arousal he felt, yet she'd backed away, her rejection clear.

He shrugged as he turned onto the highway that would take him back to Manhattan. He probably wouldn't see her much now that Alice and Derek were off on their honeymoon trip around the world. Dawn and Leland's wedding plans were still in the preliminary stages, so there'd be no reason for them to be together anytime soon.

He'd just go back to his fantasies. Only this time he could add a few more lust-enhancing details.

Chapter 4

After running her routine Sunday errands while trying not to think about the brush of Tully's fingers against her cheek, Natalie tromped up the stone steps of her front porch with a couple of plastic bags in her hand. A flash of white tucked under the doormat caught her eye—probably a flyer for window replacement or a cleaning service. She bent and yanked the paper out from under the mat, unlocked the door, and went inside.

When she got to the kitchen, she set the bags down and flipped the paper open to find two lines typed on it:

Beauty is only skin deep. What's underneath your skin?

The muscles in her throat tightened. She dropped the paper on the counter as though it were a snake rattling its tail.

It had to be from the same person who had sent her an email every day since Tuesday. They were all on the theme of beauty, which she had assumed was a reference to her hair salon. She had tried not to think about them since she didn't want a shadow hanging over her pleasure in Alice and Derek's wedding, but the messages were seared into her brain.

Beauty is in the eye of the beholder. No one sees beauty in you.

Pretty is as pretty does. What you do is ugly.

Beauty is power. But who has the power now?

A thing of beauty is a joy forever but you won't be around that long.

She had deleted the first email without paying much attention to it, assuming it had some kind of malware attached, although there was no apparent link to click on.

The second one made her stop and check the sender's address but it was not one she recognized.

The third email made her go back and dig the other two out of the deleted list so she could see if they were from the same address. They were not, which made her nervous. Whoever was sending them was hiding their identity.

When the fourth one arrived—on the morning of the rehearsal dinner—her stomach had knotted. The short message with no greeting, no closing, and no recognizable source radiated menace. That was when she'd checked all the locks on the windows in her house and called a locksmith to upgrade the locks on the hair salon's front and back doors, something she'd meant to do for years.

She had considered calling the police, but Natalie knew from experience how little they could do when a threat was not immediate and clear. At the salon she'd heard far too many stories of how useless restraining orders were against ex-boyfriends and ex-husbands.

Furthermore, how could she convince the police that a few sayings about beauty constituted a danger to her? The anonymity and frequency were sinister but the threat was only implied.

Now that she thought about it, she hadn't gotten a message on Alice's wedding day. Someone had known she wouldn't be checking her email that day. She braced her hands on the counter, closed her eyes, and concentrated on breathing in and out slowly as fear turned her knees to jelly.

The ice maker in her fridge dumped new cubes with a muffled clatter. Her knees functioned just well enough for her to jump sideways while her heart tried to wrench itself out of her chest.

She had to do something, or she would be a basket case before it got dark. After that, she wouldn't be able to sleep. In the old days, she would have spent the night at Dawn's apartment, but her friend had moved into Leland's penthouse in the city.

She looked down at the sheet of paper with its words that weren't quite a threat but sent claws of terror ripping through her.

Maybe the chief of police would believe her. After all, his wife came to the Mane Attraction every week for a mani-pedi. But what could he do? Send a patrol car by every hour?

She needed someone who could help her figure out how to stop the messages because she couldn't live in fear every time the ice maker did its job.

And she knew who that someone was.

Tully shoved the rolling chair back from his desk and walked over to the wall of windows that faced the Hudson River. A tugboat wrestled a barge upriver against the swift current while a couple of graceful white sailboats tacked back and forth behind it.

He'd knocked off a couple of proposals and modified the antikidnapping training program for the Hazeltons to include protecting their three golden retrievers. A smile tugged at the corners of his mouth. The changes had been a pain to work in, but how could he fault the family for worrying about their beloved pets?

However, he still had more to do than he had expected because his mind kept drifting away to the electric charge of having Natalie in his arms when they'd danced. And her nipples under that flimsy white T-shirt she'd had on this morning.

His cell phone vibrated on his desk, making him turn away from the view to pick it up. He glanced at the caller ID.

Natalie.

Anticipation shot through his veins. Maybe she'd changed her mind about what sizzled between them. "Hey, Nat. Are the security bars giving you trouble already?" he joked.

"No . . . no, they're fine. Something's happened. I need your help." He could hear panic making her voice tremble.

"Are you in immediate danger?" His tone was harsh but he had to know how bad the situation was.

"No, I don't think so. I have the alarm set and the doors and windows locked. I have my pepper spray. And I have you on the phone."

His level of concern eased slightly. "That's all good. Now tell me what's going on."

"I've been getting these weird email messages every day for almost a week . . . except yesterday." Her breath hitched before her voice went on. "They've all come from different addresses and have just a short message in them, always something about beauty. Sort of a reference to my salon."

"Give me an example of what they say."

"The first one was 'Beauty is in the eye of the beholder. No one sees beauty in you.' Then they got worse, like, 'A thing of beauty is a joy forever but you won't be around that long.'"

"Did you tell the police?"

"No. What could they do? Issue a restraining order against an unknown emailer?"

She wasn't wrong. "Okay. Did you get another one today?" She said she hadn't received an email on Alice and Derek's wedding day. Whoever was sending the messages knew she'd be too busy to read one. That showed a worrisome familiarity with her activities.

"N-no. Worse." Her voice quavered. "I went out for a couple of hours and when I got back, someone had left a piece of paper on my front porch. It says, 'Beauty is only skin deep. What's underneath your skin?'"

Shit! His gut tensed. "Typed or handwritten?" He headed for the elevator.

"Typed."

"I'm on my way. Just to be on the safe side, go upstairs to your bedroom and wedge a chair back under the doorknob. Don't come out until you get a text from me that I'm at your front door."

"Oh, God! Is it that dangerous?"

He hated to scare her, but criminals rarely surprised him in a good way. "He's most likely gone, but better not to take a chance."

As soon as he got in his Maserati, he gunned it out of the garage.

Chapter 5

Natalie stood at her bedroom window, watching the road in front of her house and feeling like a coward. She didn't regret calling Tully. Hearing his voice had knocked her fear down a notch. Although she still jumped at random noises, she no longer felt like her heart was trying to batter its way out of her chest.

While she waited, she had searched the internet for information about stalkers. What she learned had not been reassuring. Most stalkers knew their victims. She racked her brain to come up with someone familiar who might fit the average stalker's profile: *Unemployed or underemployed. Male. Above-average intelligence. Thirty to forty years old. Often delusional. Suffers from personality disorders.*

Added to that, most stalkers were ex-spouses or ex-boyfriends. That pointed to her ex-husband, but would Matt suddenly decide to torment her three years after their divorce?

The rumble of a powerful engine drew her attention back to the road. A wave of relief washed over her as the Maserati pulled into her driveway. Tully unfolded his long legs from the sleek black car, and a wave of pure, shocking sexual heat seared through her. She inhaled sharply and fought down the desire suffusing her body. That was a complication she didn't need in this already-fraught situation.

But she didn't turn away from the window as he stood by the car and scanned around him. After a few moments, he strode across her front yard, so she unhooked the chair from under her bedroom doorknob and ran down the stairs. She started to disarm the alarm before she remembered that he'd said not to leave her room until he sent her a text. Her fingers stilled on the keypad.

She waited, wondering what the hell was taking so long.

When her phone chimed in the silence, she started, even though she'd been waiting for it.

I'm on the porch.

Her fingers flew over the alarm keys and she flung open the door. "Thank you so much for coming!"

She had the urge to throw herself into his arms so that she could wrap herself in the protective bulwark of his strong, capable body. Then she saw his expression and the impulse died a speedy death.

His mouth was a thin, hard line. His jaw was set at an uncompromising angle. His dark-gray eyes held about as much warmth as an iceberg. And he seemed even larger than she remembered, probably because controlled menace radiated from him. In his hand was a medium-size black duffel. She wondered if it held a gun.

She took two steps backward, and his expression softened a fraction.

"You were right to call me," he said. "Cyberstalking is bad enough, but when the stalker invades your private space, it's time to get help."

"I'm not sure if I'm glad or upset that you don't think I'm overreacting."

He shook his head. "I'd like to see the emails you received."

She led the way to the kitchen island, where her laptop sat. He stood beside her, close enough that when she shifted to touch the trackpad, her elbow brushed against his arm, the brief contact sending a ripple of awareness across her skin.

She focused on the screen, bringing up the succession of messages that she'd saved in a folder she'd labeled "Crazy," in reference to both the emails and how they made her feel.

"May I?" Tully gestured toward the keyboard and she shuffled sideways to give him access.

He scrolled through the messages, his brows drawn down so deeply that a line formed between them. Pulling his cell phone from his back pocket, he tapped it and brought it to his ear. "Leland, I've got a problem I'd like you to take a look at ASAP. I'm sending you some email messages that Natalie received this past week. Let me know what you can find out about them." He listened a moment. "Yeah, this is clearly cyberstalking, but it escalated today with a letter on her front porch." Another pause on his end. "I plan to discuss that with her. Keep me posted."

She almost voiced her objection to roping Leland into her problem on a Sunday when she remembered that it was Tully's day off as well, yet here he was. She pressed her lips together.

Tully pulled a pair of thin rubber gloves and a plastic bag from his duffel and gestured toward the sheet of paper lying on the other side of the counter. "I assume that's the message you found under your doormat."

She wrapped her arms around her waist. "Yes."

He snapped on the gloves before he picked up the sheet, handling it by the corners as he examined it. "I'm going to send this to a lab to check for fingerprints and analyze the paper, ink, and printer." He looked up at her. "Honestly, I don't think we'll get anything useful, but it's worth a try." He inserted the single sheet into the plastic bag and peeled the gloves off.

"*My* fingerprints will be on it," she said apologetically.

He scooped up his phone and swiped a few times before holding it out to her. "If you just press your fingers on here, we can eliminate your prints. I promise to erase them immediately after we establish which are yours on the paper."

"No promises necessary. I trust you." She placed her fingers on the squares glowing on the phone screen, surprised that she'd given him her trust so easily.

"Okay, now we need to talk," Tully said.

Natalie headed for the sectional. "I've been trying to figure out who might be doing this." She perched on the edge of a cushion while Tully settled into an armchair, his elbows braced on his knees as he focused on her face.

"It's most likely a man," he said. "The majority of stalkers are male, particularly when a woman is being targeted." His gaze gentled. "I don't like to bring this up, but it's often an ex-husband."

There it was. All the ugliness in her past. "I know. I read that online. So I've been thinking about my ex." She hated to share the details of her private hell, but since Tully was here to help her, she needed to be honest with him. Taking a deep breath, she said, "I can see Matt playing this kind of cruel mind game because frankly, that's what he did to me in our marriage. He manipulated my thoughts and emotions until I reached a point where I . . . I could no longer recognize myself." She fought the sense of failure that still lingered from those bleak, destructive years. "So psychological torture is right up his alley."

Tully's hands curled into fists. "Did he ever hit you?"

"No." She stared down at her fingers, which were twisted in her lap. "Sometimes I wish he *had*. That would have made it crystal clear to me that I was in an abusive relationship." She might have left before so much damage had been done to her soul.

"He was clever. He knew that would make you leave." Tully flexed his fingers open. "So we need to take a long hard look at Matt. What's his full name?"

"Matthew Walter Stevens." Natalie shook her head. "But it doesn't make sense. We've been divorced for three years. He's got a live-in girlfriend who's fifteen years younger than he is, which gives his ego the strokes he needs. He has no reason to suddenly come after me."

"You can never tell what will trigger someone. Maybe the girlfriend dumped him. Or she's pressuring him to get married. Maybe he lost his job or someone got promoted over him."

"But what would be the point of tormenting *me*? I have no contact with him anymore. Frankly, I think he's done his best to erase me from his life because he feels he was the loser in that situation."

"Okay, what about anyone you've dated since the divorce? Or turned down?"

She shook her head. "No dates. No rejected suitors."

He sat up straight, shock written on his face. "In three years you haven't even been *asked* on a date? That's unbelievable."

She smiled while she tried to decide if he meant it or was just being polite. "I'm not interested and guys pick up on that . . . for the most part."

"So someone *has* asked?"

"It never gets that far." She gave him a wry look. "There are ways to stop the conversation before it reaches an actual invitation."

One corner of his mouth twitched upward for a moment before he asked, "Anyone who seemed especially unhappy that you halted the conversation?"

"I've tried to come up with someone who gave off that kind of . . . I don't know . . . obsessive vibe, but no one sticks out."

He was silent for a moment. "Okay. Let's move on to other possibilities. Disgruntled customers? Competitors?"

She shrugged. "I'm sure there are a few, but are they unhappy enough to stalk me? No." Then a thought struck her, one she hadn't considered before. "Oh!"

"What?" He leaned forward again, his attention focused.

"There's this other thing I do that maybe . . ." She tapped her bottom lip with her index finger before she gave him a level look. "It's not something I talk about, for reasons which will become obvious, so I'll ask for your discretion."

He nodded. "You've got it."

She knew that already but she had to hear him say it. "Hairstylists are kind of like bartenders. Our customers tell us things—sometimes deeply personal things. My clients know that I'm divorced, so they sometimes open up about their marital issues." She shifted on the sofa. "There are times when I recognize that they might need some help. I take them into my office at the salon and privately offer them my guest room here whenever they might need a safe place to stay, no questions asked. That's one reason I bought this house. It's private and has the self-contained guest suite."

Because she'd had no safe place to run to when she had needed it.

"You're courageous to do that," Tully said. "But it opens up a whole new field of possibilities. How many women have you housed here?"

"Here? Three. However, I used to let them stay with me in the apartment over the salon before I moved into this place. There were two who took me up on it back then."

"So five potentially angry husbands or ex-husbands." Tully blew out a breath and ran his hand over his hair. "How many ended up divorced?"

"All but one." The one wife had gone back because she had small children and her husband had agreed to intensive marital counseling. When she came into the salon now, she looked drawn and exhausted, but she said they were making progress. "You can see why I don't talk about it. I don't want those angry husbands showing up on my doorstep, terrifying their wives."

"Besides the five women, who knows you've done this?"

"Alice and Dawn, of course. One of my stylists, who's completely trustworthy." Gino had been her mentor when she started working at the Mane Attraction as a new stylist. He would never breathe a word of her secret.

“Any of the husbands?”

Natalie considered for a moment. “I don’t think so. None of them have confronted me. I ask that no one reveal where they stayed, but you never know what might come out in the heat of a divorce proceeding.”

“Can you ask them if they let it slip?”

“I can try. I don’t know if they would be honest with me. They might be embarrassed that they told their ex-husbands.”

“However, if they do admit to giving away your secret, that would give us a starting point,” Tully said. “Make sure they understand the urgency of your question. I’ll need their names, their ex-husbands’ names, and their current and/or previous addresses. All to be kept in confidence, of course.”

She nodded, thinking of the five women who’d spent time with her. Two had moved away after their divorces, so she no longer saw them. Another had remarried very quickly, and Natalie prayed that she hadn’t gone from one bad marriage to another. Her most recent guest had left eight days ago. “I’ll email you as much information as I have.”

“I’m guessing you didn’t have anywhere to go when you left Matt,” Tully said, his tone gentle.

“Oh, I went home to my mother,” Natalie said. “She didn’t understand.” In fact, she’d subjected Natalie to a barrage of criticism and pressured her to return to Matt. Natalie had nearly buckled under the stress of getting it from both sides because Matt had tried to woo her back too. He couldn’t believe she had actually had the nerve to leave him.

“Different generation,” Tully said.

“No, unsupportive mother,” Natalie said bluntly. “Why would I leave a good provider who didn’t physically abuse me?” She laughed without a trace of humor. “Another reason it would have been easier if he’d hit me.”

“That’s rough,” Tully said with a sympathetic wince. “Your mother should be there for you, no matter what.”

"I didn't stay with her long." Fortunately, the tenant in the apartment at the salon was leaving in a few weeks, so Natalie had gritted her teeth and toughed it out until she could move in there. Those weeks had felt like an eternity of being battered by a whirlpool of conflicting currents.

"Sounds like that was a good thing." Tully's expression sharpened again. "We need to talk about where you're going to stay until we get this resolved."

"What do you mean? I can't leave. I have a salon to run." But she frowned as she realized she would be alone in the house that the stalker was watching.

"It would be safer if you changed locations."

"Maybe I could stay with one of my stylists." She shook her head as a thought struck her. "No, I won't do that. It might put them in danger too."

"You can't stay here alone. It's too isolated and the stalker has proven that he's watching you." He gave her a gimlet stare. "I'm going to send a bodyguard to stay with you. You don't have anyone else who needs your guest room now, do you?"

"That's a nice offer, but I've got the alarm system and I'll make sure the police know what's going on. The chief's wife is a client of mine. I also have pepper spray and I'm not afraid to use it. Dawn has made sure of that with all her self-defense classes." She gave him a smile to soften her refusal.

"You asked for my help. You need to accept it." Tully's tone brooked no disagreement.

Shock and a touch of irritation straightened her spine. "You're right. I asked for your help and I am very appreciative of everything you're doing. However, now that I know what I'm dealing with, I will take precautions."

He made a slashing gesture that brushed her words aside. "Most stalkers are not violent, but I'm not going to have it on my conscience if you get hurt."

She should have guessed that he would take personal responsibility. But although it might be sincere, his statement was also a touch manipulative. She'd learned to recognize that from her experience with Matt. "Look, if you insist on sending me a bodyguard, I insist on paying for the service."

He shook his head. "This falls under KRG's Small Business Initiative. Free assistance to small- business owners who need it. And you need it."

She could tell his answer had been prepared ahead of time, but she had a response for him. "This is personal, not business."

"We haven't established that. Besides, if you are out of commission, your business will suffer. You're the key person."

"Do you have an answer for everything?" she snapped in exasperation.

She caught a twitch of amusement at the corner of his mouth. "If I did, I'd be able to tell you who your stalker is."

"You must annoy the hell out of your partners," she said, her own lips starting to curl upward.

He snorted. "I'll text you the bodyguard's name and photo as soon as I get things set up. But I'm going to give you a series of code phrases to confirm identity when the guard arrives here."

"I don't remember agreeing to the bodyguard."

"You said you wanted to pay for it." He tried to look bland but didn't quite pull it off. "Do you have a piece of paper so I can write down the codes?"

She retrieved a pad and pen from a kitchen drawer and walked back to where Tully sat. Handing them to him, she stayed by his chair as he wrote. When he finished, she bent slightly to read what he'd jotted down, his closeness bringing that hum of physical awareness back to life.

Bodyguard: I'm here to take a look at the toilet you're having a problem with.

Natalie: I didn't expect you to come on a Sunday.

Bodyguard: The boss says you're a good customer, so you get special treatment.

"Okay," she said, although she wanted to make a disappointed comment about how mundane it was. She'd expected something more exotic.

"The bodyguard will use those exact words. You should too. No variations from either of you." Tully folded the paper in quarters and handed it to her, their fingertips brushing so her skin tingled. "Read along as you both talk."

"I understand." She straightened and slipped the paper into the back pocket of her jeans.

"You think I'm being overly cautious," he said, "but I've learned from hard experience that you can't be too careful. So humor me." He smiled fully for the first time since they had started talking about the stalker, accentuating the indent in his chin and the slight dimple in one cheek. It was such a contrast to his stern professional demeanor that it sent another thrill of heat through her.

"Now that you've foisted a guard on me, what next?" she asked.

"We'll see what Leland finds out. You report any new messages to me immediately. You contact the ex-wives to see what you can find out." He pinned her with those intense gray eyes. "But your main job is to stay safe."

She sat down on the sofa again. "I didn't mean to sound ungrateful about the bodyguard because I really appreciate your concern. I just"—she waved her hand in a gesture of frustration—"find this whole situation so surreal. I'm a hairstylist in a small suburban town in New Jersey. Why on earth would anyone stalk *me*?"

"You don't give yourself enough credit. You're a successful businesswoman who had the strength to escape from a bad marriage. You help other women escape from bad situations." He hesitated a moment before continuing. "You're beautiful and desirable. Any of those things can trigger a stalker."

His words exploded around her like fireworks, igniting every inch of her body. For a long moment, she didn't breathe. He found her desirable. She somehow gave him a sideways smile. "I think that might be a compliment, so thank you."

"It's definitely a compliment." His gaze roamed her face in a way that sent the heat up a notch.

She thought again about asking him to stay. He could be her bodyguard . . . with an emphasis on the *body*. No, bad idea. She was still recovering from one domineering man. She didn't need another one in her life, even just for sex.

When she didn't respond, he looked away. "I'd better get back to the office. I'll let you know when Leland has answers for us."

"I'll let you know what the ex-wives say as soon as I reach them."

He nodded. "Everything locked, all the time, including your car doors when you're driving. Only open the door to people you know and trust one hundred percent . . . and the bodyguard, of course. Do you work tomorrow?"

"The salon is closed but I go in to do paperwork, check supplies, and generally prep for the week."

"Alone?"

"Yes, it's everyone's day off."

"Except yours."

"You know what owning a business is like." She gave a smile. "No one works harder than the boss."

"The bodyguard goes with you and stays with you."

"While I'm inside the salon? It has an alarm." Just as well he wouldn't let her pay for the guard. She couldn't afford all those hours anyway.

"Set the alarm as well."

He wasn't joking, and a tremor of fear ran down her spine. She had to remember that paranoia was a professional necessity for Tully. He would think of her stalker in the same way he thought of a drug lord or a gun dealer. Whoever was sending her the messages couldn't be on the same level of scariness.

"Okay," she said. "You win, even if it seems like overkill."

"Good decision." He reached out to feather his fingertips over her cheek again. "I don't want anything to happen to my dance partner."

His touch reverberated through her long after he walked out the door.

As Tully pulled his Maserati onto the road in front of Natalie's house, he activated the car's voice recognition system. "Call Pam Santos," he commanded. When she answered, he said, "I need you for a bodyguard job in Jersey. A woman is being stalked but we don't know by whom or how dangerous the stalker might be. You're with her 24-7. You up for it?"

"You know it, boss. Just give me the info."

He filled her in on Natalie's situation. "Use the plumber code phrases. Natalie's expecting them."

"How long should I pack for?"

"Say three days. We should be able to catch the son of a bitch by then." Tully hoped three days would be enough.

"I'll be at Natalie's within two hours." Pam disconnected.

"Call Leland," Tully commanded the car next.

"I don't have much good to tell you," Leland said as soon as he answered.

Tully swallowed a frustrated curse. "Lay it on me, partner."

"I've tracked all but one of the emails. The stalker isn't a total amateur. He bounced his message through a couple of extra servers on the dark web."

"Child's play for you to follow," Tully said.

"Yes, but they all lead back to internet cafés scattered around New Jersey. Never the same one twice. Always paid for in cash so there's no money trail."

"They might have security cameras," Tully said, but Leland would have thought of that too.

"I contacted three and the answer is no. They feel every citizen has the right to use the net without being watched by Big Brother." Leland's tone turned sardonic.

"You hackers are all paranoid," Tully poked at his partner.

"With good reason." Leland's southern drawl was unruffled. "Sorry I don't have better news."

Tully huffed out a breath. "I hate smart perps." Unfortunately, many stalkers were of above-average intelligence. It made them that much harder to capture. "Thanks for letting me steal time from your day off."

"Don't be ridiculous." Leland sounded annoyed. "I'll keep working on the last email. Maybe he slipped up somehow."

"I appreciate it." Tully disconnected and smacked the steering wheel with the heel of his hand. "Damn!"

Back to basics, then. Currently, his money was on the ex-husband, who sounded like a rat bastard. The puppeteer wouldn't want to give up control of his precious puppet. Even though it had been a while, Natalie's ex might suddenly feel the need to pull her strings again. Tully would get his best investigator to dig deeply into what Stevens's personal and financial life looked like right now. Also if the guy knew anything about computers.

The ex-wives' club was more complicated and less probable, in his opinion. The divorced husbands were more likely to stalk their former wives than the woman who gave them a temporary sanctuary, especially an anonymous one. He supposed it was possible that the ex-husbands might stalk both their former wives *and* Natalie. He would check into any reports of stalking filed with the police.

He would also give the police chief of Cofferwood a call, just to reinforce Natalie's report.

Finally, he needed to get his own reactions to Natalie under control. He'd gone too far when he'd told her she was desirable, even though it was true and pertinent to the situation. She'd vividly demonstrated to him—he winced at the memory—that she had ways to shut down a conversation before she needed to say no.

Yet he could have sworn she'd felt the pull between them too. He was pretty damn good at reading body language, partly from training and partly from natural ability. So he trusted his instincts. But she wasn't acting on it, so he needed to let it go. He just wished regret didn't twist in his chest quite so hard.

That scumbag Stevens had probably soured her on men permanently.

"Or maybe she just doesn't like you as much as you think," he said to his reflection in the rearview mirror. "So try not to be an asshole about it."

Chapter 6

A tall red-haired woman wearing a navy blazer over a simple white blouse and jeans looked into the camera at Natalie's front door. "I'm here to take a look at the toilet you're having a problem with."

Natalie had to suppress a giggle before she read from the script, "I didn't expect you to come on a Sunday."

The woman said her next line in such a normal tone that Natalie's giggle escaped as she pulled open the door. The woman looked surprised.

"I'm sorry, but you don't look anything like a plumber," Natalie said, struggling to stifle her laughter as she waved the woman inside. It was partly nerves and partly relief that had her chuckling. "I guess you know I'm Natalie." She held out her hand.

"Pam Santos." The woman gave her a firm handshake and then grinned. "Okay, I think Tully's plumber routine is kind of funny too."

"Would you like me to show you where you'll be staying?" Natalie asked, eyeing the leather duffel bag Pam held in her left hand.

"First, I'd like to familiarize myself with the layout of your house." Pam set the duffel down at the foot of the stairs, the movement tightening her blazer so it outlined the shape of the gun she had in a holster underneath it.

"Of course." Anyone Tully sent would take the job seriously. However, it freaked her out a little that Pam was wearing a gun. Her stalker had done nothing more than send some vaguely sinister messages.

As Natalie led Pam through the house, the bodyguard checked windows, doors, and closets with the same thoroughness Tully had shown the night before. She also moved with the same noiseless footsteps, despite sporting black boots with low square heels. Evidently, stealth—even with boots on—was a job requirement.

"I looked around outside before I rang the bell," Pam said as they walked back into the living room. "There's a lot of vegetation. I'm going to talk to the boss about installing cameras."

Natalie interpreted that to mean the stalker could easily hide among the trees and shrubs. "Thank you," she said before she glanced at her watch to find it was a little after five. "Would you like coffee? Or beer or wine? Or a Manhattan?" She needed one of the latter.

"I'm on duty, so coffee would be great," Pam said. "Black, please."

As Natalie started the coffee, Pam strolled back to the sliders Tully had disapproved of and stared through them with a frown. The low-slanting sun turned her beautiful red hair to flame, and Natalie's fingers itched to give it a cut that would suit Pam's slightly square face better than the low ponytail it was pulled into.

"Have you dealt with stalkers before?" Natalie asked.

Pam shook her head. "Just studied cases about them. They can be pretty twisted."

"Twisted?" A shiver ran down Natalie's spine as she poured a mug of coffee.

"Mentally," Pam said. "They tell themselves a lot of lies, like that their victim loves them but doesn't realize it yet." She took the coffee with a smile of thanks. "It's a strange mindset."

"But most are not violent." Natalie went back to the kitchen to mix herself that Manhattan.

"Most, but better safe than sorry," Pam said. "That's every bodyguard's motto."

The next morning, Pam helped Natalie clear the breakfast dishes. "We'll take two cars," the bodyguard said. "I'll follow you. Don't get out of your car until I'm there beside your door and give you the okay."

"Got it," Natalie said, loading the dishes in the dishwasher. She hated to admit it but she liked having the hypervigilant Pam around.

"I'm going to check the front porch for messages. Your security camera doesn't cover low enough to see that." Pam headed down the hallway, silent as always, and Natalie held her breath. "Nothing here," the other woman called out.

Natalie exhaled in a whoosh. There'd been no email either. Maybe Pam's presence had scared the stalker away.

When Natalie pulled into the small parking lot beside her salon, Pam's big black SUV came right behind her, a comforting presence with its menacing size and color. Natalie felt a little foolish as she waited until Pam signaled she could get out. With the sun flickering through the spring leaves, the shoppers strolling along the brick-paved sidewalk, and the constant stream of passing cars, it seemed ridiculous to take such precautions.

Pam insisted on going first, her stride long and athletic as they walked around to the back entrance of the two-story Victorian that was home to the Mane Attraction. Natalie had painted the house a soft shade of lavender with butter-yellow trim to make it eye-catching. She got out the keys and unlocked the glossy purple back door, which led into a small back foyer with access to the stairs to the apartment and to the basement. Pam went in first, sweeping through the small space and checking the staircase. "It's clear," she said as she tried the door to the basement and found it locked.

Natalie stepped in and unlocked the door that led to the bright open kitchen, which the staff used to eat and relax in. She disarmed the alarm—placed inside the kitchen door so her upstairs tenant didn't have to deal with it—and relocked the door while Pam prowled through the salon. There were a lot of rooms to check, so Natalie set up the coffee machine while she waited, tracking Pam's progress by the sound of doors opening and closing.

"Shit!" Pam's voice came from somewhere up front.

Natalie's shoulders tensed. "What is it?"

"You'd better come to the front door," the other woman called back.

Natalie walked quickly down the hall beside the front staircase with its ornately carved oak bannister. When she got to the reception desk that wrapped around the foot of the now-unused stairs, she saw Pam holding an unfolded sheet of paper by one corner. The woman looked up with a grim expression. "Another message."

All the fear she'd thought was vanquished roared through Natalie again, and her stomach tried to force her breakfast back up her throat. She swallowed hard. "What does it say?"

"'Mirror, mirror, on the wall, who's the fairest of them all? Pretty soon it won't be you.' It was on the hall floor, so I assume it was slipped under the front door."

"I guess I need to put some weather stripping along there," Natalie tried to joke until she realized something disturbing, and her breakfast started to rise again. "So my stalker must know that I come to the salon on Monday even though it's closed."

"It's not uncommon for a stalker to be familiar with his victim's daily routines," Pam said in a soothing voice. "It doesn't mean he's going to interfere with you physically."

"But it means he's watching me." A shudder ran through Natalie. "He's like one of those indestructible masked killers from a slasher movie. A faceless bogeyman."

"I have to admit that the anonymity isn't typical. Most stalkers want your attention. That's the point. This one is taking care not to be identified." Pam laid the paper down on the reception desk. "I don't want to leave you alone to go to my car to get an evidence bag. Do you have a plastic baggie I could use to protect the letter?"

Natalie fetched a bag and looked at the paper after Pam had carefully sealed it. It was exactly like the one from her front porch except for the words. Now that the shock was past, rage boiled through her veins. The stalker was playing with her, trying to make her afraid of her own shadow because she didn't know whom the messages were coming from. "Damn it, I'm not going to curl up in a ball and shake with fear! I'm going to find out who this creep is."

Pam shook her head. "Please don't do anything to endanger yourself. That would get me in trouble with the boss. Let him do the investigating. He's good at it."

"I won't be stupid but I'm going to contact my previous houseguests right now and find out what they told their ex-husbands. Even Tully said that was okay."

An hour later, Natalie leaned back in her desk chair and let her gaze travel around the small, familiar room with its cream-painted desk and pale blue carpeting. It was feminine and restful—her retreat from the constant noise and movement of the salon.

Honestly, she found the Monday silence somewhat eerie, even when she wasn't being stalked. The whir of blow-dryers and the continual twitter of voices represented life and success to her. Without them the salon felt a little desolate.

She looked at the legal pad with all the contact information she'd gathered about the ex-wives. She'd reached two of the women. Both had sworn—up, down, and sideways—that they hadn't mentioned her name to anyone. She was inclined to believe them because they were grateful, and they didn't want to screw things up for the next person who needed a safe place to stay. She'd left voice mails for the other two, just simple requests to call her back.

Regina Van Houten, her most recent refugee, was a problem, though. Her cell phone was no longer in service, and Natalie had no new address for her. However, Natalie would bet money Regina hadn't told her husband where she'd taken refuge. The young woman was terrified of him, saying he'd threatened to throw her down the stairs and tell the police it was an accident. He'd convinced Regina that no one would believe her version of the story because he was the scion of a wealthy family who had been in the area for generations, while she was a newcomer he'd plucked off a farm in Nebraska and married a year before.

Natalie's cell rang, making her jump. The fact that her cell phone could scare her pissed her off. She checked the caller ID to discover it was Tully, and her anger turned into an entirely different kind of heat. "Hello, Tully. Thanks for sending Pam. She's not only a great bodyguard but good company too."

"I figured you'd be more amenable to being protected if you liked your guard." He sounded pleased. "I sure slept a lot better last night knowing Pam was with you."

Oh, God! There was that image of Tully's well-muscled body draped in nothing but bedsheets again. He needed to stop talking about his sleep. "Honestly, I slept better too."

All softness drained from his voice. "Yeah, but Pam told me about the new message."

"What did Leland find out about the emails?" Natalie asked.

Tully huffed out a breath. "Nothing useful. The stalker is paying cash at internet cafés without video cams to send his messages. And there were no prints on the letter." His tone gentled. "But I didn't really expect much this soon, so there's no need for concern. We'll catch him."

Knowing he was focused on solving her problem loosened the knots in her shoulders. "I don't have good news to report either. Two of the women swear they didn't tell their ex-husbands. Two I left voice mails for. The last one I have no way of contacting because her cell phone service has been shut off, probably to avoid her husband. However, I'm almost certain she wouldn't even tell him the time if he asked."

"Give me her name and I'll see if I can track her down."

"Regina Van Houten. Married to William Van Houten. His nickname is Dobs, for some reason. She lived in Manorville, about forty-five minutes from here, although she's originally from somewhere in Nebraska. She's not close with her family, though, so I don't think she'd go there. I always ask them not to tell me where they're heading so I can't be pressured to reveal their whereabouts."

"You are a very smart woman. But I knew that already."

His approval sent a glow of gratification spiraling through her.

"I'm going to check up on what's happening in Matt's life too," Natalie said.

"No!" Tully's response was emphatic. "Let me handle that. He could be your stalker, so I don't want you going near that SOB."

"I won't have to. I own a beauty salon." She smiled. "I have a web of informants I can tap at any time."

Tully's chuckle was a dark rumble that vibrated low in her belly. "And to think I was going to waste time by hiring a private detective." However, there was no amusement in his voice when he said, "But that could prod him into doing something worse, so I'm asking you to leave that to me."

He was putting a lot of resources—which cost money—into solving this. She massaged the bridge of her nose as she wondered how to repay him. Free haircuts for life as long as he trekked out to New Jersey? She dropped her hand onto the legal pad. "This stalker is jerking my chain and I'm tired of it. I'm not going to spend my days looking over my shoulder in fear."

"That's strong, but don't put yourself in danger because of it. Listen to Pam when she's with you."

"She can't stay with me indefinitely. It's too much. And don't feed me that line about the SBI covering all this."

"Hey, Derek chartered a private jet to fly Alice to Texas when they were tracking the computer accounting fraud."

"That affected thousands of people. This is just about me."

"You've got it backward. All those people were going to lose was their money. This is about your *safety*." His words were rock hard with conviction.

"Okay. I won't object anymore . . . for now." His implication sent a shiver though her. Despite all the reassurances, he wasn't sure the stalker was nonviolent.

"I'm going to come by your house later in the day to install outside security cameras on more than just your front door. That way we'll catch him on video if he comes there again. Or scare him off with the added surveillance. Either option works for me."

Her heart did a flip of anticipation, and she slapped her palm against her chest in a ridiculous attempt to calm it. "Remember what I said about too much? I'll get the alarm company to do it. Just tell me where you want them."

"I want to check on you too. See how you're holding up."

Now a different part of her body was doing a happy dance. "You're coming whether I agree or not, aren't you?"

His chuckle added the accompaniment for the pulse beating between her legs. "Now you're getting the idea."

She'd sworn never to have her decisions overruled by a man again. But that didn't mean she would be stupid when Tully suggested sensible precautions.

Especially when the prospect of seeing him made her body hum like a two-thousand-watt hair dryer.

Tully walked into Leland's computer lair, which was known as Mission Control due to its massive array of computer screens. "You should see the safe I found for the Meier house in Connecticut. It makes Fort Knox look like it's built out of tissue paper."

“That will make Mrs. Meier happy. All those diamonds to protect,” Leland said, just as Tully noticed there was a third person in the room.

“Hey, Tully!” Dawn swiveled her chair around, her glossy dark hair lit by the glow of the screens, and jumped up to give Tully a hug. Then she put her hands on her hips. “I’m going to stay with Natalie tonight.”

Behind her Leland shook his head. As if Tully needed that cue.

“Natalie won’t let you do that,” Tully said. “She’s concerned that you’d be in danger.”

“I’m an expert in self-defense.” Dawn was a personal trainer, but she also taught women to protect themselves from attack. “I can help.”

In addition, she was as tenacious as a bulldog.

“It’s not my call. I already suggested that Natalie stay with a friend and she refused because she didn’t want her stalker to target anyone else. So I sent a professional bodyguard to protect her.” Tully shrugged. “But if you think she’ll let you come . . .”

Leland gave Tully a thumbs-up behind Dawn’s back.

Dawn assessed Tully with a narrow-eyed stare. “You’d better not be messing with me.”

“Call her yourself,” he said.

Dawn flopped back down in the chair. “It sounds exactly like what Natalie would decide. She won’t budge if she thinks she’s protecting her friends. She can be stubborn.”

“Of course, you don’t have a stubborn bone in your body,” Leland said.

Dawn nudged his sneaker with hers. “And your slow southern drawl doesn’t fool any of us into thinking you’re a pushover.”

“There’s no lack of strong personalities in this room,” Tully said with a grin. “Keeps life interesting.”

“Is the bodyguard really good?” Dawn’s gaze was pinned on Tully again.

"One of my best." He propped his hip against a desk. "I'm also going to install some additional security cams at Natalie's house. Leland, I want to set up a feed that my people can monitor from here."

Leland looked at him with an odd half smile. "Why don't you let Jackson or Sarah take care of it? They just finished some continuing education on that very topic."

Tully was about to tell Leland to stuff it when he realized his partner was baiting him. "I need to check out the security at the salon too."

"Okay, I'll hook up the monitoring from this end," Leland said, his smile deepening.

Tully would have wiped the smirk off Leland's face with a few choice words if Dawn hadn't been present.

"I'm coming with you when you install the cams," she said. "I want to see how Nat is doing and meet this bodyguard."

"Let me ask you something," Tully said. "Did she tell you about the email messages?"

"No, and I'm not happy about that. She should have."

"Maybe she doesn't want you involved because it would add to her anxiety." Tully kept his voice gentle. "We don't know what this stalker is after yet, so it's risky introducing people Natalie cares about into the equation. It makes her more vulnerable, not less."

"But I'm her friend," Dawn said. "Friends are there for each other in bad situations."

"Do you trust me?" Tully looked at her straight on.

"Yes, but—"

"Then trust me."

Dawn held his gaze for a long moment. "All right, but I'm going to call her to see how she's doing."

"I'd be surprised if you didn't." Natalie was lucky to have such a fierce ally—just as lucky as he was to have his two partners. But then, Natalie helped women she barely knew. She would be an unwavering friend. "What do you know about Natalie's ex-husband?" he asked.

"You mean Matt the narcissistic douchebag?" Dawn's lips twisted into a grimace. "He's a pro at psychological abuse, so I could easily see him being a stalker."

"But he's left her alone for three years," Leland said. "So why now?"

"Good question," Tully agreed before he turned back to Dawn. "Would he hurt her physically?"

"Well, she always said he didn't hit her." Dawn considered for a moment. "It was more stuff like gaslighting. When no one else was around to hear it, he would criticize her in a horrible, nasty way. If she brought it up again, he would look at her like she was crazy and deny he'd ever said it. If she pushed harder, he would backpedal and claim he didn't *remember* saying it." Dawn looked thoughtful again. "That might have been even worse—to forget you'd said something so devastating."

Tully felt an urge to plant his fist in Matt Stevens's face.

Dawn continued. "He's very worried about what people think of him—he plays the funny, charming guy in public—so that might stop him from physical abuse. If he injured her, it could become public. He would hate that."

Dawn's analysis reinforced Natalie's, so Tully reduced his concern about her physical safety by half a degree. The ex's anxiety about public disgrace could also explain why he was working so hard to remain anonymous.

Assuming the stalker was the ex.

Tully had put an investigator on Stevens to see what might have sent him into stalker mode. Now he was thinking that he might pay a visit to Stevens himself just to get a vibe from the man.

"What about Natalie's sanctuary for abused wives?" Tully asked Dawn. "Anyone come to mind who might be so angry about his wife leaving him that he would punish Natalie for it?"

"I guess she had to tell you about that, but it's a big secret. It took her a year to trust me with it, so I don't think any of the ex-husbands know." Dawn rolled her shoulders. "If they did, yeah, they could be pissed off. One of them trained at the gym in Cofferwood, and he was a real lowlife. But I'd see him more confronting her and yelling than sneaking around writing cryptic emails."

"That's useful," Tully said with a nod of encouragement. "How about competitors? All the quotes are about beauty, so the stalker is referring to her work." Or her appearance. She was exactly as he'd told her: stunningly beautiful and sexy as hell.

"She'd know more about that than I would," Dawn said before she leaned forward. "But people respect her. She's really good at her job, and she hires people who are the same and then mentors them. Customers come from a couple of hours away to get their hair done at the Mane Attraction. That might make someone jealous, but would they stalk her because of it?"

"If they thought she was stealing business from them, they might," Leland said. "Money makes people do strange things."

A shadow crossed Dawn's face, and she reached for Leland's hand where it rested on the arm of his chair.

Tully suspected she was thinking of the arms dealer she and Leland had uncovered at the gym where Dawn once worked. They had nearly lost their lives as a result of their discovery.

"Okay, I'll let you get back to work." Dawn scooted her chair over to give Leland a quick kiss and stood. "I've got clients." She tossed a sassy glare at Tully. "And I'm going to call Nat."

After Dawn left, Leland said, "It doesn't sound like you're any closer to finding the stalker than you were before."

"My first priority is getting Natalie protected. That's handled. I've got investigators looking into her ex and the other possibly disgruntled ex-husbands."

"That's a lot of investigating." Leland's look implied a question.

"The SBI will take care of it." Tully crossed his arms.

Leland steepled his fingers. "Knowing Natalie, I'm surprised she will accept all this. She strikes me as a very independent woman."

"It's taken some persuasion." Tully shifted against the desk. "And she doesn't know about everything I've done."

Leland's eyebrows lifted. "You think she won't find out?"

"As long as we catch the stalker, I don't care."

His partner lifted one shoulder. "It's your funeral."

"As long as it's not hers."

Leland gave him a level look. "Agreed." Then he tilted his chair back. "Did you see the latest message from our favorite client?"

Tully pinched the bridge of his nose in frustration. "If you mean Henry Earnshaw at Dexcorp, yes. I'll set up *another* meeting to reassure him that his corporate security is state of the art." Tully gave a knife-edged smile. "But this time I'm going to charge him for my time. That may convince him that he's been reassured enough so he'll forgo the meeting."

Leland nodded his approval. "If we ever do another proposal for them, we'll build in an excessive meetings surcharge."

Tully snorted and pushed away from the desk. "No amount of money is worth dealing with Henry Earnshaw ever again."

Leland laughed as Tully walked out of the room.

He would have to get on the phone with Earnshaw before he could head to New Jersey. The delay in seeing Natalie just made him more irritated with the time-wasting senior vice president at Dexcorp. He couldn't even tell himself that he was worried about Natalie's safety, because he trusted Pam implicitly.

No, he just wanted to feel that buzz between them. It was like a drug that he had become addicted to.

Chapter 7

As Tully pulled into the parking lot next to the Mane Attraction, he surveyed the decorative shrubs under the salon windows and wished they didn't offer so much opportunity for concealment. There was no video camera on the wide front porch with its fancy carved railings. He knocked a code rhythm on one of the purple double doors. At least those were solid oak. Kicking them down would take some doing and make a hell of a racket.

Pam opened the door. "Hey, boss. I wasn't expecting you here."

"I wanted to check out the salon. Get the layout. Not that I don't trust your report." He smiled briefly before scanning the space. Through the right-hand archway, a big room held styling chairs, a seating area, a coffee bar . . . and many windows, tall and with multiple panes, spilling light onto the polished wood floor. At least Pam had reported that they all had alarm contacts. The place was neat as a pin, but he would expect nothing less from a business Natalie ran.

He pivoted to his left to look through the archway there. A small waiting area filled the front of the space. Bulky pedicure chairs sat along another multiwindowed wall, the tops of the damn shrubs blocking part of the view onto the parking lot. At the back were two doors opening into rooms furnished with what looked like massage tables, as well as a narrow hallway. Too many places a psychopath could hide.

"The hallway leads to Natalie's office," Pam said. "She's there now."

"Where's the latest communication from the stalker?"

Pam picked up a plastic bag from the reception desk. "I touched the upper-right corner but that's all."

"We won't get any prints anyway." Tully took the bag and scanned the message. "What do you make of all the sayings?"

"If she didn't own a beauty salon, I'd think this was a rejected admirer," she said. "But her job muddies the picture."

"Exactly." Tully flicked the paper back onto the desk. "Why don't you take time off until after dinner? Say, nine o'clock. I've got to install cameras at the house, so I'll be around anyway. It'll give you a few hours' break."

"My husband will love you. He just got back from a business trip."

"Why didn't you tell me that? I wouldn't have put you on this assignment if I'd known."

"Because then you wouldn't have put me on this assignment." She grinned as she exited.

Tully threw the dead bolt on the front door behind Pam. Savoring the sense of anticipation, he strode into the left-hand room and down the hallway.

When he got to the open door of the office, he knocked on the frame before he stepped in. Natalie sat at a desk with her back to the window, her short, sleek blonde hair painted with sunlight. She wore a simple white shirt unbuttoned just enough to tantalize his imagination with the shadows it cast in the V. He felt the now-familiar buzz vibrate through his body.

When she looked up from whatever she was reading, her blue eyes widened in surprise. "Tully! I thought you were coming to the house later."

"I wanted to take a look at the salon." He leaned his shoulder against the doorframe. "I can tell you've put a lot of thought into it. It's real nice."

She folded her hands on the desktop. "Thank you. I'm very fortunate that the previous owner took a liking to me when I worked for her. She sold the business to me when she retired."

He suspected that Natalie had earned it with her talent and hard work and not just luck. He sat down in one of the small blue chairs in front of her desk. "I gave Pam time off until after dinner."

"I'll be fine alone with all the equipment you're installing."

He shook his head. "Not happening. It's a subtle progression but the messages are becoming more threatening. The one you just got is from a fairy tale with an evil queen who tries to kill her stepdaughter."

Natalie's full lips tightened. He noticed that today she wore pink lipstick. He was still partial to the Natalie with no makeup—and no bra—of yesterday morning. "I thought I might have imagined that the quotations have become more menacing, but I guess not," she said.

"He's also escalated from email to hand delivery in two locations. He's showing that he knows your routine. That's a power play."

"What does he want from me?" Natalie asked, an undertone of anger and fear in her voice.

"I'd say your attention, but the anonymity undercuts that." Tully looked at her slender shoulders, her elegant hands, and the fine bone structure of her face. She should appear fragile, but instead she radiated strength. So he told her the truth. "He's trying to make you afraid. To keep you off-balance. The question is why."

Her hand went to her throat to fiddle with the fine silver chain she wore. What would the skin there feel like against his lips? Her blue eyes clouded. "I don't understand who would hate me enough to do this."

He didn't want to tell her that it could be a total stranger, a psychopath who had become fixated on her for no reason other than that she had crossed his path. And that she was beautiful.

He needed to stop thinking about her beauty.

"We'll figure it out soon," he said.

"I hope so because my conscience is already bothering me about how much time you're spending on my problem."

"Would it help if I told you that I'm doing this because I don't want to risk getting on Dawn's and Alice's bad side? They'd rip me to shreds if I let something happen to you." He gave her his best shit-eating grin.

For a moment she answered him with a cool, measuring look. Then the corners of her lips curled upward. "I'm not sure about Alice, but Dawn might kick your butt."

Her smile arrowed right down to his groin. "How much longer do you need here?" he asked.

"Honestly, my concentration is shot," she said with a glance at the laptop in front of her. "I might as well admit it and go home."

A door slammed at the back of the salon and Tully tensed. "Who's that?"

When footsteps sounded on the stairs that ran up the wall beside her office, she said, "It must be Deion. He rents the apartment upstairs."

"Let's go talk to him. See if he's noticed anything out of the ordinary around here." Another long shot, but some people observed more than they realized. It just took the right questions to draw the knowledge out of them.

Tully shifted into what Natalie had come to think of as "FBI mode." His eyes took on a glint of purpose, the angle of his jaw hardened, and he exuded a coiled energy that sent a sexual thrill zinging down to her belly. She forced her gaze back to her laptop, shutting down the accounting program and closing the computer.

"Give me a quick background sketch on your tenant," Tully said.

Natalie pulled her focus back to Deion. "He's young—in his midtwenties. He works a lot of odd hours at the Harper Court Mall selling men's suits. He's saving up to travel to Patagonia because he's an outdoor lover. As a landlord, I couldn't ask for a better tenant. He keeps his place immaculate and always pays the rent on time."

He also had been arrested for shoplifting when he was a teenager. The social worker he'd been assigned was one of Natalie's clients, and she was the one who'd suggested Deion as a tenant when the apartment became vacant. Natalie admired him for working hard to change his life, so she'd rented to him for below market rate. However, she wasn't going to share all that information with Tully.

"How long has he lived here?" Tully asked, his attention focusing like a laser.

"About eight months." She gave him back an equally level gaze. "He's not my stalker."

Tully held up his hands. "I didn't say he was."

"You have that look in your eyes." She stood up. Deion didn't need to deal with being treated like a suspect.

He nodded and rose, standing aside in her small office so she could go through the door first. "Actually, I want to recruit him," Tully said. "Everyone around you should know about the stalker so they can keep an eye out for someone who behaves strangely. He's an excellent candidate because he's familiar with what's normal around the salon at all different times of day."

Natalie felt a pang of guilt for misjudging Tully's intentions. "I hate people knowing about this whole stalker thing. It's so . . . melodramatic. Sometimes I think I must be imagining it."

She'd felt that way about some of the things Matt had said and done to her as well. She was just an average, everyday person. How did she get involved in these crazy situations? What did she do to attract such awful people? The questions shook her and she inhaled sharply.

Tully stepped in front of her and pivoted, his head tilted downward so she could easily look into his eyes. "You're *not* imagining it. Your reality has just shifted for a short time because you are the victim of a crime. This is not melodrama. This is real."

"I hate that word, 'victim.' I don't ever want to be a victim." *Again.* She'd allowed Matt to crush her into a person she barely recognized. She refused to let that happen to her now for any reason.

Tully cupped his hands over her shoulders, their strength and warmth seeping through her blouse to her skin. "Bad choice of word. You're the stalker's target, his prey. But prey can be smart and lead the predator into a trap."

The concern that softened his face brought a prickle of tears to her eyes. She blinked them back hard. "Then let's set that trap."

He dropped his hands, the loss of his touch more noticeable than she wanted it to be. "We're working on it." He fell into step beside her, his gaze sweeping back and forth as they walked down the hallway beside the front staircase and through the door to the kitchen. He winced. "I hate french doors. They're worse than sliders."

Natalie smiled. "Pam wasn't crazy about them either. But they're alarmed and there's a glass-break detector in the corner there." She pointed.

He just shook his head. She knew he was thinking what Pam had voiced—that the alarm only discouraged amateur thieves. Someone who really wanted to get in would know that it took at least ten minutes for the phone calls to go out and the police to arrive.

"It's not as though I sleep here, you know," she pointed out, opening the door to the back foyer. The back stairs were narrow, so she went ahead of Tully, marveling at the fact that her footsteps made more noise on the oak treads than his, despite his cowboy boots. By the time they reached the landing where the steps turned, her whole back fizzed with a delicious tingling. She could almost feel his eyes resting on her. She had to control her primitive urge to put an extra sway in her hips.

She knocked and turned her head to watch Tully's reaction to his first sight of Deion. She heard the door open and caught the slight widening of Tully's eyes before she looked at her tenant.

Deion was flat-out gorgeous and the sight of him never got old. He had huge brown eyes, glorious high cheekbones, a perfect jawline, and spectacular dreadlocks. Since he'd just come from work, he was still wearing one of the tailored suits that emphasized his trim, fit build, although he'd discarded the necktie.

"Hey, Nat," Deion said while eyeing Tully warily. "What's up?"

"This is my"—she stumbled over what to call him—"friend, Tully Gibson. He's helping me with a problem I have. May we come in?"

"Sure." Deion led them into the living area, which was furnished with the inexpensive furniture Natalie had left behind when she moved to her new house. Except Deion had rearranged things and added little decorative touches that jazzed it up. "You want something to drink?"

"We're good," Natalie said, sitting on the beige sofa while Tully took the knockoff of a Danish modern chair, and Deion sat on an overstuffed ottoman. "I need your help with a . . . well, an issue in my life."

Deion nodded. "Sure. Anything you want."

"I have a stalker," Natalie said.

"A what?!" Deion rocked back on his ottoman. "Like what kind of stalker?"

"He—we think it's a man—started out by sending me emails," Natalie explained, "but now he's taken to delivering letters. One was put under the door here at the salon."

"Shit!" Deion winced. "Sorry."

"I've heard the word before," Natalie said. "And it's exactly the way I feel."

"What kind of messages?" Worry creased Deion's forehead. "Like threats?"

Tully spoke for the first time. "Sayings about beauty. Not overt threats but delivered in a menacing way. Have you noticed any people hanging around the salon who seemed out of place or were here at an unusual time of day?"

Deion tugged on one of his dreads as he considered the question. "I can't think of anyone, but I haven't been paying close attention. Now I will."

Tully smiled. "That's what I was hoping you'd say. If you see someone suspicious, don't approach him or her," Tully warned.

"I'll take a photo with my phone," Deion said. "I want to catch this motherf . . . monster. I don't want anyone hurting you, Natalie."

"No photos if he can see you. I don't want you to get hurt either," Natalie said, her heart touched by his desire to protect her.

"She's right. Don't draw attention to yourself." Tully looked around the stylish apartment. "You've got a good eye for detail. Just memorize the face and any other distinguishing characteristics so you can describe it all later. Get a license plate number if there's a car." He took out a business card and handed it to Deion. "Anything at all, any time at all, you call *me*."

Natalie caught the emphasis on the last word. Tully didn't want her to get the news first. It irritated her but it made sense. He would have a better idea of what to do.

"No one's going to bother her when I'm around." Deion's beautiful face was taut with resolve.

"I'm counting on that." Tully pushed up from the chair and held out his hand.

Deion rose with his usual grace and gripped Tully's hand. Natalie saw one of those looks pass between them that meant "We men will protect our women." It was very caveman, yet it caused her heart to do a little flip. It was her safety they were joining forces to ensure, so how could she object to that?

Chapter 8

"Deion's a good guy," Tully said as they walked back into the kitchen. "Why the hell is he selling suits instead of modeling them? He could make a fortune."

"He says he doesn't want to depend on his looks for a job. He's a fantastic salesman and earns the highest commission payout in the store virtually every month."

"I have news for him—people buy suits from him because they hope they'll look like him when they wear them."

Natalie chuckled. "That's a partial truth but his boss says he's amazing at upselling. He doesn't stand around and pose to make that money."

"You said he likes the outdoors?"

"He does intense activities like free climbing and sleeping in a hammock clipped to a cliff face."

"Hmm, I might have a job for him at KRG." Tully went over to the french doors and inspected the lock with a disapproving frown. "I feel better knowing he's fully informed about your problem."

"Would you really hire him?" She would love to see Deion get a better job.

Tully swung around. "He'd be a great asset. He likes a physical challenge and he's got the protective instinct."

Excitement bubbled up inside her until she remembered Deion's record. "There's something I didn't tell you. He was arrested for shoplifting more than once when he was a teenager. Your fancy clients might not be happy about his past if they found out."

A grimace twisted Tully's lips, and Natalie's heart sank. "You said he got in trouble for shoplifting. No drugs, no violence, no gangs, right?"

"Definitely not," Natalie said.

Tully shrugged. "I did a lot of stupid and illegal things when I was a teenager. The only difference is that I didn't get caught. I won't hold some adolescent shoplifting against him."

Profound gratitude—and surprise—welled up inside her. She would have understood if Tully had rescinded his offer. He had KRG's reputation to protect. His willingness to give Deion a chance melted a barrier. "I expected you to have been an Eagle Scout."

"Not even close." Tully's voice was flat. "I was never good at following rules."

"Yet you joined the FBI."

"A miscalculation." He stared past her into some memory before he shook his head. "I wasn't cut out to work in a bureaucracy. But that's history. Let's head out."

He escorted her back to her office to collect her laptop and purse. She didn't stop him—not because she was afraid but because she savored the occasional brush of a hand or shoulder as they maneuvered down the narrow hall. Even better was the brief press of his palm against the small of her back when he wanted her to go in front of him through the doorway. She could read new feelings into that moment of contact—protectiveness, compassion, and bone-deep decency. That small touch rippled through her body and then deeper, where she didn't want to feel it.

"I'm just going to check that everything is secure," he said as they came back into the front hall. He put her laptop case, which he had taken from her, on the reception desk and prowled through the salon, examining window latches, testing the front door, and sweeping his gaze around the rooms. She shifted her position so she could watch him, his body encased in jeans and a dark-green T-shirt, his male presence a striking contrast to the feminine decor. When he ran his fingers over a cracked windowpane, she imagined them skimming over her bare skin. That sent a bloom of arousal through her body.

He pivoted and caught her staring. In a startling change from his flurry of purposeful motion, he went entirely still, his gaze locked with hers.

She should have looked away but she didn't have the willpower.

She swallowed and he moved again, coming toward her with a different kind of purpose.

"Nat?" he asked as he stopped two feet away from her, his eyes scanning her face with a heat she knew was answered in hers.

She stepped into him, pressing her hands against the cotton of his shirt so she could feel the wall of his chest muscles underneath. "Yes."

But he moved back so her hands hung in thin air as he shook his head. "You're just scared."

"That's the thing. I'm not scared at all." She should be. Not of her stalker, but of her desire to have this man kiss her.

She closed the distance between them and ran her hands up his chest to rest on the hard curves of his shoulders, tilting her face up and waiting. He let her stand that way for a stretched-out moment as if he expected her to change her mind.

She held on to her patience. Why had he decided to have an attack of scruples just when she'd gotten hers to shut up?

She breathed a silent sigh of relief when his hands came up to rest just above her hips. Then he lowered his mouth to hers so slowly that she could see tiny details on his face. A small scar at the corner of his right eyebrow. The striations of silver, black, and gray in his irises. The faint glint of whiskers along his jaw line.

Her breathing grew shallow as his lips touched hers with a light pressure, almost a question. She leaned in, pleasure running through her veins like lightning as her breasts met his chest.

No longer were his hands gentle on her waist. Now one cupped her head and the other slid down to palm her butt, bringing her hard against him. And his mouth! He angled it to fit hers, teasing with his tongue, grazing with the edge of his teeth. She opened her lips to flirt with that tongue, making him moan, the sound spiraling down between her legs.

His fingers massaged her scalp, threading into her hair, while he shifted so his thigh was between hers. The friction against the V between her legs made her gasp and arch her neck backward.

He bent farther so he could drag his lips down her bared throat, swirling his tongue in the indent at the base. Her nerve endings danced with arousal. "Yes!" she said, digging her fingers into his shoulders and pushing her hips against his thigh. She couldn't believe how close she was to an orgasm.

His mouth was on hers again in a too-brief, too-soft kiss before he raised his head. His eyes blazed as he gave her a crooked smile. "Nat, I want like hell to keep going, but I need to be sure you're not just . . . reacting to the situation."

"My reaction is to you and only you." She was a little pissed that he would imply she didn't know her own mind.

"I like that answer." His smile went scorching. "But let's take this back to your house where it's more comfortable."

She could see that his decision was made. Maybe her common sense would reassert itself on the drive home.

No, her body was humming with anticipation in a way she hadn't felt for years. Just this once, she wasn't going to let good judgment and bad experiences interfere with that.

When his hand stayed on her butt, she let a satisfied little smile curl her lips.

His eyes narrowed. "What's the joke?"

"You haven't let go of me."

"Because I don't want to." However, he gave her bottom a squeeze and slid his hands off her. "I've been waiting a long time to do that."

"How long?" she fished.

"Let's just say that six months of wedding planning have had their bonuses."

"So all those meetings with the wedding party weren't only to get the logistics worked out?" More heat poured through her veins at the revelation of his long-standing attraction.

He lifted an eyebrow. "I work at one of the world's top consulting firms. We could have organized that wedding in twenty-four hours flat. Well, maybe not the dress stuff."

She laughed.

He took her wrist to pull her against his side and hold her there before he grabbed her laptop. "Let's head out the back. I want to take another look at those french-door locks."

"That's what got me hot and bothered the first time," she said, enjoying the power of his arm around her waist as they walked toward the kitchen. "You're sexy when you go into security mode."

His grip tightened fractionally. "I'll keep that in mind." His voice held the edge of a rasp.

He released her long enough to let her set the alarm and lock the kitchen dead bolt behind them. But his arm went back around her for the short walk to her car, giving her the double buzz of his protectiveness and his hard-muscled body moving against hers.

She hit the unlock button on her key and turned to stand on her tiptoes for a quick kiss to tide her over for the drive home. Even that brief contact zinged into her private places.

When she opened the door and leaned in to sling her bag across to the passenger seat, she hissed in a breath.

A hand mirror just like the lavender-framed ones she used in her salon lay on the driver's seat. The reflective glass was webbed with cracks and a few of the smaller fragments lay on the leather seat.

"Did you leave that there?" Tully asked, his voice harsh from behind her.

"No!" she said as fear clawed at her chest. "How did he get into my car?" She swung around to look at Tully. "We were in the salon the whole time. Why didn't we hear the car alarm?"

He took her by the shoulders and gently shifted her away from the open door before he inspected the lock. "First, are you sure you locked the car?"

"I always lock it." But it was so automatic, she didn't remember doing it this time in particular. "Pam was here, so she would have noticed if I hadn't."

"Did you use your key fob to lock it?"

"Yes, of course. How else would I do it?"

Tully leaned into the car and snapped some photos with his phone. "He probably had a code reader and picked up your code when you pressed the button on your fob."

"It's that easy? Why do we bother to have locks?" Her stalker had been inside her car. A shudder ran through her at the violation.

"If you lock the car manually, they can't steal the code." He straightened. "There won't be any prints, but I'm going to call one of my investigators to double-check. He had to touch more than one surface to plant the mirror there." He used his elbow to close the door. "Go ahead and lock it again."

She hit the button on the fob and the car beeped at her.

"Let's get you out of here," he said, putting his arm around her and guiding her to his hulking black SUV.

He held her hand to help her up the high step into the car. It was hard to let go of him once she slid onto the black leather seat. After he closed the door, the silence in the car seemed thick and ominous. Yet when he opened the driver's door, the normal, everyday sounds of cars and birds and rustling leaves made her sense of being trapped in a bad dream even worse.

He must have felt her tension, because he turned to her. "Are you okay?"

"I'm fine," she lied. "I just hate the idea that the stalker was *in* my car. It gives me the willies."

He reached across the console to squeeze her hand where it clutched her purse. "He knows that. Our car becomes an extension of our bodies, so he's deliberately invaded your personal space."

"He's also made a mockery of my idea that locks will keep him away." There. She'd said it. She felt helpless in the face of her tormenter.

"Car locks are easy," Tully said, his fingers still wrapped around hers. "He can't get past your home and salon security systems like that."

"I place more confidence in you and Pam," she said.

He smiled in a way that flooded her with heat because it wasn't just an "I will protect you because that's my job" smile. It was an "I will protect you because I lust after you" smile. That worked even better to chase away her terror.

He released her hand but kept his eyes on her face. "Don't freak out but I'm going to take my gun out of its safe. As a precaution. Nothing more."

She nodded and he pressed his thumb to a square set into the console, where a lid lifted and folded down. He reached into the opening and extracted a dull black handgun, pulling back the slide and checking something before he set it back in the safe, leaving the lid open.

"That makes it seem scarier," Natalie said. The gun added a third presence in the car.

"I don't expect to need it," Tully said, bringing the engine to life with a rumble. "It's just a habit from my FBI days."

As he deftly maneuvered the big SUV onto the street, Natalie tried to wrap her mind around the strangeness of her life. Her car broken into, a broken mirror left as a threat, a loaded gun stowed within a few inches of her hand. How the hell had this happened?

Her hands began to tremble, so she fisted them around the straps of her handbag. "I don't want to live this way," she said. "We have to find him and stop him."

"We will." Tully's tone was grim but steely. "Trust me." A muscle ticked in his jaw.

She did trust him, but she felt like the shards of broken glass in her car were slicing through her, leaving an open wound of fear. It was a different intensity from the daily grinding trepidation of living with Matt. What wasn't different was the strain of never knowing when the next shock would occur. The constant tension wound her shoulders and neck into a knot of nerves.

"Have you had any luck tracking Regina Van Houten? I'm a little worried about her."

"We found a used-car dealer in Pennsylvania who sold her a junker for cash several days ago but nothing after that. She's done a good job of disappearing."

Natalie had helped with that, cutting Regina's long, thick blonde hair into a nondescript style and dying it an unremarkable brown. What was hard to disguise was her height since she stood close to six feet tall. She'd practiced slouching while she stayed with Natalie.

"I wonder if she has friends in Nebraska who she might go to," Natalie said.

"That's a long drive. You really changed her appearance, by the way. The only reason the car dealer remembered her was because she had the same kind of designer handbag his wife wanted for her birthday."

"Damn! I told her not to use that Gucci bag but she wouldn't leave it behind," Natalie said. "She said it was the first piece of designer anything she'd ever owned. But I feel better hearing your pro can't find her. That means she's safe from her husband."

He threw her a sharp look. "Don't assume that. Her husband knows far more about her than we do. He may have a better idea of where to look. How bad was he to her?"

"Awful. I offered her my guest room when I saw bruises on her wrists, but she didn't take me up on it for a couple of months. She left when Dobs dragged her to the top of the stairs and threatened to throw her down them and then claim she'd fallen. He said no one would question his version of the story." Natalie grimaced. "He kept her isolated, only socializing with his little circle of friends, so she figured he might get away with it."

His knuckles went white as he gripped the steering wheel. "I hate domestic abuse. It's hard to prove even when you know damn well it's happening."

Natalie looked down at the tense shape her hands had twisted into. It was even worse when you didn't realize you were being abused until it was almost too late.

"Sorry," Tully said, glancing down at her pretzeled fingers. "I didn't mean to hit so close to home."

"No apology necessary. That's behind me." But it never was. She still questioned her judgment. Including about Tully.

He swung the car into her driveway and stopped. "Let me have your keys so I can check the house."

She unhooked the keys from the ring in her purse and handed them to him. "The alarm code is 2-5-9-5-8."

Then Tully did something that sent a shock through her. He took the gun out of the safe.

Chapter 9

As soon as Tully exited the car, the locks clicked shut with a beep. Natalie watched him tuck the terrifying gun into the back of his jeans and stride past the front porch steps, his head swiveling as he scanned the surroundings. Watching him do his job with such expert intensity, she felt that familiar deep, primitive pull low in her belly. It twined with the fear, leaving her slightly breathless.

When he disappeared around the corner, she surveyed her house too. There was no stark rectangle of white paper visible on the porch, so she breathed more easily. Of course, now the stalker was leaving objects, so his latest gift might be on the back patio or tucked behind the screen door. But Tully would find it first and that would lessen the shock for her.

He came around the garage and mouthed, "All good," before he walked onto the porch, his jeans stretching tight over the muscles of his thighs as he climbed the steps. He examined the porch thoroughly before he pulled her keys out of his pocket and disappeared inside the house.

She felt exposed and vulnerable in the car, despite the locked doors. She was almost afraid to look around for fear the stalker would loom up at one of the windows.

To break her own tension, she spoke out loud. "It would be *good* if the stalker showed up. Then Tully could catch him and stop the torment."

The sound of her voice steadied her. As did imagining Tully searching every room in the house to make sure she was safe. Until Tully walked back onto the porch with that smooth panther's stride of his, looking hard and fearless and sexy as hell. Desire overlapped dread, so she couldn't tell which one had a stronger hold on her.

She closed her eyes as she remembered how his big masculine hand had looked splayed on top of her velvet comforter.

Desire overwhelmed all else, sending a bolt of arousal through her body.

When he opened her car door, she wanted to hurl herself into his arms, to wrap herself in his strength and warmth. Instead, she took his hand to climb down from the SUV as though his presence was merely a convenience.

"The house appears undisturbed," he said. "Not surprising, since he was focused on the salon and your car today."

"I'd ask how he knows so much about my routine, but it's not hard for someone to figure it out." She made a wry face. "I don't vary it much. Or ever." She liked her predictable schedule. The salon gave her plenty of social interaction, after which she could retreat to the serenity of her quiet house to recharge.

He held the front door for her. "Exactly the opposite of what we advise our high-profile clients to do. They take different routes to work every day in different vehicles. They leave and come home at variable times. Predictability is a kidnapper's—and a stalker's—best friend."

"I'd hate to be that rich and famous," she said, dropping her purse on the foyer table while he locked the door. "Alice says even you and your partners take certain precautions."

He placed her laptop case beside her purse. "Mostly because I'm professionally paranoid. And in some cases, I've been right."

She'd just been making conversation until his hands were free. As he turned away from the foyer, she stepped into him so their bodies touched from knee to chest and skimmed her fingers up the ridged muscles of his arms and over his shoulders to tangle in the rough silk of his hair.

His eyes lit up as she lifted her face and tried to tug his head downward. But he stood straight with his arms at his sides again.

"Nat, I know we started something back at the salon, but I need to make sure I'm not taking advantage of what's going on." He cupped her shoulders to move her a few inches away from him. "Fear activates the fight-or-flight instinct. If you can't fight and you can't flee, the energy has to go somewhere."

If she hadn't felt him harden against her before he pushed her away, she might have considered this a rejection. "I know what I want," she said, feathering her fingers along the rim of his ear. "I've known since we danced the two-step at the wedding."

His eyebrows went up. "You hid it well."

Because she had been battling against it with every ounce of her common sense. "I needed to be sure of who you are."

"Sweetheart, you don't know anything about me." Shadows dimmed the blaze of his eyes.

"I know enough to do this." She stood on the tiptoes of her ballerina flats and managed to reach his lips, flicking her tongue along the lower curve of the bottom one.

With a deep groan, he yanked her against him and lowered his mouth to hers. She felt like dry tinder touched by a torch as flames seared through her, turning liquid between her thighs.

He wrapped one arm around her shoulders and banded the other across her waist so that she felt engulfed by his body. Her nipples hardened against his chest, the pressure sending exquisite sensation sizzling along her nerves. She could smell the clean cotton of his shirt, the woodsy scent of his soap, and the deeply masculine tang of arousal on his skin.

He slid a hand up her back to tilt her head so he could kiss the soft spot behind her ear before he blew a breath on it. She arched into him as a delicious tingle danced over her skin. When her pelvis pushed into his erection, he moaned her name before he splayed his other hand over her butt and sank his fingers into the soft flesh to hold her hard against him.

She bent her knee and skimmed it up the outside of his thigh to press herself against the length of his cock outlined by the denim of his jeans. "The sofa," she gasped as sparks shimmered through her belly.

"The bed. I want to do this right." He tugged the gun out of his waistband and placed it on the table beside her purse. Even the grim reminder of her stalker couldn't dim her desire.

Hooking one hand under her thigh, he lifted it higher. She took the hint and hopped so he could catch her other leg and bring it around his waist. Locking her ankles behind his back, she wound her arms around his neck to hold on as he headed for the stairs.

"Are you sure you can carry me up a whole flight of stairs?" she asked as he planted his boot on the first step.

"I could jog up the stairs with you, but I don't want to make you nervous." He squeezed her thigh as he walked steadily upward, his lips curling into a cocky smile.

"Am I supposed to swoon now?"

"That would be damn inconvenient since I want you awake and responsive for what I'm planning next."

Anticipation bubbled through her like champagne. "Then don't be so manly."

He took one step past the top of the stairs before he locked eyes with her. "I'm pretty sure manly is a requirement here."

"Good point. Keep moving, cowboy." She tightened her legs around his waist and he started toward her bedroom.

“I’m tempted to make a bad pun about riding, but I don’t want to ruin the mood,” he said.

The mental image of her astride his naked body made her hiss in a breath of anticipation. “I think you just improved my mood.”

He strode through the door and laid her down across the bed, bracing his hands on either side of her shoulders so that his biceps swelled under his T-shirt. He stood between her thighs and stared down at her. “God, you’re amazing.”

She reached up to brush her fingers over his short-cropped hair, wishing it were longer so she could better feel the texture of it. “I want to *feel* amazing,” she said, dropping her hands to unbutton her blouse.

He took one of her wrists and tugged it away. “That’s my job.”

“I’m just trying to move things along.” The ache between her legs intensified as her craving to feel his hands on her built with every touch.

He put one knee on the bed beside her hip, his weight making the mattress dip. “Some things need time. This is one.” He slipped his fingers around her rib cage so that his thumbs rested on her nipples. He began to stroke in slow circles, moving the silk of her blouse over the lace of her bra with an exquisite friction that made her arch up for more. The man knew what he was doing and she appreciated that.

“Beautiful,” he breathed as her nipples hardened to points of need.

He increased the pressure and she gasped as electric desire shot down to her belly. Then his fingers were at her buttons, swiftly opening the blouse and easing her bra up to expose her breasts. He leaned down to suck one sensitized nipple into his mouth while he cupped the other in his big hand. She grabbed fistfuls of the quilt as the heat and the wet and the suction on her skin twisted the coil of longing tight inside her.

“More,” she begged, pushing her breast farther into his mouth.

He let her feel just the slightest scrape of his teeth—adding an edge of intensity to the sensations ricocheting through her—before he skimmed his hand down to the top of her thighs. She gave him enough room to work his fingers down where she wanted them and then she rocked her hips into his hand. He rubbed hard, his strength compressing the denim against her throbbing clit.

"Yes! Yes! Yes!" she breathed as everything fed into the pinpoint of pure longing deep down in her body. He pulled on her nipple with his mouth and wedged his hand tighter against her and then she exploded into orgasm, bowing up from the bed as her muscles and nerves convulsed with the power of her release. Then she convulsed again and a third time before she collapsed back down onto the bed, delicious aftershocks shivering through her.

When she opened her eyes, Tully was lying on his side next to her, his head propped on one hand, looking down at her with a bemused smile quirking the corners of his lips.

"You'll have to go slowly with the next one," she said. "That one couldn't wait."

"It's good to take the edge off." He leaned over to kiss her. "And that was very, very hot."

She could feel his erection against her hip, so she believed him. She smiled and reached up to trace the scar in his eyebrow while satisfaction hummed through her lax body. "Where did that come from? Chasing bad guys?"

The corners of his eyes crinkled. "Falling off a horse when I was thirteen. I hit a fence post on the way down."

"Ouch." She saw a jagged patch of scar tissue she hadn't noticed before low on the side of his neck. She touched it. "And this one?"

He grimaced. "That was from a bad guy."

She followed the edges with her fingertip. "Not a bullet, I hope."

"A broken bottle. Surprising what a good weapon that makes." He took her hand and kissed her palm. "I should warn you that there are a few more under my clothes."

"I'm not surprised, given what you do for a living." She slid her hand under his T-shirt, running her palm over his abdomen before she gave him a siren smile. "I'd like to find out where the rest of them are."

"All you have to do is ask." Using those impressive abdominal muscles, he curled his body up just enough to get his back off the bed, crossed his arms in front of him, and yanked his shirt up over his head before he settled back onto his side.

His chest was lightly furred with brown hair that arrowed down to his waistband. His abs were ridged exactly like a washboard, and he had those sexy indentations that came around each hip before swooping toward his groin.

She whistled. "Well, that's quite a sight." His massive shoulders were sculpted with muscle that flexed and jumped as she touched the warm skin.

There were scars too, but nothing shocking, as though he'd managed to dodge the worst of whatever came at him. "I won't ask," she said as she ran her finger over a two-inch-long line that slashed across two ribs, surprised at how much the thought of his pain bothered her.

"As long as you keep touching, I'll tell you anything you want."

She rolled onto her side and kissed the scar. When she ran her tongue along the raised skin of the old wound, he sucked in a harsh breath. "What about the ones under your jeans?" she asked against his skin.

His laugh was part groan. "You have a unique way of getting a man to undress."

"It's working, isn't it?"

She reached for his belt buckle but he dodged her hands and stood to pull off his boots and strip away his jeans and briefs. His erection stood high and proud above the carved stretch of his powerful thighs.

The longing to have him inside her surged like a tidal wave. She pushed upright to slide off her blouse and unhook her bra.

As the lacy fabric fell away, he curved his palms under her breasts to lift them. "I could spend hours just enjoying these," he said, his gaze locked on them. The bruises Matt had left on her confidence faded under his obvious admiration.

"I'm hoping you can enjoy two things at once." She grabbed his biceps to pull herself to her feet and unbuttoned her jeans.

"Sweetheart, let me have the pleasure." He drew down her zipper and peeled the denim down her hips and legs, leaving her pink-lace panties in place. She kicked off her flats so she could step out of the jeans he held for her. Then he knelt in front of her so he was at eye level with her navel.

She held her breath as he hooked his fingers in the waistband of her panties and slowly dragged them down her thighs, her calves, and her ankles to pool on the floor, his fingers leaving a trail of phantom fire over her skin.

He brushed his palms up her legs to her butt, which he cupped hard to bring her closer so he could kiss one hip bone before he moved his mouth lower. When he kissed her just above her mound, his touch seemed to spiral down to the craving within her.

"Sit on the bed," he said, his breath whispering over her skin. "I want to taste you."

She sat and leaned back on her hands. He pushed her knees apart so he could find her clit with his tongue, flicking it and then sucking on it before he slipped the tip of his tongue inside her. The pleasure of it sent fireworks bursting through her. "Oh, God, Tully!" she moaned as she fell backward onto the bed because her arms wouldn't hold her up any longer. "Please, yes!"

He huffed a warm gust of air against her before he pulled at her clit again, making her spine arch upward. She had just climaxed, yet here was a new one building.

She sat up and reached down to pull his head away from her. "I want you inside me when I come."

"I love a demanding woman," he said, looking up at her with a glaze of lust over his face even as he grinned. He reached for his jeans and fished a condom out of his wallet.

She held out her hand. He ripped the envelope open with his teeth and handed it to her before he rose to his impressive height. His cock tempted her into licking the salty little bead of semen off the tip and then putting her mouth over the head to flick her tongue against it.

When she sucked at him, he inhaled sharply before he pulled out of her mouth. "You might want to put that condom on now," he said, his voice hoarse.

She smiled to herself as she rolled the condom down the length of him. He wasn't as patient as he claimed to be. She gave him an extra stroke as proof.

Before she realized what was happening, he had seized her waist and moved her toward the center of the bed as though she weighed nothing. He followed her, driving one knee between her thighs and then using the other to spread them so he could fit his hips in their V. He laced his fingers with hers beside her head and braced himself over her on his forearms, his chest just grazing the hard tips of her nipples so the hair tickled deliciously.

He eased his cock inside her, her wetness allowing him to slide deeper. He was big, and she hadn't had sex in three years, so she felt the stretch and reveled in it. The hollowness was filled and her nerve endings danced with electric delight.

"Are you good?" he asked.

"So good!" She rocked her hips to prove it.

He began to move slowly, pulling nearly all the way out before plunging back in. The hard length of him felt so perfect within her she felt tears filling her eyes. She blinked them back because she knew he would stop if he thought he was hurting her. And she did not want him to stop. A light, wonderful feeling was blooming inside her.

Except he did stop, driving into her and then curling himself down enough to find her nipple with his lips. When he sucked it into his mouth and rolled his tongue over it, she felt like a pinball machine being lit up by a ball careening in every direction. "Yes! Like that!"

He shifted to her other breast, pulling hard on it so her muscles spasmed around his cock.

That drew a groan from him that vibrated right through her. He released her nipple and locked his eyes on her face while he began to thrust again, this time faster and harder.

The motion ratcheted her arousal higher and higher.

"Come for me, baby," he commanded. "I want to watch you come."

She wrapped her legs around his hips to tilt her pelvis against him. When he drove in, he hit her clit and she shrieked as every molecule of her body contracted and then blew apart, her muscles pulsing around him.

"Oh yeah, Nat!" he shouted as he pumped inside her, the tendons of his neck taut with exertion.

They arched and shuddered in unison, their bodies locked together as they propelled each other to climax and then melted back onto the bed, lax with release. Tully's full weight came down on her for a second before he rolled to the side, bringing her with him to rest on top of his rock-hard body. She closed her eyes and rested her cheek on his chest, the bang of his heartbeat loud against her ear.

"That was really something, sweetheart," he said, blowing out a long breath and stroking one hand down the length of her back to rest on her buttock, his palm warm against her bare skin.

"Define 'something.'" She smiled without opening her eyes.

"The hottest sex I've ever had in my life," he said without missing a beat.

She found that hard to believe, but it was gentlemanly of him to say so. "Ditto."

He pretended to be insulted. "*Ditto?!* That's the best you can do?"

"Brain fried. Can't form sentences."

His chuckle rumbled through her. "Good recovery."

It felt so good to be skin to skin with this man, the angles and curves of his body pressing against hers in interesting ways. She grazed her fingers over the hair sprinkled across his chest, the texture uniquely masculine somehow. Or maybe that was just because the hair was attached to an overwhelmingly male body. The outside of his thigh lay against the inside of hers so she could feel the hard bulge of muscle there. And he radiated a delicious heat that made her nestle into him.

His other arm wrapped across her back. "You cold, sweetheart?"

"Not with you under me," she said.

He chuckled. "I run a little hot."

"It feels good. You feel good." She wanted to lie there—her body sated and relaxed—for as long as she could.

His stomach growled.

"Ignore that," he said.

"You're hungry."

"Only for you." He gave her butt a squeeze.

She propped her hands on his chest and lifted her head to look at him. "Did you have lunch?"

He squinted in thought. "I don't remember."

"That's a no. Let's get you something to eat." She tried to sit up but he didn't release her.

"Give it a few minutes," he said. "I like having a blanket of satisfied woman draped over me."

"You need to keep your strength up so we can do, er, *this* again." But she settled back down onto his chest.

"I don't need food to do this again." He kissed the top of her head. "You inspire me to superhuman efforts."

"Superhuman? You think highly of your skills," she teased.

"Only when combined with yours." He was silent a moment before he said, "It makes me real happy that you want to do *this* again."

"Did you think I was a one-hit wonder?"

"No, ma'am. Just that I'm one lucky cowboy."

She laughed and let herself relax into him again. When was the last time she'd felt this good in a man's arms? Matt had stopped holding her after sex years ago. He would finish and roll to his side of the bed, leaving her to bring herself to orgasm. He told her it was her fault that he found her so sexually uninteresting that he couldn't be bothered with her pleasure.

The insidious sense of failure began to creep through her again, twining its ugly black tentacles through her mind and soul, so she shoved Matt back into the box she'd built for him. The black tentacles weren't as easy to remove. Except when Tully was looking at her like she was the best thing since sliced bread.

Bread. Tully needed to eat. "Okay, cowboy, let's get you fed."

He sat up, hauling her with him. "I can cook for myself."

"We'll make it a joint effort." She leaned off the bed to scoop up her panties and jeans from the floor.

"Nothing could taste as good as you," he rumbled against her skin before he kissed her shoulder.

"And I'm low cal too," she joked, but pleasure swooped through her. He chuckled and bent to pick up his clothes. She admired the expanse of skin that rippled over the flexing muscles in his back. "I don't suppose I could convince you to leave off the shirt."

"As long as I don't have to stand over a frying pan."

"I promise to do all the frying." She skimmed her panties up her legs and stood to put on her jeans. She looked around for her bra.

"Can I make the same deal with you?" he asked with an interested gleam in his eyes.

She laughed. "Not if I'm cooking."

He stood up behind her and snaked his arms around her rib cage to cup her breasts, sending another shot of pleasure sparkling into her core. "I could protect your bare skin from splatter like this."

"Nice try, but you just wanted to cop a feel." She brushed his hands away with a certain reluctance.

"Busted." True to his word, he dressed in just his briefs and jeans, not even bothering with his boots.

He leaned one shoulder on her doorjamb, his gaze appreciative as she finished dressing. She could feel the weight of it like a brush over her skin. After she ran a comb through her hair, she turned and let her eyes take in the sight of him. Sex-tousled hair. Gray eyes lit with residual lust. Door-filling shoulders roped with muscle under bare skin. Ridged abs under the soft dusting of brown hair. Long denim-wrapped legs crossed at the ankles. Wide, strong bare feet.

"I'm putting *you* on the menu," she said.

He pushed away from the door and prowled over to her to hook his fingers in her belt loops. "I was thinking that you would be dessert. On the counter. Legs open while I lick you."

His words tickled over her, setting little fires everywhere.

"But first the main course." He used one hand to spin her into his side so he could hustle her toward the bedroom door.

Tully sat on a stool at the counter, slicing and dicing the various vegetables Natalie put in front of him. It felt strange to cook half-naked but worth it for the admiring heat in her eyes. Everything else about the situation felt good. Maybe too good.

But watching Nat move around her kitchen, throwing together a chicken dish of some sort, made him happy. It could be the way her blonde hair swung against her cheek, reminding him of its silky texture when she rested her head on his shoulder. Or maybe the glimpse of her delicate little feet with their pink-polished nails. She'd disappointed him by putting on a bra, but her T-shirt still outlined those beautiful breasts that he'd sucked to hard points while she arched into him. His cock began to stir, so he brought his focus back to the tomato he was slicing for the salad.

"You've gotten quiet," Nat said, looking up from the sink as she washed more vegetables.

"Basking in the afterglow, sweetheart," he said. "And enjoying the sight of you."

"Oh, I understand enjoying the sights." She gave him a sexy slant of a smile.

"Am I being objectified?" He raised an eyebrow. "Because I'm fine with that."

"Let's just say that I would cook a lot more if you were always my sous-chef."

He chuckled, feeling that dangerous sense of rightness again. He usually avoided this kind of domestic scene. It made him want things he couldn't have. He needed to remind himself that he was here to protect her.

"After we eat, I'll get the cameras installed," he said.

She went still, staring down at the water running over her hands. "I'd actually forgotten about the stalker." She shook her head. "Did you make love to me to distract me?"

"I made love to you because I've wanted to for weeks." He realized he sounded pissed off, so he softened his tone. "And it was worth the wait."

"That was a joke," she said with a wry look. "Mostly."

He wanted to drop the knife and put his arms around her, but she started messing with the raw chicken.

He hated that she was afraid of the stalker but he felt confident he would catch the culprit soon. What he couldn't fix was her lack of confidence. Here was this beautiful, passionate woman who believed he would take her to bed as some sort of professional kindness. And he'd caught that same undercurrent of self-doubt in other comments she'd made.

Her SOB of an ex-husband must have really done a number on her. His grip on the knife tightened until his knuckles went white. Yeah, he would have to pay a visit to Matt the Dirtbag. Maybe scare him just a little as payback. Of course, if he turned out to be the stalker, Tully would do a lot more than scare him.

He whacked the hell out of the tomato and piled the slices on a plate. "Got something else I can hack up?"

She tossed him a green pepper before she braced her hands on the counter and said, "I don't get it. You're rich, successful, fantastic in bed, and you chop vegetables. Why aren't you married?"

He placed the pepper carefully on the cutting board, even as her words expanded in his chest. "Is that a proposal?"

"You're a great guy but I have no intention of ever marrying again." Her voice rang with conviction before she smiled. "So no need to panic."

"I'm not the marrying kind." His standard brush-off. Then he realized he wanted to be partially honest with her. "When I was in the FBI, I gravitated toward the more, er, exciting assignments. That wasn't conducive to family life."

"I'm guessing that 'exciting' is code for dangerous." She threw a bunch of ingredients in with the chicken. "But now your job is less hazardous."

He shrugged. "I got out of the habit of thinking about marriage." Again, partially correct. The real truth was that he refused to have children. He'd seen his parents pass on their problems to his siblings and, in a way, to himself. Not a chance that he was going to do that to another generation.

She gave him a sideways smile. "It only takes two months to form a new habit. You'd make such a wonderful, overprotective dad."

A sense of loss jabbed at him. He liked kids but he would make do with being a Big Brother. "Emphasis on the 'overprotective,'" he said with a wry grimace. "It's a tough world to raise kids in."

"Is that why you shy away from it? You've seen too much of the underbelly of life?"

"I'm an adrenaline junkie. That's not a good way to be, if you're a father." He'd admitted his addiction to her and that was enough on the topic. He scraped the chopped peppers into his hand. "Where do you want these?"

She slid a small glass bowl across the counter. "Sorry. That was a personal question."

"It's fine, but I'm curious about why you asked," he admitted.

"Seeing you there at my kitchen counter, with a knife in one hand and a pepper in the other, made me look at you in a different way, I guess. I'd never imagined you at home before. You seem as comfortable here as you are with a gun in your hand."

She was way too right about that. "You make me comfortable." Nope, that was the wrong thing to say because he didn't want to acknowledge the truth of it. "Besides, I figure the faster I chop, the faster I'll eat."

She laughed, a low musical sound. "The chicken is going in the oven now. Let me add some shrimp to the salad so you can dig right into that."

While she plated the salads—one large, one tiny—he admired her slim, elegant fingers, remembering how they felt on his skin. It struck him that she felt free to prod him about marriage because she meant it when she said she would never marry again. That gave her the freedom to discuss his marital status because she had no interest in his answers for herself. Anger at her ex-husband roiled up again. Natalie shouldn't be alone for the rest of her life because of that asshat.

Natalie laid her hand on Tully's solid shoulder—regrettably, now covered by his T-shirt—and leaned over to peer at her laptop. The screen was split into four quadrants, one for each side of her house. "Wow! You covered everything."

He shook his head. "I need to adjust camera three. There's still a small blind spot just below it. If your stalker is tech savvy enough to use a key-fob reader, he could figure out the blind spot."

Natalie's stomach lurched. Tully had made sure she had the number for the local police dispatcher on speed dial. He'd also followed up her call to the police chief to make sure the cop took her stalker seriously.

She'd finally reached the fourth ex-wife, who confirmed that she had not mentioned a word about Natalie to her husband. Regina Van Houten was still in the wind. That worried Natalie but it also made her believe that Regina hadn't discussed her sanctuary with her husband.

Tully took her hand and turned it to kiss the palm, his lips making her skin tingle. Then he twisted in his chair to look at her. "Okay, what's the drill when I'm not here?"

"My laptop stays on and plugged in at all times so the surveillance software is running. If it sounds an alarm, I call the police first and then you. If I'm not at my house, I make sure to stay away from it. If I'm in my house, I go to my bedroom and wedge a chair under the doorknob. Then I go in the bathroom, lock the door, and wedge another chair under that doorknob. Oh, and I have a container of pepper gel in every room." She glanced at the black plastic cylinder sitting on the kitchen counter.

Tully had unpacked an array of security supplies from the giant black duffel bag he'd hauled out of his car, including a box of police-grade pepper gel canisters with dye to mark the stalker. He'd also put smaller versions of pepper spray in her purse and laptop bag.

"And?" he prompted.

"If he confronts me, use the pepper gel without hesitation. Aim for the face. Don't talk to him. Just escape in whatever way possible. My imperative is to get away," she repeated his instructions. He'd already taken her outside to spray the stuff so she could get a feel for how hard she had to squeeze the button.

"Good." His voice was crisp with approval. "Can you do that?"

"Yes." She meant it. "It helps to have a plan mapped out."

"We'll go over it with Pam as well before I leave."

Disappointment crashed through her. She'd somehow assumed that he would spend the night after they'd had sex. She *wanted* him to spend the night, to fall asleep and wake up with his big, powerful, naked body beside her in her bed.

Something of her feelings must have shown in her face, because he stood and hooked his fingers in her belt loops to pull her against him. He brushed a soft kiss over her lips. "I have an antikidnapping training session scheduled with a client tonight. And it's the kind of client who requires that I be there."

"Of course," she said, feeling like an idiot. He had a high-powered position. He couldn't spend all his time with her. "I completely understand."

"No, you don't." His voice was deep and resonant. "I want to spend the night making love to you—first fast, then slow, then somewhere in between. I want to wake up to see your hair all messy from sex and sleep." He released a belt loop to take a lock of her hair and tuck it behind her ear, his fingertips tracing the whorls so she shivered. "I want to peel the sheet back from your beautiful breasts and suck them to make you wet before I slide into you first thing in the morning."

"Tully!" She was getting wet without his mouth being anywhere near her breasts. She grabbed his biceps to keep her shaky knees from folding.

"There's something about morning sex that makes it different from every other time of day. It's low key and sleepy and slow." He skimmed his fingers down her neck and over the outline of her now-hard nipples. "Which is why I intend to spend tomorrow night here." His smile was a seduction and a question. "If I'm invited."

"Consider this an invitation," she said as she stood on her toes to lick the indentation at the base of his throat. She flattened her palms over his nipples, rubbing in tiny circles. She wasn't going to be the only one who went to bed frustrated tonight.

"Here's my RSVP." He tilted her head up so he could slant his lips over her mouth, teasing the seam with his tongue until she opened to him. When he broke the kiss, it made her feel a little better that he was breathing hard too.

"Back to work." He set her away from him. "Before I forget what I need to do."

She copied his methodology and hooked one finger in his belt loop to hold him there. "Before Pam arrives, I'd like to ask you something. When I'm at the salon with customers, is there any reason for Pam to be there? I mean, the stalker isn't going to walk in with all those people there, is he?"

Tully frowned. "I'd feel a lot better if she was there."

"But is it necessary?" She felt like a bodyguard was overkill when she was surrounded by staff and clients. "She can come with me to open and return just before closing."

"Your stalker might be one of your customers," Tully said. "Or even one of your employees."

"Not one of my employees." Every member of her staff had been with her for at least two years. She trusted them because she didn't continue to employ anyone who didn't live up to her standards. "They have a vested interest in keeping me happy and healthy."

He shook his head. "I don't like it."

She crossed her arms. "I don't like wasting Pam's time." And she felt like she was taking advantage of what was now a personal relationship with Tully.

"As long as there are no more messages from the stalker, I'll allow it for tomorrow." He pinned her with his gaze. "But you have to swear to tell me if you receive anything new."

She raised her eyebrows at his wording but decided not to argue since he'd agreed to "allow" it. "Of course I will."

He grazed her cheek with his fingertip. "Camera three isn't going to reposition itself."

Chapter 10

When Tully dropped into a chair in his partner's computer room after a long night without Natalie, Leland swiveled around, looking surprised. "I didn't expect you in so early this morning. Didn't you have a training session with the Hazelton family?"

"Yeah, and they're a smart bunch. They won't make stupid mistakes in a bad situation." Tully yawned. "But I've got a call to make today, so I need you to give me some leverage on Natalie's rat bastard of an ex-husband." He couldn't wait to put the fear of God into the man. Ferreting out if he was her stalker was almost secondary. "He's my prime suspect as of now."

"Because?" Leland did that thing where he touched his fingertips together without looking ridiculous.

"Because a high percentage of stalkers are exes of some kind. And he's manipulative and narcissistic. Right up there on the stalker-personality charts."

"I haven't seen anything to indicate changes in his financial or professional status. God knows I've looked."

"If you've looked, then there's nothing to find on the grid." But that didn't mean the slime bucket was innocent. He'd just been clever enough to keep whatever might have triggered him off the radar.

"Are you still going to see him?"

Tully stood up. "Damn straight. I'm going to use my old FBI strategy of getting in his face and seeing how he reacts."

"You no longer have a badge to flash at him, so it would seem less effective," Leland observed.

"But I still have a gun." Tully bared his teeth in a feral smile.

Two hours later, he walked up the steps to Matt Stevens's office, located two towns over from Cofferwood but in a Victorian house much like Natalie's salon. The building sported fresh gray paint with crisp white trim. Prosperous and solid—a good look for an insurance agency.

Tully adjusted the shoulder holster under his charcoal suit jacket. He would make sure Stevens saw it when he sat down.

"I'm Tully Gibson, here to see Matt Stevens," he said to the receptionist seated at the oak desk just inside the front door.

"Do you have an appointment?" the youngish woman asked with a smile.

Tully winked at her. "I was hoping he might have a few minutes open." Leland had hacked into Stevens's computer, so Tully knew he had no scheduled appointments at this hour.

"Let me check." The receptionist spoke on the office phone while Tully scanned the waiting area. Comfortable chairs around a glass-and-wood coffee table scattered with magazines. A wall of bookcases that held a coffee station, some framed photos and industry awards, and a few rows of matching books, probably obsolete insurance regulations. Nothing to indicate a man in financial trouble.

"Mr. Gibson? I'm Matt Stevens."

Tully focused sharply on the man who walked into the room with his hand held out. He wanted to see what had led Natalie to marry him.

Stevens's smile was practiced but not insincere, his teeth even and too white—probably bleached. He was medium height and fit. He wore gray trousers and a blue dress shirt with a purple-and-pink tie that was too garish for Tully's tastes, but he figured the new girlfriend had picked it out. He wore his brown hair long enough to curl over his collar. His demeanor was that of a man who liked himself more than a little.

While Tully was sizing up Stevens, he knew the other man was doing the same to him, evaluating his expensive suit and custom-stitched boots.

Tully took the man's hand in a strong grip, which Stevens returned. "Thanks for seeing me without an appointment."

"Would you like some coffee?" Stevens asked, his smile still in place.

"I'm good, thanks."

"Please, come back to my office and tell me what I can do for you." Stevens gestured toward the door he'd emerged from.

Tully preceded him through it, finding the decor much the same. His gaze caught on a large silver-framed photo of Stevens with his arm around a slim, young blonde woman with a big smile. Evidently, the man had a type, although his new girlfriend lacked Natalie's air of elegant composure.

"Have a seat." Stevens gestured toward the fake-leather-and-wood chair in front of his oak desk. He settled into a matching high-backed swivel chair behind it.

Tully waited until he was sure Stevens's attention was on him before flicking his jacket button open so his holster would be visible as he sat. He caught the jitter in the other man's eyes with satisfaction.

"I have a confession to make," Tully said with a thin smile. "I'm not here to buy insurance."

Stevens swallowed but folded his hands on his desktop. "Then why *are* you here?"

"Where were you yesterday between twelve and four p.m.?"

"If you're with law enforcement, I'd like to see some kind of identification," Stevens said.

Tully leaned forward and locked his gaze on the other man. "I'm conducting a private investigation because I think you would prefer not to have this made public."

"I have no idea what you're talking about." His anger was mixed with confusion that Tully judged to be genuine.

"Answer my question and I'll tell you," Tully said.

"Yesterday was Monday, so I was here at the office."

"You didn't go out for lunch?"

"No, I had it delivered."

"Can your receptionist vouch for your presence here during that time period?"

"This is bullshit. You need to leave." Stevens stood and reached for the phone.

Tully leaned back and let his jacket flap open even farther so the gun would be obvious. He'd brought his big Glock for intimidation purposes. He said in a flat voice, "Don't."

The other man sat down slowly. "Who are you?"

"Have you ever been in an internet café?" Tully shot at him.

"Why would I? I have my own internet here." Stevens waved a hand at his computer. The man's hand shook slightly, which brought Tully great joy.

"Have you broken up with your girlfriend?"

Stevens frowned. "What? No."

"Have you had any financial losses in the past six months?"

Sweat glistened on the other man's forehead. *Good.* "Nothing significant. The usual ups and downs of any business."

"How far down?"

"Shit, it's no big deal. I've had worse months."

"Then why are you stalking your ex-wife?" Tully gave him a hard, threatening look as he bit out the words.

"My ex . . . Natalie?" Stevens looked baffled. "Stalking her?"

"Sending her emails, leaving her letters."

Stevens shook his head. "I'm not doing those things. I haven't spoken to Natalie in months." A cloud of bitterness darkened his expression. "She and I aren't exactly friends."

"Which is why you're stalking her. To punish her."

He looked almost relieved. "I swear I'm not doing anything to Natalie. I have a new life. I don't even think about her."

That pissed Tully off, but he read Stevens as telling the truth. Of course, the problem with narcissists was that they often convinced themselves of their own bullshit. That made them believe they weren't lying even when they were. They could fool a lie detector test on a good day.

Tully changed tacks. "Do you have any idea who might stalk her?"

"She's not the kind of person who makes enemies." Stevens considered for a moment. "What kind of emails and letters? Threats?"

"Yes." He wasn't going to mention the broken mirror. He decided to stroke Natalie's ex to see if he could add information. "You're a businessman, so you understand local economics. Does she have a jealous competitor? Anyone whose business she might have hurt?"

"Natalie bought the salon from its owner, so it was already a going concern." Stevens's tone was dismissive. "She didn't have to build up a clientele or anything. It was just handed to her. So I don't see anyone getting bent out of shape over that."

Tully wanted to hit the other man in his patronizing nose. He knew Natalie had taken a faded hairstyling studio and turned it into a sleek high-level salon. But he'd learned long ago not to let his emotions control his actions. He nodded.

"Who are you?" Stevens asked again.

Tully reached for his wallet, smiling when Stevens flinched. He drew out a business card and flicked it on the desk. Tully stood, deliberately looming over the desk and Stevens. "If I find out you're the stalker, you will be very, very sorry."

The man spread his hands in a gesture of abject surrender and stammered, "I'm n-not. I swear."

Tully turned on his heel and walked out.

~

Natalie rolled a section of her client's hair around her brush and aimed the blow-dryer at it. The voices of customers and staff, the drone of hair dryers, the bright pop tunes playing through the ceiling speakers, and the occasional ring of the office phone hummed in her ears. It was the best kind of music, spreading a soothing balm over her frayed nerves. Her work had kept her sane during the disintegration of her marriage and it would calm her until her stalker was caught.

Once she'd convinced Tully that her stalker couldn't be a staff member, he'd insisted that she and Pam hold a meeting that morning to inform her employees about Natalie's stalker. They'd given out Pam's cell number to call if anyone saw anything suspicious. One of the shampoo girls was so upset Natalie had sent her home. Natalie had been embarrassed to share her strange situation with her staff; it made her feel weak and not in control of her life. However, everyone had rallied around her, their shock turning to anger and a determination to protect her. Their loyalty had brought tears that she'd turned away to hide.

Pam had been especially pleased with the presence of Gino. He worked out at the gym on a regular basis, so he had impressive muscles, and he had appointed himself Natalie's friend and protector from the day she'd started at the salon. Pam felt he would be a deterrent to any stalker.

"Sir, do you have an appointment?" The raised voice of her receptionist, Bianca, cut through the pleasant swirl of sound.

"Excuse me, please," she said to her client as she set down her brush and hair dryer.

As Natalie walked toward the front desk, she scanned the tall, thin stranger standing in front of it. He wore a navy suit and white shirt with a red-and-blue-striped tie pulled loose at the neck. His blond hair was receding from his high forehead, but he was probably only in his thirties. He had a bland, round face that seemed at odds with his lean frame.

"May I help you?" she asked as she stepped in front of the desk.

"Please tell me that you're Natalie!" His slightly nasal voice shook.

"Yes, I am. May I ask who you are?"

He thrust out his hand. "Dobs Van Houten. I'm Regina's husband. That's what I came to talk to you about." He took a breath and spoke almost on a sob. "I'm hoping—no, praying—you know where she is."

A steel band seemed to wrap around her chest and squeeze while she stared at his outstretched hand. It had finally happened. A husband had somehow connected her with his wife's flight. Now she had to pretend to be nothing more than a concerned but uninvolved bystander.

Although it made her nauseated to do so, Natalie shook his hand, finding his grip surprisingly firm. She kept her expression neutral and said in her most sympathetic tone, "Oh dear, I wish I could help you, but I wasn't aware she was missing." She turned to Bianca. "Could you check the last time Regina was here for an appointment?"

Fortunately, she knew the appointment had been at least three weeks before Regina had requested her assistance. Bianca gave her the date. "She hasn't been here since then," Natalie said. She was trying to picture this man angry enough to threaten to throw his wife down the stairs. He seemed too vapid to generate that much emotion.

But she knew how deceiving appearances could be. Everyone assumed her marriage with Matt had been ideal.

He rubbed his forehead. "She told me she was going to New York City to sightsee with her cousin, who was visiting. They were supposed to stay in a hotel for a few days. When she didn't answer her cell phone, I called the hotel. I found out she never got there."

"That sounds scary. Did you call the police?" What Natalie really wanted to ask him was if there might be a good reason that his wife ran away from him.

"Not immediately. I thought there must some reasonable explanation." He looked up at her, his eyes a pale, watery blue. "They haven't found her, so I'm trying to contact anyone who knows her." He looked around at the busy salon. "Could we go somewhere more private?" he asked.

"Why don't you sit down in the lounge over there?" She gestured to an empty chair on the mani-pedi side, where it was less crowded. She had no intention of being alone with him since she knew he was capable of hitting a woman.

He hesitated before nodding.

"Just give me a moment and I'll join you." She returned to her waiting client. "I'm so sorry, but I have a very upset man here whom I need to calm down. Is it all right if I have Gino finish blowing you out?" The ladies loved Gino, both for his muscles and his charm. Her client gave an enthusiastic assent, so Natalie waved Gino over before she walked back to where Dobs Van Houten sat slumped in the chair.

"I'm so worried about her," he said. "I'm afraid she's in some kind of trouble."

Natalie forced herself to arrange her face in an expression of dismay and concern when she really wanted to slug him. "Did you check with her family to see if her cousin knows anything?"

His gaze dropped to his hands where they rested on his thighs. "She wasn't close to her family. They don't know where she is."

That was an oddly indirect answer. "What about her friends?"

"She isn't from around here, so she hasn't had time to make a lot of friends."

Because like many abusive husbands, he had done his best to isolate her so she would have no one to talk to and no one to support her.

He lifted misery-laden eyes to her. "Something bad must have happened to her. Why else would she just disappear?"

Because his wife was terrified he would injure her or even kill her.

Regina had come to Natalie's house with her clothes stuffed in a gym bag, shaking and sobbing. So Natalie had given Regina the guest room, fed her, and let her use her phone and computer to set up her escape. She'd warned Regina to erase whatever searches she'd made and not to tell Natalie anything about where she was going.

That way Natalie only had to lie about her guest staying there, not about where she went afterward.

"Did you have a fight?" Natalie asked, trying to behave as though she knew none of this. "She might have gotten upset about that."

He shook his head. "No, of course not. I adore her."

He probably believed he did. Matt had always told her how much he loved her, even as he did everything he could to crush her into nothingness. That was the insidious part of psychological abuse—she had trusted him because of that love.

"I'm sorry I can't do more to help you," Natalie said. "But your wife has been a client of mine for less than a year."

"I think you *could* do more to help me," he said with a brief flash of anger. He held up his hand in apology. "She always spoke so highly of you. I think she looked up to you as a role model."

"Me? That's kind of you, but we didn't have that kind of relationship. She was just my customer." This was getting weird now. She and Regina had been nothing more than client and stylist until Natalie had seen the bruises on the other woman's forearms. As she had snipped the ends of Regina's hair, she'd quietly offered her sanctuary if she ever needed it. Natalie had not asked for a response nor gotten one. Until Regina's appearance on her front porch.

His eyes flickered. "I had hoped . . ." He rubbed his forehead again. "I don't want to share this with anyone else, but Regina was pregnant." His voice cracked on the last word. "I would be destroyed if something happened to her and to our unborn child. There are two lives I'm trying to protect."

Shock ran through Natalie. Was it possible Dobs thought Regina had cheated on him and now she was pregnant with another man's child? That could be why Dobs was so angry he'd threatened her with extreme violence. Regina had never said a word about her condition to Natalie. The young woman hadn't been showing yet.

Or maybe Dobs was lying about the pregnancy in an effort to pry more information out of Natalie.

She reined in her spiraling thoughts. "I can understand why you would be concerned, but I don't know what I can do for you. The police are the ones you should be talking to."

"You're right." His tone was listless. "Please let me know if you hear anything from her."

"Of course I will," Natalie lied without a qualm. She slid a piece of paper and a pen toward him on the desk. "May I have your phone number?"

He pulled out his cell phone. "If you tell me yours, I'll send you a text so you'll have my number."

His request sent a shudder through her. She didn't give out her cell number to abusive men. "I'd prefer that you write yours down."

Another spark of anger came and went in his eyes, but he scrawled a number on the paper.

Natalie stood. "Will you let me know when she returns so I won't worry about her myself?"

"*If* she returns." He pushed himself up from the chair, his shoulders slumped.

He walked beside her to the reception desk with his gaze on the floor and his hands dangling at his sides as though he didn't know what to do with them. When she pulled the front door open, he seized her free hand between both of his, his grip slightly clammy now. "If you think of anything else . . ."

"I promise I'll call you." She pulled her hand away, forcing herself not to wipe it on her smock. "Good luck."

After the door closed behind him, her knees felt shaky. "Bianca, I don't have an appointment for half an hour, so I'm going back to my office to take care of some paperwork."

Once she got into her cozy private domain, she sagged into her comfortable chair, letting her head rest against the high back.

Dobs Van Houten seemed pathetic more than anything else but that didn't make him less dangerous. Often, weak men abused their wives because they had no power anywhere else in their daily lives. She'd seen the flashes of anger in his eyes that lent even more support to Regina's story. It was anger he couldn't unleash on the outside world, so he would use his young, lonely wife as his scapegoat.

But he'd gotten too close to the truth about her role in Regina's escape. She didn't want her sanctuary exposed, because that would prevent her from helping other women. Even Dobs's visit might bring too much attention to her salon.

The question was why he'd sought her out. She knew Regina had not considered her a role model. So what connection had Dobs made that brought him to her doorstep? She hoped it was just desperation that drove him to visit anyplace that his wife had frequented.

If Regina was really pregnant, that upped the stakes in the situation. Dobs would have some rights as the father, although maybe not until after the baby was born. But it would certainly make the man pursue his fleeing wife with more determination.

Would it also make him send Natalie threatening messages?

She massaged the back of her neck where the muscles had knotted themselves.

Tea. She got up to turn on the electric kettle she kept on her credenza and plopped a bag of herbal tea in her favorite mug.

Gino stuck his head in the door. "You okay, Nat?"

"I'm fine. Thanks for finishing the blowout."

He waved away her thanks. "What did the guy want?"

"He's trying to find his wife."

Gino knew about Natalie's secret sanctuary, so he caught on right away. "Shit! So she's one of your rescues."

"But he can't find her, so she didn't tell him that. He says he's just talking to everyone she knew." Which could be the truth.

"Do you think he could be the stalker?" Gino looked worried and angry.

"It's possible. But I feel like he wouldn't have come here if he was also sending anonymous messages. They don't seem to connect. I'm more concerned that he's going to expose my secret." She would figure out a way to keep sheltering women, though.

"If he comes here again, you let me handle him," Gino said, his voice hard.

"It's a deal." Natalie didn't want to see Dobs ever again. Her teakettle whistled and she reached over to turn it off.

"I'll leave you alone to chill," he said, disappearing from the doorway before she could thank him.

She steeped her tea and decided to jot down a few notes to share with Tully when he came to her house for the night. The thought of having his hard-muscled body in her bed sent such a wash of heat through her that she nearly choked on her drink.

"Oh my God, what is going on with you?" Her friend Dawn strode into the office, looking like a warrior princess with her dark hair scraped back in a ponytail and her lean body sheathed in skin-hugging workout clothes. "First a stalker and now a distraught husband. You've got to get out of here and stay with me in the city."

"How on earth—?" Natalie sputtered.

Dawn sat in one of the chairs in front of Natalie's desk. "The gym receptionist called for a hair appointment, and your receptionist told her you'd been accosted by some man looking for his missing wife. So the gym receptionist told me. Was his wife one of your—you know?"

"Yes, but I don't think *he* knows that. He's just looking everywhere he knows his wife went." Natalie took a sip of her tea. It figured that

Dobs would show up on the day that Dawn was at the gym to teach her self-defense classes for women.

"It's a little too close for comfort, though," Dawn said, her brown eyes filled with concern. "Come back to Leland's place with me tonight."

Natalie almost laughed. "I already have a professional bodyguard staying with me." She wasn't going to mention that it was Tully.

"That makes me feel better, but why isn't there a bodyguard here at the salon too?"

"Because it's ridiculous to waste a bodyguard's time when I'm surrounded by people who will protect me. Dobs Van Houten wasn't going to hurt me anyway. He was almost in tears." She didn't want Dawn worrying about her.

Dawn made a little huff of dissatisfaction. "At least come to my self-defense class tonight and refresh your skills."

"Thanks, but I still have bruises from the last refresher." An exaggeration, of course, but she wasn't going to miss a minute of her limited time with Tully. "Besides, the last time you told me I had all the moves down pat."

"You went after your attacker with conviction, I admit. I figured you were imagining it was Matt so you could give him what he deserved." Dawn leaned forward and braced her elbow on her thighs, her tone coaxing. "We could have a girls' night with action movies, popcorn, and that nasty drink you like."

"I'll take a rain check on that. I have to be here early tomorrow. Alice's wedding festivities ate into my schedule, so I'm catching up on my clients." She smiled at Dawn. "But I'll look forward to it soon."

Dawn rose. "Okay, but you be careful and listen to your bodyguard. I know how stubborn you can be."

Natalie raised her eyebrows at her friend.

"I know. Birds of a feather." Dawn grinned. "I have to get to my class."

She'd just turned toward the door when Tully stormed through it. "Damn it, Natalie, I shouldn't have let you talk me out of having Pam stay with you." He came to a halt when he noticed Dawn. "Hello, Dawn. What brings you here?"

Thank God Tully was focused on Dawn, because the sight of him obliterated any coherent thought Natalie could muster. He wore a dark-gray suit that had clearly been tailored to his wide shoulders, trim waist, and muscular thighs, fitting his body like a fine wool glove. A deep red tie glowed against a snowy-white shirt. His presence ran through her veins like a swallow of fiery scotch.

Too bad he had been scowling when he blew through her door.

"Probably the same reason you're here," Dawn said. "The crazy husband?"

"How the hell did you hear about that so fast?"

"The receptionist grapevine," Dawn said. "How did *you* hear about it?"

"One of the stylists called Pam." He pivoted toward Natalie and said in a milder tone, "Are you all right?"

"Are you carrying a gun?" Dawn interrupted, eyeing his suit jacket.

"Yeah, I needed to intimidate someone this morning." Tully smiled in a terrifying way. "Sometimes I really love my job."

Natalie was glad she wasn't the person he wanted to scare because he looked downright dangerous.

"Nat, did he threaten you or frighten you?" Tully persisted, buttoning his jacket.

"No, but he nearly cried." Natalie folded her hands on the desktop. She didn't want to get into this in front of Dawn. "I would have felt sorry for him if I didn't know he deserved every second of his suffering."

Tully's scowl returned. "So she was one of your guests."

"The one who's dropped off the radar," Natalie said.

"You know about her guests?" Dawn asked Tully.

"I told him because of the stalker," Natalie explained. "Their ex-husbands fit the typical profile in a sort of twisted way."

Dawn nodded. "Makes sense. Well, now that I know you're in good hands, I've got to get back to the gym." She pinned one of her steely trainer looks on Tully. "You keep her safe, or you'll answer to me."

"Yes, ma'am," Tully said with false meekness.

The moment Dawn spun out of the room, Tully was behind the desk, his hands on Natalie's shoulders, pulling her to her feet. He wrapped his arms around her so that she was pressed against his warm, hard body, then looked down into her face. "Are you really all right?"

"Trust me, I've dealt with much worse in my years at the salon. Generally related to weddings. Bridezillas, you know." She smiled at him.

He gave her a little shake and didn't answer her smile. "Not a joke when there's a stalker after you."

"Seriously, what would have been different if Pam had been here?"

"I'd feel better."

The tension in his voice softened her resistance. "Okay, Pam can stay at the salon tomorrow." She relaxed into him, his protectiveness sending a sexual buzz through her. She had to remember that protecting people was just his job. "This situation is so strange that it seems unreal. I can't wrap my mind around the fact that someone out there wants to do me harm. Or at least make me believe that he wants to."

He brushed his fingers through her hair, his touch featherlight, a disarming contrast to his powerful physical presence. "You're a strong person, so you keep living your life. It's a positive response to a bad situation, but you have to temper it with caution. The threat is real. Maybe this Dobs guy isn't your stalker, but you have to assume he could be and act accordingly." His expression was grim as he asked, "Do you understand me?"

She avoided his gaze by laying her cheek against his chest with a sigh. "Yes. I just wish this was over." Although that meant Tully would go back to his skyscraper in Manhattan while she stayed in New Jersey. At least she had tonight to look forward to.

"Sweetheart, I'm doing my best to make that happen." He tightened his embrace, and she felt the hard edge of the gun nudging her rib cage.

"Who did you scare this morning?" she asked, allowing herself to feel safe in his arms.

"I'll tell you later." He put a finger under her chin to tilt her face up so he could kiss her in a way that promised more. Then he eased her away from him, making sure she was steady before he released her. "Did Van Houten say anything I should know about?"

He was back in security mode. Natalie shook off the fog of sensual contentment he'd enveloped her in and decided there was no point in keeping Regina's secret any longer. "He says his wife is pregnant."

Tully's eyebrows rose. "Did you know that?"

"No. She didn't mention it and she wasn't showing at all, so it must be early in the pregnancy." She looked a question at Tully. "Or Dobs is lying to try to get me to tell him where she is."

"Yeah, I thought of that too. What's your take on it?"

Surprised gratification flickered through her. He respected her enough to ask her opinion about Dobs's truthfulness.

"It would explain why he's so desperate to find her. Regina told me that he was obsessed with having a son to carry on the family name. She said that after they got married, she felt like a brood mare because of the way he talked about her hips and how she was built for childbearing. He became angry and frustrated every time she told him she wasn't pregnant."

"Obsessed. Angry," Tully repeated. "That's moving into stalker territory, especially if he feels that you helped his wife take his unborn child away from him. Have you checked your email today?"

"There was nothing this morning, but I've been too busy since." She flipped open her laptop and logged in, skimming through the list of messages. There was an email from an unfamiliar address that hadn't gotten dumped in her spam folder. "Crap!"

"Let me look at it first," Tully said, using a big shoulder to edge her away from the computer.

"Why?" She could handle a random quotation about beauty.

He turned his head to look her in the eye, so close that she could see the black ring around his irises. "The broken mirror was a major escalation. I have a bad feeling."

A quiver of nerves ran through her. "Okay. It's the one from dk2118. It came in about two hours ago. So it was before Dobs came here and got nothing from me."

She watched his face as he swiped into the email message and flinched when she saw his expression change from focus to fury. He muttered a curse, typed something, and turned the computer completely away from her.

"You don't want to see that," he said. "I've sent it to Leland, but it will probably be another dead end."

She wasn't sure how she felt about him deciding what she should or shouldn't see. "Did you delete it?"

"Not yet. That has to be your decision." The taut angles of his face softened as he moved into persuasion mode. "Nat, it will upset you and I hate for that to happen."

At least he understood that she had to decide. "So it's not just a quotation?"

He shook his head. "It's an image. One that pops up the moment you open the email. Which means he coded it to get through any photo blockers."

"A photo?"

"A disturbing one. Let me describe it to you instead. Then you won't have the actual picture smeared across your brain." His voice held a note of entreaty that she'd never heard from him before.

"I know you're trying to protect me but I think I need to see it." She'd worked too hard to build herself back up again. She couldn't let a man make her decisions for her, even with the best of intentions.

He put his hand on the computer just as she reached for it. She was about to snap at him when he said, "Let me prepare you first. It's a photo of you. It looks like a professional headshot, but your hair was longer. The photo is pinned to a wall . . . by knives. They're positioned on the eyes, the mouth, and the throat. Streaks of red paint run down from the knives."

Natalie fought the urge to cup her hands over her eyes to protect them. She noticed how Tully had described the picture in the most objective terms he could in an attempt to undercut the horror of it. She swallowed hard and nodded. "Okay. Let me see it."

He blew out a breath and slowly rotated the computer toward her, his reluctance clear. For a moment she was tempted to let him carry the burden of the image, to keep the ugliness out of her brain, as he had advised. But she straightened her spine and shifted her gaze to the screen.

Horror sucked her breath out of her lungs. Tully was right. It was much worse to see it in high-resolution color on her computer screen. The knives were large, vicious-looking hunting implements with nasty serrations along one side of the black blades. The paint Tully had described as red was blood colored and had been gobbed onto the picture so it dripped like blood as well. Even worse, each of her eyes had been entirely cut out before the knife was plunged through it. A dripping red line was drawn across her throat beside the impaling knife.

She suddenly realized that one of her hands had drifted up to touch her throat exactly where the red line would be. She dropped it abruptly, and then her knees gave way so she had to sink into her chair.

"That is . . . a definite escalation," she finally said, her voice coming out with a quaver.

“That’s a threat,” he said. “We’re taking all the evidence to the police.”

She dragged her gaze away from the vile email to look at him. “But they can’t do anything if we don’t know who sent it.”

“We’re getting it all on official record so that when we catch this son of a bitch, he’ll be locked away forever.” His voice held an icy determination. “From now on, you do not spend one second alone. Not one single second.”

“Yes . . . no. I mean, I agree.” She didn’t want to be alone with the terror that snarled through her chest and her gut and her mind.

Whatever the expression on her face was, it must have been bad, because Tully knelt in front of her chair and wrapped her hands in his warm, strong grasp. “Nat, we’ll get him. Don’t worry.” His eyes were lit with a gentle concern. “I won’t let anything bad happen to you.”

“I just—” She had to stop and clear the tightness in her throat. “I just don’t understand what I’ve done to make someone hate me that much.”

He lifted one hand to cup her cheek, his calloused fingers tender. “Sweetheart, you haven’t done anything. We’re dealing with a psychopath. He doesn’t need a reason to hate you. Somehow you happened to get in his path, so he picked you as a target.”

Tully was so big and so close and so comforting. She echoed his gesture and laid her palm against his cheek. His skin was smooth from his morning shave. She could see the crinkle of lines at the corner of each eye and the way the scar twisted a few hairs of his eyebrow. His brown hair caught flecks of gold from the sunlight coming through her window. If only she could wrap herself in him until the stalker was captured, she would feel no fear.

She leaned forward, shifting her hand to the back of his neck and finding his mouth with hers. His grip moved to her waist and he eased her off the chair so she was on her knees and crushed against him while his lips slanted across hers. Then his hands were in her hair, tilting her head so he could kiss her more deeply. All the horror that had twisted through her body transformed to a desperate yearning to meld herself with Tully, to let physical pleasure blast away the clench of panic.

She yanked open the buttons and slipped her hands under his jacket, stroking over the fine cotton of his shirt so she could feel the dense muscle underneath. When she encountered the body-warmed metal of his gun, the brutal rigidity of it shocked her out of her mindless seeking.

Leaning back, she withdrew her hands and laid them against his lapels. "I'm sorry."

"For what?"

"Using you for comfort."

The corners of his eyes crinkled as he smiled and stroked the pad of his thumb along her jaw. "You can use me anytime, sweetheart."

She shook her head. It was too tempting to let him carry the whole burden of her stalker. She lifted herself back onto her chair. "Okay, what do I tell the police?"

Tully searched her face, the small crease between his eyebrows evident. "You wait until I can go with you. We need to take all the evidence to them—emails, letters, mirror. I'll have them messengered here." He pushed up from the floor to lean his hip against her desk and glanced at his stainless steel watch. "I already called Pam, so she'll be arriving soon. I have to get back to the city for a couple of meetings I can't cancel, but I'll return as soon as those are finished."

Guilt jabbed at her. "Do whatever you need to do in the city. As long as Pam is here, I'll be fine. Please don't rush back."

He gave her a sizzling look. "I'm not rushing back for *your* sake. I'm rushing back for *mine*."

He was trying to distract her from the horrible image on her computer.

"Natalie? Sorry to bother you." Bianca hesitated halfway in the doorway. "Your next client is here."

"Of course." Natalie rose. Work would be almost as good a distraction as Tully. Okay, that was a lie, but work would help. "I'll be right there."

Bianca nodded and vanished.

"You really don't have to stay until Pam arrives," Natalie said to Tully. "Gino has already offered to deal with Dobs if he comes back."

"I could use a cup of that coffee I smelled out in the lounge," he said, gesturing for her to precede him.

"You are an obstinate man." Natalie sighed as she walked out the office door.

He grinned. "I hear that a lot."

Chapter 11

Once he'd checked the perimeter and the interior, Tully allowed Natalie to walk into her house after they'd returned from filing the stalker complaint with the police chief. She went straight to her kitchen while he paced behind her, thinking wicked thoughts as he watched the way her hips swayed.

"Would you like a drink?" she asked, pulling bottles out of her pantry. "I'm making a rye Manhattan for myself, but I've got bourbon, scotch, beer, or wine if you prefer."

She'd held up like a champ during the ninety minutes of presenting their evidence, describing her encounter with Dobs, and answering the chief's probing questions. Tully had seen strong men break down under that kind of pressure, but not his Nat. She was like an elegant china doll with a spine of pure steel. Even the chief had been impressed with her calm, rational attitude, telling Tully he wished all his witnesses were like Natalie.

But Tully could hear the edge of a tremor in her voice and see the tension in her slim shoulders. He put his arms around her waist from behind and gently kissed the side of her neck just under her ear, savoring the satin of her skin. "You're exhausted," he said. "Let me make your fancy drink. I worked as a bartender in college."

Satisfaction spread through his chest when she leaned back against him without hesitation, saying, "I find it soothing to do something normal."

"I'll have a Manhattan too, then." Even though he would have preferred straight scotch. No, he would have preferred to stand like this, her body pressed to his, her light feminine scent infusing the air he breathed. But he needed to take care of her. "You got any crackers and cheese? I'll get those out." He figured she could use some food to soak up the alcohol. Otherwise the effects might hit her hard. Although maybe it would be a good thing after what she'd been through.

She reached into the pantry to pull out a box of wheat crackers, which he took from her. "Cheese in the fridge drawer," she said. "Platter under the island. Knife in the top drawer by the range. Also, would you grab two martini glasses from the cabinet by the sink and put them in the freezer?"

"Sure thing." He stripped out of his suit jacket and yanked off his tie. He'd ditched the gun before he went into the police station. Cops didn't take kindly to civilians with firearms, even former law enforcement officers with a license to carry. Of course, he'd brought the Glock with him into the house in his overnight bag.

Finding the martini glasses, he wedged them into the freezer drawer. When he stood up, he caught Natalie's gaze on him, a slight smile playing around the corners of her soft lips as though she liked what she saw. His groin tightened and he gave her a wink.

Her smile went wider before she looked back at the vermouth she was measuring. God, he wanted to take her to bed. Instead, he rummaged around in the fridge to find cheese and grapes, piled them on the platter, and arranged the crackers around them.

When he heard the cocktail shaker plunk down on the counter, he looked up. "You ready for the glasses?"

She nodded without saying anything. He could see the shadows of fatigue under her eyes, making their blue seem darker. Now he wanted to fold her in his arms and swear that no one would hurt her. Because no one would on his watch.

He carried the platter to the coffee table in front of the sectional sofa while she balanced the drinks. When she sat, he settled close to her and snaked an arm around her waist to tuck her against his side. Contentment warmed him when she scooted over willingly. He held up his glass. "To the confusion of our enemies!"

"I'll drink to that," Natalie said, clinking her rim gently against his. She took a sip, closed her eyes, and let her head fall back against his shoulder. "Ahh."

The sensual melody of her voice vibrated through him, making him shift on the couch. "That sound reminds me of last night. In a very good way." His words came out with a rasp.

She hummed. "A perfect Manhattan is almost as good as sex."

"Maybe in your opinion, but I prefer a perfect woman." He brushed his mouth against her temple, the silk of her hair tickling his cheek.

"Your compliment is over the top but I'll take it," she said, her lips curled in that little smirk of a smile again.

To keep himself from devouring her, he said, "The police chief thinks you're pretty amazing."

And the chief had taken the threats to Natalie seriously. Tully had made sure of that.

"Chief Borland is a good guy." She took another sip of her drink. "But he admitted that he doesn't have the resources to track down a stalker."

"But I do." He put every ounce of his determination into his voice to reassure her. The latest email had taken this situation to a whole new level of bad. He was clearing his calendar so he could catch this bastard.

"You know, I feel sorry for Regina Van Houten, out there all alone, terrified that her husband will find her and drag her back." Natalie opened her eyes and angled her head to meet his gaze. "While I have all your strength and expertise guarding me. I'm very lucky."

He would be flattered except that her eyes swam with unshed tears and her words were the smallest bit slurred. "Just doing my job."

"No, you're doing far more than your job." She searched his face, her brows drawn down in a tiny frown. "Pam could handle things. She's very good . . . but you already know that, of course. Why have you taken such an interest in my problem? And don't tell me it's for sex. You could get that on your own. I know that for a fact."

He snorted. "You give me way too much credit." Okay, she wasn't wrong if she meant one-night stands or women who were turned on by his bank account. He'd lost interest in those kinds of liaisons, though. He was old enough to want something real and that was Natalie. The real deal. He wasn't even sure what he meant by that, but he knew in his gut it was true.

And she had no intention of ever marrying again, so that fit right in with his life plans.

"Never mind that," she said. "Why are you helping me?"

He rubbed the back of his neck with his free hand. "Because you need help." Because he admired her grit and her integrity and her sexy little smile. "I hate stalkers. They're psychopathic bullies, preying on innocent people who don't have the weapons to fight back."

"Sort of like the big guy beating up the little guy in the schoolyard. Did you ride to the rescue back then too?"

"Maybe." He'd been in his share of fights as a kid, but not all of them were for noble causes.

She curved her hand against his cheek, sending a ripple of awareness down to his belly. "You are a very good man, Tully. The knight on his white charger."

"You have a rose-colored vision of me," he said. "I do it because I like to, not because I'm noble."

He was an addict like everyone in his family, except his particular addiction was the adrenaline rush of kicking ass. He'd just learned to channel it into kicking the ass of bad guys.

A tear rolled down her face. He stopped himself from licking it off, using his thumb to brush away the warm liquid instead. "That's the alcohol hitting you. We need to get you some food."

He eased his arm from behind her to stack a slice of cheese on a cracker. When he offered it to her, she surprised him by leaning forward to bite into the morsel as he held it, her lips grazing his fingertips so he could feel the chill of the Manhattan on them. The contact was like cold fire on his skin.

He waited for her to swallow before he lifted the remainder of the cracker to her mouth again. This time her tongue flicked out to touch his thumb.

As much as he wanted what she was offering, he couldn't take it when she was so vulnerable. "Sweetheart, you've had a rough day. Let me order us some Chinese and then you can go to sleep."

"Sleep?" Her face turned bleak and she shook her head. "If I don't have something else to think about, all I can see is that horrible photograph. I won't be sleeping without some help." She gave him a seductive smile and skimmed her index finger down the center of his chest.

He seized her hand and lifted it to his mouth, kissing her small, warm palm. "After you eat, we'll see how you feel." But her words and touch had brought his cock to full attention. He adjusted his position to ease the pressure.

Her gaze dropped below his waist and her smile grew even more scorching. "I can see how *you* feel."

"Yeah, but the advantage of being a mature male is that I know better than to act on it right now." He pulled his cell phone out of his pocket. "What's your favorite Chinese restaurant that delivers?"

She let out an exaggerated sigh. "I guess I'm not as irresistible as I thought."

He twisted to kiss her chilled lips in a way that warmed them right up. When she made an eager little noise in the back of her throat, he nearly lost his grip on his good intentions. Pulling away, he said, "My resistance is very short term. After dinner, I will ravish you thoroughly."

"That's more like it," she said, peeking at him sideways through her eyelashes. "Look up Zhang Wei for dinner. The tangerine beef is excellent."

~

Natalie had to admit that dinner had improved her mood. She was embarrassed at how weepy she'd been earlier. She'd sworn off needing a man for comfort . . . or for anything other than sex. They were useful for that.

And for not thinking about things she was trying to avoid.

She put her chopsticks down beside her empty dish. "You never told me who you went to scare this morning."

"I'm not sure you want to know," he said, scooping more food onto his plate. "You're right about this tangerine beef. It's damn good."

Realization struck her, and the food in her stomach soured. "You saw Matt, didn't you?"

"Yeah." He stowed the serving spoon back in the rice and glanced at her from under his eyebrows. "You want to know what I think?"

She nodded, her throat tight with a strange combination of fear, anticipation, and residual rage toward her ex. If he was her stalker, she would be tempted to do him real physical damage.

"I don't think he's your stalker. Not because he's a decent person but because he was relieved when I accused him of it."

"Relieved?" She didn't understand.

"I had a gun. He had no idea why, so he was afraid. When I told him the reason I was there, he became less afraid. Fear is fundamental, so I believed his reaction, even though I wouldn't trust a single word he said otherwise." Tully took a bite of beef and rice and chewed.

Natalie watched the strong muscles of his throat as he swallowed, feeling a little charge of heat run through her. "So if not Matt, then who?"

"Well, I've moved Dobs Van Houten to the top of the suspect list after today. I've arranged for one of my people to keep an eye on him."

"Dobs? He was so pathetic." Natalie shook her head as she tried to picture him jamming knives into her photograph. "I could see him sending emails and maybe even dropping off letters. But breaking into my car? And that horrible picture?" A shudder caught her unawares. "He seems too . . . bland for that."

"He threatened to throw his wife down the stairs." Tully's voice was as hard as granite.

Natalie's fingers curled into a fist. "Men do things in their own homes that they wouldn't dare do outside them."

Tully reached across the table to lay one of his big hands over hers, his warmth and strength coaxing her fist to unclench. "You're not wrong, but stalking is cowardly too."

"I suppose." She turned her hand to wrap it around Tully's. "I want to take a break from worrying about my stalker. Let's talk about you."

Tully gave her fingers a squeeze before he went back to his second helping of dinner. "There's not much to talk about."

"I don't believe that." He might affect a simple cowboy vibe, but she saw the shadows in his eyes. However, those were his secrets to keep. For now. Tonight she didn't have the strength to pry. "What was your favorite subject in high school?"

His laugh held a note of relief at the easy question. "Nothing. I didn't much like school. I cut whenever possible."

"Because you were bored." He was too smart to have found it difficult.

"Didn't see the point. Until I realized I could get out of town if I went to college. So I worked my tail off to get the grades." He took a sip of the beer he'd switched to and grinned. "Still didn't like it, though."

"You liked school enough to get an MBA." And he'd gone to a very prestigious school.

"A means to an end. The red tape of the FBI didn't suit me. I needed to learn how to start my own business."

"You met Derek and Leland in class?" She would have loved to have seen that first meeting between the three men. Derek, with his movie-star good looks and his sharp financial acumen. Leland, the preppy-faced computer genius who refused to don a suit. And then Tully, the former FBI agent who sported cowboy boots and a gun. "How on earth did the three of you decide to join forces?"

"Derek and Leland were roommates by pure random chance. We all got assigned to the same first-year learning group. That's where we discovered that we had one powerful connection."

"What was that?"

"We hated learning groups."

Natalie grimaced in sympathy. "Are those like group projects?"

"Yeah, where ten percent of the group does ninety percent of the work. And you have to pretend that everyone's contribution is equally valuable. Not only that, it was the same group for every project." He harrumphed. "We didn't give a shit that everyone got the same credit but we got real tired of babysitting the lazy-ass members of the group."

"So what happened?"

"Well, it became apparent early on that Derek was a wiz at numbers, and Leland was on a tech level so far above the rest of us that we didn't speak the same language. So I made the executive decision to give them sole responsibility for those areas of all our projects. Then I kind of ran interference for them."

So Tully had taken over the leadership role. She could imagine that his confident physical presence and his FBI mystique had intimidated the rest of the students into obedience. Derek had told Alice that he and Leland had originally been a little afraid of Tully.

"When our first project came back with a high grade, everyone kind of settled down about the division of labor." Tully smiled reminiscently.

"So you decided that the three of you would make good business partners?" She loved this glimpse into the dynamics among these men she'd come to care about.

Tully leaned back in his chair, his plate once again empty. "That came about in our second year. We'd all done internships at big companies at the top of their industries." He winked. "Because only the best would do for us."

"That goes without saying."

"And we hated them. The bureaucracy, the politics, the waste of time and talent. We decided that we had to be our own bosses." He chuckled. "We might have been a little drunk the night we made a pact to start a consulting firm. But it still seemed like a good idea in the sober light of morning, so here we are." He shrugged.

"Now all the business school students want to work at KRG because it's at the top of its industry." She echoed his words with a touch of amusement. "Do you hire interns from your alma mater?"

"Yeah. We all believe in lending a helping hand." He shrugged again. "It's not so easy to get started in the world."

It was even harder to found a company and grow it into an international powerhouse. The three partners had tremendous drive. She knew something of Derek's and Leland's histories, but Tully didn't talk about his much.

She was about to ask him another question when he stood and stacked his dirty dishes. "I'm on KP duty. You sit and relax."

Evidently they'd reached the limit of his revelations for the evening. She pushed up from her chair and grabbed a couple of cardboard containers. "It will take five minutes to clean this up if we do it together."

Once the dishes were racked in the dishwasher and the leftovers stowed in the fridge, Tully stretched and gave a yawn that made his jaw crack.

That reminded her that he'd done some sort of nighttime training session with a client the night before, and she felt a stab of guilt. "How late did the training go?"

"Long enough not to bother with sleep," he said, rubbing the back of his neck.

"You must be exhausted." Natalie glanced at the microwave's clock. It was eight forty-five, but what the hell? "Let's go to bed."

He went from good-natured drowsiness to laser-focused lust in a nanosecond, his gray eyes smoky, his smile lascivious, and his body against hers before she even realized he had moved.

He lowered his mouth to within an inch of her lips. "Now that's the best idea I've heard today, sweetheart." Then he kissed her in a slow sensual dance that sent desire spreading through her body like a warm tide.

She grabbed fistfuls of his shirt, a faint aroma of starch rising from it, and tried to wrap herself in him. He seemed to understand because his arms came around her and he pulled her into him so that they were locked together from knee to chest. He felt like strength and safety and sex all rolled up into one.

One of his hands slid down to her behind, his palm flattened to bring her pelvis even closer so she could feel his cock harden against her. The need to have him inside her ripped through her like a tornado. She tore her mouth away from his to say, "Lift me onto the counter."

He went still. "Are you sure about this, Nat?"

She worked her hands down between them and found the zipper of his trousers, yanking it down so she could stroke the length of him through the confining fabric of his briefs. "Is that a good-enough answer?"

"Better than a lie detector test. But let's get some clothes off you first." He found the button on her trousers and flicked it open before he returned her favor by sliding down her zipper. She kicked off her flats and shimmied out of her pants, leaving just a blue-lace bikini.

"These are real pretty," Tully said, skimming his fingers along the fabric's top edge where it stretched over her hip. "But they're blocking my view." With a single motion, he stripped them down to her ankles. Then he seized her waist and boosted her onto the island's quartz top as though she weighed nothing.

The stone was cold and hard under her butt, but she didn't care. "Your shirt. Off," she said, grabbing his placket to start unbuttoning it. He worked up from the bottom, and when the last button flew free of its hole, he shucked the shirt off so that she could run her hands over the bare skin that covered his beautiful, flexing muscles.

"God, you feel good," she said, exploring the ridges of his abs and the bulge of his upper arms.

He closed his eyes and groaned, but he stood still for her. Until she skimmed her hands down to his belt buckle. He circled her wrists and gave her a sinful smile. "Not yet, sweetheart. It's time for dessert."

He knelt in front of her and pushed her thighs open. For a moment, she felt strangely shy, but then he leaned in and kissed her between her legs and she forgot to care.

"You taste better than steak, apple pie, and beer all rolled up in one," he murmured against her clit, the vibration of his words sending spirals of delight sizzling through her.

He lifted first one of her knees and then the other to hook them over his bare shoulders. The feel of his skin on the backs of her legs and the tickle of his hair against the insides of her thighs stoked the fire glowing in her belly.

When his tongue licked into her, she lay down on the island, closing her eyes and giving herself over to the sensations because she trusted him with her body. She arched and twisted and moaned while he tasted her from different angles and with different pressures, pushing her closer and closer to climax.

But she wanted him there when she came so she could clench around him. "Tully, stop! I'm going to come."

"And I want to taste you when it happens." His voice rumbled against her, winding her tension even tighter.

"But I want to come around you." She curled up from the now-warm stone to put her hands on either side of his head and pull him up from between her thighs. "It feels intense."

"I'm not going to argue with a lady's wishes," he said, his lips glistening and his eyes heavy-lidded. He came to his feet with Natalie's legs still draped over his shoulders, tilting her pelvis upward. He pulled a condom out of his trouser pocket and rolled it on before he eased the head of his cock inside her.

He grasped her buttocks, his fingers imprinting the soft flesh, and thrust inside her in one smooth movement. She was so wet that he slid in easily and the angle of her hips let him seat himself deeply.

"Oh, yes, Tully!" she said as her body tightened in anticipation of his next stroke.

But he surprised her by releasing her butt and leaning farther into her so he could unbutton her blouse and shove up her bra. Her nipples were already hard and sensitive, so his touch sent an electric streak of sensation down to where his cock impaled her. She used her legs to rock her hips against him.

He made a guttural sound. "Let me play with these beauties a little longer." He rolled her nipples between his calloused thumbs and forefingers, the dual abrasion pushing her over the edge. She arched up off the countertop as her orgasm crashed over her, squeezing hard around Tully's cock.

He started to move and that sent her into another paroxysm of mind-bending pleasure so that she screamed his name as she held on to his forearms like a lifeline.

And then he was stroking into her in perfect synchronization with the clench and release of her muscles until, with a wordless shout, he hit his own climax.

Slowly, she became aware of Tully's big hands splayed on either side of her hips as he braced himself over her with his eyes closed. He huffed out a breath. "That was really something, sugar."

He opened his eyes, still glowing with desire. He shifted his weight to one arm so he could feather his finger over her cheekbone. "Your skin gets this pretty flush when you come," he said.

She could feel the tight heat in her face. "That's because you set fire to my blood."

"That might be the hottest thing anyone's ever said to me. Pun intended." He started to withdraw but she tilted her pelvis to stop him. "Sweetheart, you've got to be uncomfortable on that hard countertop. Let me take you to bed."

"I just want to savor the feeling a little longer." Although her shoulder blades were a little sore from being pushed against the stone, she liked having Tully over her and inside her and looking down at her as though he wanted to do it all over again.

And it kept her from remembering terrible things.

Natalie sat in bed, watching Tully brush his teeth in her bathroom in his gray sweatpants. His torso was bare, so the lights outlined every curve of his muscles as they flexed with the movement of his arm and shoulder. She liked that he hadn't closed the bathroom door while he washed up. It seemed homey and normal and she needed that right now.

Although it was strange to have his very masculine presence in her private space. She'd never had a man in this bedroom. It had been a place meant to belong entirely to her, arranged and decorated to her taste and no one else's.

Yet he fit right in. A soft chime of warning pinged in her brain but she shut it down. This whole relationship was about nothing more than comfort and safety and sex. Once the stalker was caught, it would be over.

Tully finished up, drying his face on the powder-blue towel she'd given him, He looked up from it to catch her gaze on him. "You're supposed to be asleep, sugar."

"Not while I have such a spectacular show to watch," she said.

He looked genuinely surprised. "Me washing?"

"You washing without a shirt on. All those muscles flexing." She put a purr into her voice.

He chuckled and struck a bodybuilder's pose, with his arms curved in at his waist so his shoulders bulged and his abdominal muscles rippled like a washboard.

"Yum, makes me want to lick those abs."

He released the pose and prowled to the bed, crawling onto it to give her a quick kiss as he hovered over her. Then he rolled to the side and slipped between the sheets. "Tomorrow. Tonight we both need rest."

He pulled her down beside his body, pillowing her head on his shoulder while his arm went around her back.

His weight dented the mattress so gravity pressed her into the solid mass of him, her thin cotton nightshirt offering very little barrier to the feel of his muscle and bone and body heat. Tully was larger and fitter than her ex-husband, so it felt different when she snuggled against him. That was a good thing. Yet it also felt easy. And sexy when she crooked her knee over his thigh, her bare leg brushing against the hair that dusted his skin.

She hesitated to damage the sensual mood, but she'd been thinking about Regina ever since Dobs had told her his wife was pregnant.

"Tully, I'm worried about Regina. If she's really pregnant, Dobs is going to keep looking for her." And Regina had no one to help her. "Who knows what he'll do if he finds her?"

His arm tightened around her. “You’ve got enough problems on your own plate and now you’re worrying about someone else’s?” His lips were warm against her temple. “I’ve already sent out my best investigative team. They’ll find her.”

Hope and admiration flooded through her. He was as concerned about the other woman as she was. “And then what? She can’t come back here because Dobs is already suspicious.”

“We’ll find her someplace safe to stay until she can sort out the situation with Van Houten. He won’t abuse her ever again. I promise.”

She laid her palm on his chest so she could feel the beat of his heart against it. “I believe you one hundred percent.”

He blew out a long exhale. “I didn’t want to mention this tonight, but it’s something you should know. I asked the police chief if Van Houten had filed a missing person report. The answer was no.”

A tendril of dismay wound through her. “Why wouldn’t he?”

“I have to assume he doesn’t want the police involved.”

She wrestled with the implications of that. “Because he’s afraid they’ll find out he abused her? Or because he wants to capture her himself? Or because he’s my stalker?”

His shoulder moved under her cheek in a shrug. “Possibly all three.”

“You’re saying it’s not a good sign.”

“It’s just another piece in the puzzle. But we’re going to forget about it until morning.”

As she lay beside him, his heartbeat slow and steady beneath her palm, gratitude welled up in her chest. Big macho Tully had shared disturbing information with her instead of withholding it and using the excuse that it would worry her. He thought she was strong enough and smart enough to handle it. A few of the cracks in her soul knitted back together.

Chapter 12

Natalie jolted awake to find Tully already out of bed. She had the sense that there had been a noise that awakened her, but all was quiet now. In the dim light, she saw Tully bend to take something out of his overnight bag from where it sat on the floor beside her bed.

"What is it?" she whispered and then jumped when the doorbell chime sounded through her electronic virtual assistant.

"Stay here," Tully said. She heard the unmistakable sound of a firearm being cocked. He'd gotten his gun out of the bag.

He moved soundlessly to the bedroom door, stepping through and closing it behind him.

Natalie grabbed her phone from the bedside table. It was 4:45 a.m.

Would her stalker ring the doorbell? Had he gone that insane?

She didn't want to face whoever it was in her nightshirt, so she got out of bed and retrieved her clothes from the chair she'd dropped them on. She had her trousers almost buttoned when she heard a cut-off shriek from downstairs. It sounded feminine.

She fastened and zipped her trousers at high speed before she tiptoed to the door, laying her ear against it. Now she could hear the rumble of Tully's voice, so she eased the door open and pressed herself against the wall while she sidled to the top of the stairs.

"It's all right. I'm a friend of Natalie's," Tully was saying in a soothing tone. "If you promise not to bolt, I'll go get her."

Natalie started down the stairs just as Tully appeared at the foot, his pistol held in one hand by the side of his thigh. "Good," he said with a nod. "I believe our visitor is Regina Van Houten."

"Thank God!" Relief rushed through her as she trotted down the stairs. "But why did she come back here? Did Dobs find her?"

Tully shook his head. "I scared the hell out of her, so I don't know yet. I figured she'd rather talk to you."

Natalie dashed past him and into the living area. Regina sat on the sectional with her hands between her thighs, her shoulders slumped, staring straight ahead. Her dyed-brown hair was rumpled and she had a yellow stain on her white T-shirt.

"Regina. I'm so glad you're safe." The other woman turned to stare dully at her when Natalie sat down next to her. "Would you like something to drink? Maybe some coffee?"

Regina nodded, and Natalie saw Tully already moving toward the kitchen, that scary but reassuring gun still in his hand.

"Are you okay?" Natalie asked gently.

Regina nodded again.

"Did Dobs find you?"

The other woman's face crumpled and tears poured down her cheeks. "I ran."

"From Dobs?" He'd been at Natalie's salon in the afternoon, so how had he found Regina so fast?

"N-no. A guy was at the motel, asking the clerk if she'd seen me."

Tully set mugs on the counter beside the coffee maker. "Can you describe him?"

Regina flinched, clearly still unnerved by Tully. "I hid behind a door, so I only heard him. He had an accent, like he was Spanish or something. I ran," she repeated.

"What did he ask the clerk?" Natalie asked.

"He must have had a picture because he asked her if she'd seen this woman. And he offered her money to tell him." A shudder ran through

Regina, making the couch vibrate. "He said I had escaped from a mental hospital. I know I shouldn't have come here but I couldn't think of anywhere else."

"No, it's good that you came here. We were looking for you anyway," Natalie said. "Did the clerk tell him you were there?"

"I don't know. I ran." Her voice quivered as she said it a third time.

"That was smart. You did the right thing," Tully assured her from the kitchen.

Regina grabbed Natalie's forearm in a grip that nearly cut off her circulation. "Don't let him catch me. I didn't tell you something important . . . so you wouldn't have to lie." She inhaled on a sob. "I'm six weeks pregnant. If he finds out, I'll never get away from him."

"Wait! You didn't tell him that yourself?" Natalie asked.

"No, I packed my bag and left as soon as I got home from the doctor. If Dobs knew, he'd lock me in my room until I had the baby. After that, I don't know what he'd do to me."

Natalie hesitated. She hated to upset the already-distraught Regina but the woman needed to know the truth. "Don't worry, we won't let him get to you. But I have some bad news. Your husband already knows that you're pregnant."

"No! No, no, no!" Regina wailed and shook her head back and forth, her hair flopping wildly.

"Shh!" Natalie said, stroking Regina's back. "You see my friend Tully over there? He used to work for the FBI. He knows how to keep you safe."

Regina quieted and clearly started to think. "How did Dobs find out?" She turned to Natalie with her eyes wide and frightened. "How do *you* know that he knows?"

"He came to the salon yesterday, hoping I would tell him where you were. I wasn't sure if he was telling the truth when he mentioned the baby or whether he was trying to gain my sympathy to get more information out of me." Natalie smoothed Regina's disheveled hair. "Are you feeling all right?"

"My stomach is kind of messed up. Morning sickness, I guess, except it hits me at all different times of day." Regina curved her hands over her abdomen protectively. "I don't want Dobs anywhere near my baby."

Tully carried over a tray loaded with three steaming mugs of coffee, sugar, cream, and some crackers. "We won't let that happen," he assured her.

"Can the FBI help stop him?" Regina asked, grasping her mug in both hands.

"I don't work for the FBI anymore, but I know the right people to handle this." Tully sat in the armchair across from them. Natalie noted that the gun was now on the occasional table beside him. He must be worried that Dobs or the guy with the Spanish accent might show up.

Tully leaned forward. "Ma'am, can I ask you a few questions, things I need to know to keep you from harm?"

Regina nodded.

"I didn't see a car outside. How did you get here?"

"I was afraid to use my car. The clerk at the motel knew it was mine. I took the bus."

"Where were you?" Tully asked.

"Wheeling. West Virginia." Regina looked at Natalie. "Is it okay to tell you where I was going?"

"You need to tell us *everything* so we know the best way to proceed from here," Natalie reassured her.

"I was going to Kentucky. My second cousin lives there. I haven't seen him in years, but he's a nice guy. I figured he could help me go somewhere else."

"Did he know you were on your way?" Tully asked.

Regina shook her head. "I planned to just show up. So my cousin wouldn't have to lie if Dobs called him."

"Good move," Tully said. Natalie could see Regina's confidence returning under Tully's compliments. "Now we need to get you out of here."

"Can I stay in the guest room?" Regina's eyes filled with tears again. "Just for tonight?"

"Not a good idea." Tully said gently but firmly. "Your husband has already confronted Natalie at her salon. How did you get here from the bus station?"

"I took the PATH train to Newark and a taxi from there to the end of Natalie's road and then I walked. I paid cash."

"You are a very resourceful woman." Tully picked up his gun and stood. "I'm going to make some phone calls. Nat, could I talk to you a minute?" He tilted his head in the direction of the foyer.

Natalie pressed a cracker into Regina's hand. "Eat something. It will help your stomach."

She followed Tully to the foot of the stairs. He was in tactical mode. Eyes like steel, jaw tight, and gun in hand. "Could you put the gun down on the table while we talk? It's a little frightening."

"Of course, sweetheart." He laid it on the foyer table, the barrel pointed away from both of them. "But when it's in my hand, this gun is your friend."

"I get that but it makes the whole situation seem even more like a scary movie. And I don't want to be the star." Natalie tried to smile at her weak joke.

Tully skimmed the back of his hand down her cheek. "This will all be over soon."

"God, I hope so! Where are you going to take Regina?"

"To my place in the city. However, I don't want her to be there without a friendly face because she's nervous, exhausted, and pregnant. Would you be willing to go with her? I know you have to work and I'll get you back in time for that."

"I could get Gino to open up for me and reschedule my appointments." Natalie didn't want to leave Regina alone, either, and she trusted Gino to take good care of the salon.

Tully thought for a moment. "I'm afraid that might tip Dobs off that something is up."

"Then let's take her to Dawn and Leland's. Dawn is in and out with her personal training appointments. I know it's safe because you supervised the security system." She gave him a slanted smile.

"I like it." Tully nodded before he grinned. "And it'll be a pleasure to wake up Leland before the crack of dawn."

"This is good coffee," Tully said, taking a swig from a steaming mug as he sat down on one of the ergonomic chairs in Leland's home office. He'd left Natalie and Dawn to settle Regina into the large guest suite in Leland's Manhattan penthouse.

"It's arabica from Costa Rica." Leland swiveled his chair to face Tully, the multiple computer screens painting a glow on his face. "I looked into Van Houten's finances." He smiled. "Killion isn't the only one who can read a brokerage statement. At any rate, the man has serious bucks, so he's going to be tough to fight in court. He'll hire a battalion of lawyers."

"Did he make the money or inherit it?" Tully asked.

"It's mostly family money but he's added a little bit to the pot." Leland shot him a look of understanding. "You're trying to figure out how smart he is."

"How smart. How driven. How crazy." Tully needed to meet the man to get an accurate assessment. "I plan to pay my man Dobs a visit."

"The estate he lives on in New Jersey has a value in excess of twenty million dollars. You're not going to have an easy time getting in there."

Leland shrugged. "If he's even home. He owns a ski house in Aspen and several beach houses scattered around the world."

"Oh, he's there and he has some security." Tully's team had reported back to him about the cameras, alarms, and staff.

"Well, security won't stop you any more than firewalls stop me." Leland's eyes glinted with amusement.

"My first approach will be just a straightforward, walk-up-to-the-door visit, so no need to worry about guards."

"More a drive-up-miles-of-driveway visit," Leland said. "What excuse do you have to visit him?"

"He's a man of wealth who needs really *good* security, which he hasn't got. I think KRG might want to court his business and I'm willing to stroke his ego by making a house call."

"Ah, yes, a full partner coming to see him. He won't be able to resist that," Leland said.

"Not if he's the kind of asshole I think he is." Tully slowly swiveled his chair back and forth, holding his mug in both hands. "I'm trying to figure out how to make the connection between Van Houten and Natalie's stalker."

"Are you sure there is one?"

Tully raised his eyebrows at his partner. "You know how much I believe in coincidences."

"Well, Van Houten has enough money to hire someone to figure out which internet cafés don't have cameras and to send the messages from those. He wouldn't do that himself."

"No, he'll have minions to do his dirty work. That will make it hard to pin the stalking on him."

"If Van Houten is her stalker and he's keeping her under surveillance, won't he recognize you? You've been at her house and her salon," Leland pointed out.

"That will make it all the more jarring for him. My appearance on his doorstep could push him into making mistakes." Tully swiveled some more while he thought. "What is the point of stalking Natalie if you want to get your wife back?"

"Maybe he was simply angry and wanted to punish someone."

"Or maybe he was trying to soften her up so that when he finally came to see her, she'd be upset and off-balance. That way she might spill what she knew."

"Or both," Leland said.

"Good point. Whether it's physical or psychological, abusers like to beat up on anyone they think is weaker than they are just for the fun of it. No reason for him not to kill two birds with one stone." Anger roiled in Tully's chest. He hoped he would have a reason to punch Van Houten in his aristocratic nose.

Natalie nibbled on the buttery croissant that Dawn had set on the stainless steel tabletop in front of her as they sat in Leland's sleek, modern kitchen. "Thank you for taking in Regina."

Dawn gave her a dagger glare over her yogurt. "Seriously? You know better than to thank me. I'd do the same for anyone in her situation."

"But we woke you up at an ungodly hour to do it." Natalie glanced out the wide window, where the city lights blazed against the dark sky. "Tully enjoyed that."

"I'll bet he did." Dawn put down her spoon. "So what exactly is going on with you and Tully?"

"Sex," Natalie said without hesitation. "Very good sex."

Dawn choked on a laugh. "Yeah, I can see the glow around both of you. But it looks like more than that. He's spent a lot of time on your stalker investigation."

"He's a protector by nature and profession," Natalie said, brushing croissant crumbs off her wrinkled white blouse. She hadn't had time to change out of yesterday's work clothes before Tully had herded her and Regina into his car. "And I need protection right now. That's all."

"You seem very sure of that." Dawn stared into her yogurt bowl for a moment. "You know he refuses to get married."

"So I've been told. What I can't figure out is why. He would be a terrific husband." Natalie sipped her coffee. "And father."

Her heart gave an odd little twist as she pictured Tully with a child riding on his shoulders while a blurry, undefined wife walked next to him.

"Yeah, he loves the kid he's a Big Brother to," Dawn said. "But his family is really screwed up. Alcoholism, gambling, drugs."

"Wow! That's a lot to deal with." No wonder Tully wanted to fight bad guys. It was easier than trying to fight all those intractable problems. "But why does that stop him from getting married?"

"Something about having bad role models and not wanting to drag a wife into his family problems." Dawn shrugged. "He doesn't talk about it much, according to Leland. All I know is that his father died of liver disease due to alcoholism and his sister died of a drug overdose."

Sorrow rolled through Natalie like a gray fog, making her chest ache. Tully's broad shoulders carried a heavy burden. "That's crazy. He's not like that!" Natalie objected.

"Right?" Dawn said. "But he's made his decision and Leland says he won't budge from it."

"That doesn't surprise me." But he was depriving himself of a happiness that he deserved.

"I just thought you should know."

"Now explain why you decided to tell me that particular piece of information." Natalie pinned her friend with a sharp look.

"Look, you say that you don't want to get married ever again—" Dawn began.

"And I mean every word of it," Natalie interrupted, with all the conviction born of a narrow escape from an abusive relationship.

That didn't stop Dawn. "When I see you and Tully together, I can't help thinking that you are really good for each other. Why shouldn't you both be happy?"

Natalie wanted Tully to find a good woman to bring him joy, but it wouldn't be her. "I *am* happy, just as I am."

"You look happier when you're with Tully," Dawn insisted.

"He's a great guy," Natalie said. "I wish him all the best." She was still rebuilding herself. There wasn't room for a man in the process, especially not one as overwhelming as Tully.

"Give it a chance, Nat," Dawn said. "That's all I'm saying."

"You know, I think I'll try some of that raspberry jam on this croissant," Natalie said.

Chapter 13

"Why don't I give you a little layering in the back?" Natalie asked her client. "It would add some lift and bounce to your hair."

The woman smiled at her in the mirror's reflection. "I trust you, so do whatever you think will look best."

"Terrific." Natalie swapped her scissors and began to snip. Working with the texture and natural bend of the hair required a concentration that kept her mind off her personal problems. The feel of the scissors around her fingers, the metallic swish of the blades sliding against each other, and the fragrance of hair products were like a spa experience for her today, blissfully familiar and soothing. As her client's hair fell into a sassy curve, satisfaction spread through her. "I think you're really going to like this."

"Natalie, sorry to bother you." Bianca, the receptionist, approached with a concerned frown. She came up close and murmured, "Your ex is here. He says he needs to talk with you and that it's urgent."

For a moment apprehension balled a fist in Natalie's throat. Matt wouldn't be here if he wasn't upset about something, and she would have to deal with his displeasure. She reminded herself that she was no longer married to him, so she didn't have to live with his punishing anger. Yet she still had to take a deep breath.

"Ask him to wait in my office while I finish up with Leslie." She wasn't going to rush through her appointment because her ex had shown up unannounced.

Pam prowled over to Natalie's chair as Bianca departed. "I'll be right outside your office. Make sure to leave the door open when you go in to talk to him."

Natalie nodded, and Pam walked away.

Making Matt wait would probably increase his anger, but Natalie willed her hands to stay steady as she took her time in trimming and blowing out Leslie's hair. When she was done, she tossed her client's lavender cape into the laundry bin and then wiped her palms on her linen trousers. She hated that Matt could still jangle her nerves like this. She faced herself in the mirror, tucked her short blonde hair behind her ears, and lifted her chin, sending herself the message that she held the power now.

She stopped to tell Bianca to get her next client started with shampooing and strode down the hallway to her office, exchanging what she hoped was a steady glance with Pam as she passed. Her ex stood staring out the window behind her desk, his arms crossed. He was wearing a gray suit, so he must have come from work. She noticed that his hair was longer than he used to wear it. Trying to look young and hip for the new girlfriend.

"Hello, Matt," she said in a cool tone as she took two steps into the room and halted. "I've got a client waiting, so what can I do for you?"

He turned with a scowl. It was odd that he looked so familiar and yet seemed like such a stranger. "You can tell me why two people have come to my office asking about you. I'm concerned for you."

"*Two* people asking about me? Goodness, I'm popular." She only knew about Tully. "What did they want to know?"

His jaw tightened. "The first guy—who had a gun!—accused me of stalking you, which is ridiculous. He seemed to be investigating for you, so you must know him."

Natalie nodded. "He's a former FBI agent."

"Shit, Nat, you're really being stalked?" Matt uncrossed his arms. "Did you catch the guy?"

"Not yet, but Mr. Gibson is working on it." Natalie gestured toward the chair in front of her desk. She wasn't going to let Matt have the power seat behind her desk. "Why don't you sit down, since this sounds serious." She wanted to know about his second visitor.

"Damn straight it's serious. You could be in danger." He hesitated before coming around the desk and seating himself where she'd suggested.

Natalie settled into her desk chair with a small sense of victory. "What did the second person want to talk about?"

A look of unease flitted across her ex-husband's face. "He claimed that you're stealing men's wives."

Natalie managed to chuckle even as the half-truth struck home. "That's insane."

"I laughed too, but the guy wasn't joking. He said you talk them into leaving their husbands. Which sounded like something you'd do." Matt's expression wasn't amused. "Then he told me that you were going to get yourself in trouble and I should warn you to stop."

"Why would he think you could stop me when we are no longer married?" Natalie folded her hands on the desk to keep them from shaking with nerves.

"Right?! I told him that I can't control you anymore."

His statement hit her like a sucker punch. He had *controlled* her. And she had allowed it. *Never again.*

"What did he look like?" The information might be useful.

"I don't know. Regular height, muscular. Dark hair. Some kind of accent. Dead eyes."

"A Spanish accent?" she prodded, remembering what Regina had said about her pursuer.

"Maybe." Matt swept his hands out from the chair arms. "Look, I don't know what you've gotten yourself mixed up in but you need to stop."

"Sometimes you have to help people, even if it stirs things up," Natalie said.

"Well, it's sure as hell stirring things up for me," Matt said, his hands clenched in fists. "I don't like being threatened in my own office."

A stab of guilt hit her in the chest.

"It's upsetting for my staff and it's bad for my reputation," Matt continued before he pointed at her. "Whatever you're doing is affecting my business, so it's a big problem."

She shoved the guilt down. He hadn't come here because he was worried about her. He had come because he was worried about his image. "I can't control other people's actions," she said.

"You can tell those guys to quit bothering me." A vein stood out in his temple. "Seriously, Natalie, I have a good life now, and I don't want your shit interfering with it."

Rage boiled up in her throat. He'd blamed every problem he'd ever had on her and expected her to fix them for him. At least this time the issue really *was* related to her actions. "I will not stop doing the right thing," she said in a calm voice.

"The next time one of those goons shows up, I'm calling you to come deal with him." He must have heard how petulant that made him sound because he stood up abruptly. "Obviously I'm not going to be able to talk any sense into you."

"It must be hard for you to lose control of me," Natalie said with a serene smile as she also stood.

He spun on his heel and stomped out the door. She could hear his footsteps pounding down the hallway.

She sat back down again because her knees felt shaky. Taking a deep breath, she closed her eyes and focused on holding the air in for a count of ten before she let it out slowly. She opened her eyes and turned her chair to face the window, letting the sun's warmth soak into her skin.

She needed to tell Tully about the second visitor to Matt's office. He might be the same man who'd been asking after Regina at her motel.

Which meant that Dobs had definitely connected Natalie with his runaway wife. Even if he was just acting on a suspicion, it had the same frightening effect.

In a way, it would be a relief if Dobs was her stalker too. Then they could take action against him. But what would he have to gain by tormenting her if he was just trying to get his wife back? Was it sheer revenge?

She shook her head in frustration and pushed up out of her chair. She had a client waiting.

As she walked down the hallway, Matt's words about controlling her gnawed at her. It had taken years of subtle manipulation for him to gain that power, but she still got angry with herself. She should have been smarter, should have seen what was happening.

Now it would take more years to rebuild the person she used to be. That was why she was so sure getting involved with Tully long-term was a bad idea. She still felt tentative about herself. He would roll right over her without meaning to.

She needed to limit their relationship to sex and protection. When the need for protection was over, she'd have to give up the sex too.

Tully strode across the blood-red oriental rug in Dobs Van Houten's office to where the other man stood in front of his desk. "I appreciate your seeing me on short notice," he said, shaking Dobs's hand.

"I was intrigued by your call," Van Houten said with a faint smile. "May I offer you a drink? I have scotch or coffee."

Tully chuckled. "I like the menu, but I'm good."

"Please, have a seat." Van Houten sat in one of the two black leather armchairs positioned to face each other in front of his desk. He arranged the crease of his gray wool trousers to center perfectly on his knee and shot the cuffs of his pink button-down shirt.

Tully eased down into the other chair with its brass rivets and oak frame. Sitting in front of the desk was a calculated statement of confidence. Van Houten was saying that he didn't need the massive mahogany barricade to protect his self-importance.

Tully unbuttoned his navy suit jacket while he studied the man sitting across from him. Dobs Van Houten had the bland face, straight blond hair, and pale blue eyes of a preppy, but something seemed slightly off. The eyes were flat and set too close together and the hair was thinning, even though he was in his thirties. He looked like a wholesome apple pie with one slice missing.

Van Houten was also scanning Tully with narrowed eyes. It was the look of someone searching his memory. Tully waited a moment but there was no flash of recognition . . . yet.

"You've got some handsome horseflesh grazing in your fields," Tully said, starting with pleasantries. "I keep a couple of horses of my own out near here." Which he didn't get to ride nearly enough.

"Thoroughbreds?" Van Houten asked.

"Half Thoroughbred, half quarter horse. I like the combination of speed and agility." He'd grown up riding farm horses, so he appreciated sturdiness too—something Van Houten's overbred racehorses didn't offer.

"Ah." Van Houten put a world of disdain into the one short syllable, exactly as Tully had expected. Now Dobs was feeling smug and superior . . . which would make Tully's takedown even harder for him to stomach. "I can arrange for you to visit my stable after if you'd like. So you can see the beauty of a purebred."

Tully nearly refused, but a sudden longing to be with creatures who concealed no dark secrets overcame him. "I'd enjoy that. Maybe on my way out?"

"Of course. I'll have my head groom show you around." Thus Van Houten made it clear that he considered Tully equivalent to an employee—which didn't bother Tully at all. Being underestimated always worked in his favor.

Tully leaned back in his chair and got to the crux of his visit. "You've got an impressive security system." A lie. He'd done some scouting on foot before he'd driven through the electric gates and down the winding road to the stone mansion. "But KRG could make it better."

"Really?" Van Houten raised an eyebrow with a tiny smirk. "Tell me how."

"First, lose the hedge. It provides more protection for an intruder than for you. You don't need it for privacy because you're at least two miles from the nearest road or house."

"That hedge has surrounded this house for over fifty years." Van Houten's voice held a patronizing note, as though Tully couldn't be expected to appreciate such a heritage.

"Then it needs better lighting and a perimeter fence inside it." Tully set his left ankle on his right knee so Van Houten had a good view of his slightly muddy cowboy boot. The man glanced at it with an expression of distaste. Then something else flickered across his face that Tully couldn't quite read. He waited a second before he continued. "You've got at least two blind spots in the video surveillance on the front of the house. One's by the garage and the other is at the front left corner. You might have more but I didn't check the sides and rear."

"I'll ask my security team to rectify that."

"You're welcome," Tully said with a shit-eating grin. "And that's just from a quick glance around. A more thorough inspection would uncover additional holes." He was poking at Van Houten's pride.

The other man's lips thinned to a tight line. "I rely on my personnel more than on technology. A loyal staff is invaluable."

And it probably made him feel like the lord of the manor to command his army of serfs. "Couldn't agree more," Tully said, still trying to figure out if Van Houten had recognized him from his boots. "But I got through your perimeter on foot about a half an hour ago without anyone raising an alarm. If you check, you'll find my business card on the stone bench in that fancy gazebo by the fish pond."

Now Van Houten looked seriously pissed off. Tully had figured that the business card would get under his skin. It had been easy to get past the guards, partly because their patrol pattern was easy to predict and partly because for all their vaunted loyalty, they weren't especially alert. They clearly didn't take their assignment seriously.

"I will speak to the guards about that," Van Houten said. Tully caught the flash of ugly fury in his eyes and in the white knuckles gripping the arms of his chair.

"I'm sure your night crew is better, since that's the time of higher risk." Tully matched the patronizing tone Van Houten had used earlier.

The anger blazed hot for a second before something darker took its place. Van Houten's eyes went utterly opaque and his hands relaxed before he smiled in a way that made Tully's psycho detector whoop a loud alarm. "I'll see to it that my security staff members take their duties very seriously from now on."

Tully nodded. "KRG would be happy to train your staff."

"That won't be necessary," Van Houten said, the ugly smile evaporating into a cold blankness.

Now Tully knew. This was a man who could abuse his wife and take pleasure in it. He would also relish playing cruel psychological games, such as stalking Natalie. However, his capacity for cruelty wouldn't prove he had done either of those things.

"If you'll give me permission, I'll look around a little more and draw up a proposal for you," Tully said.

"Let me give it some thought and get back to you." Van Houten stood abruptly.

Tully took his time uncrossing his leg and rising to his feet. He stepped in closer, using his greater height to look down at Van Houten as he extended his hand. "It's been a pleasure. I hope we'll be working together soon."

"I'll be in touch. Maria will be outside the door to show you out." Van Houten did not shake Tully's hand nor did he bother to walk with Tully to the office door. Instead, he pulled his cell phone from his pocket. Tully heard the furious edge in Van Houten's voice as he ordered the person he was talking with to come to his office.

Tully smiled. He'd stirred up the hornet's nest.

After a refreshing half hour spent in the company of large, beautiful animals who didn't have a psychopathic gleam in their eyes, Tully climbed back into his Maserati. He was savoring the feel of hugging the curves on the two-lane road leading away from Van Houten's estate when a call came in from Natalie's upstairs tenant, Deion.

"Someone's watching the salon." The young man sounded angry. "I set up a camera in my apartment window aimed at the street. The same black SUV has cruised by about every fifteen minutes for the last three hours. It's a big Mercedes Benz. I have the plate number. I'll text it to you."

Tully's hands tightened on the wheel as exhilaration flooded through him. Finally, a solid string they could pull on. "Excellent work. Could you see who was in the car?"

"The windows are tinted, so no. Also my camera isn't real high resolution." His voice held frustration.

"You got the important information. This is a real break, thanks to you," Tully encouraged him. "Are you at your apartment now?"

"No, I'm on break, so I logged into my computer remotely to see if anything looked wrong."

"I'm headed for the salon now. I'm guessing Natalie has a key to your place. May I have your permission to enter and look at the video on your computer?" Tully passed a car dawdling along in front of him. He needed to get back on the highway fast.

"Sure thing, Mr. Gibson." He gave Tully his password too.

"Hey, the name's Tully. And I have an offer for you. How would you like a job with KRG Consulting? I could use someone with your smarts and motivation." Clients would love Deion's good looks too. That never hurt.

"Like a *permanent* job?" Disbelief tinged his question.

"Hell, yes. I'm not going to waste my time training you if you don't intend to stay." Tully dodged around another slow car, the Maserati's engine roaring like a big cat.

"Yes, sir! That would be awesome," Deion said with enthusiasm before he asked, "What would I be trained for?"

"Security. You've got a knack for it. Besides, I found you, so I'm keeping you in my division."

The young man laughed before he asked with some hesitation, "Is it all right if I give my boss two weeks' notice? She's been really good to me."

"I'd respect you less if you didn't." Tully smiled as he accelerated onto the entrance ramp to the highway. "I'll get HR to send you the paperwork. In the meantime, keep up the good work with surveillance at the salon."

After they disconnected, Tully called to alert Pam about the possible threat before he sent the license plate number to one of his resources who could get him the registration information. The stalker had made his first mistake and Tully was going to use it to hunt him down.

Chapter 14

Thirty minutes later, he parked on the street a couple of blocks away from the Mane Attraction. He took off his jacket, ditched his tie, and rolled up his shirtsleeves to give himself a more casual look. Then he sauntered along the street, watching for the SUV Deion had flagged. He spent twenty minutes wandering nearby, but no car matching that description appeared. Tully glanced at his watch. Four thirty. So the salon would be closing in an hour. Why had the car been cruising past?

He walked up the front steps and through the purple door.

"Welcome back to the Mane Attraction, Mr. Gibson." The pretty, young receptionist gave him a pleasant smile. "Natalie has a client right now."

"Hey, Tully!" Pam walked up to the desk. "Any luck with an ID on the SUV the tenant spotted?"

Tully shook his head. "Not yet. Let me grab a cup of coffee." He gestured for her to precede him down the hallway by the staircase to the kitchen. Even with the doors closed, the sound of hair dryers and the smell of hair products permeated the air.

"Nothing from the stalker yet today either." Pam poured a mug of coffee and handed it to him. "Nothing on the surveillance cams around her house except the UPS man."

Tully took a sip of the coffee, surprised to find it almost as good as Leland's. Natalie treated her staff well. "Was Natalie expecting a delivery?"

"Not today specifically, but she has a couple of things on order," Pam said. "He was on and off the porch fast and left a box."

"Could you see his face?"

She shook her head. "He wore a baseball cap."

"I'll check him out on the video later," Tully said with a frown. "I'm more worried about the cruising SUV."

"What do you think it was doing here?"

"That's what I'm wondering. Waiting for a chance to put something else in Natalie's car?"

"If he does, we'll have him." Pam held up her phone with the feed from the security camera she had installed to monitor the parking lot.

"Or he wants to make sure she's staying at the salon?" Tully shook his head. "No use speculating. We'll have to see what his next play is." He bared his teeth in an anticipatory smile. "In the meantime, we have his plate number."

Pam pumped her fist in victory. "Gotcha."

"I'm going to get the key to the tenant's apartment from Natalie." Tully finished his coffee and walked through the archway into the main salon, where he stopped, his gaze drawn immediately to Natalie despite the swirling motion of stylists and customers in the busy room.

Her chair was in the center of the inside wall, a position that would allow her to keep an eye on everyone in the room either directly or via the mirrors in front of her chair. He gave her kudos for good surveillance strategy.

Then he forgot all that as he watched her move around her client like a ballerina, her movements precise and graceful as she lifted swaths of hair with a round brush and aimed her blow-dryer at them. Like the rest of the stylists except the guy, Gino, she wore a lavender smock belted over her navy trousers and cream blouse. The wide sleeves accentuated the sinuous movements of her delicate wrists and hands.

A surge of desire raced through him, settling in his groin. He started toward her just as she did a scan of the room, her eyes widening when she saw him. She smiled, a private, meant-only-for-him smile of welcome and—he'd swear it—seduction. His cock hardened even more.

As he approached the chair, Natalie's customer saw him too. "Well, hello!" she said with a flirtatious note. "Do I know you? I'd like to."

Natalie choked on a laugh. "This is my friend Tully Gibson. Tully, one of my most loyal customers, Marta Cipriani."

Marta held out her hand and Tully shook it with a wink. "Pleasure to meet you, ma'am."

"Absolutely," Marta said, eyeing him with appreciation. She was probably about twenty years older than Tully and had a curly cap of dark-brown hair that Tully suspected owed its rich color to Natalie's expertise.

"Would you excuse me just a moment, Marta?" Natalie asked.

"Take all the time with him that you want, honey," her client said with a knowing look.

Natalie coughed before she led Tully partway down the hall. She lifted her hand to lay it against his chest, sending a zing of pleasure through him. "How did it go with Dobs?" she asked.

"I guess I can't kiss you at your place of business," he said, his eyes on the sweet curves of her mouth, "but I sure as hell want to."

"If I didn't have a client in the chair, I'd take you to my office and we could do more than kiss," she said, the blue of her eyes burning.

His cock got very happy at his vision of bending her over her cream-colored desk and coming into her from behind. "You are one surprising lady." He snaked a hand around her waist to give her gorgeous rounded butt a squeeze. "And I like that about you."

"It's Marta's fault," Natalie said, a delicate flush tinting her cheeks. "She put ideas into my head."

"She said to take all the time you wanted," Tully teased. "And frankly, right now, I'm pretty sure it wouldn't take either one of us very long."

Natalie gave him a slanted smile that made him want to kiss her even more. "You didn't answer my question."

"Did you ask a question?" he joked. "Oh yeah, Dobs." All the fun went out of the conversation. "He's bad news but I'll tell you more later. Right now, I'd like to get the key to Deion's apartment. He gave me permission to check the video from the security cam he set up in the window. He caught a car running surveillance on the salon."

Natalie's elegant brows drew down into a fierce scowl. "Someone's watching the salon? Why? I hope my staff and clients aren't in danger."

"I did my own surveillance before I came in. The SUV didn't show, so it's probably gone now." There was no point in worrying her any more. "By the way, I officially hired Deion to work at KRG."

The scowl disappeared, as he'd hoped it would. "You're so kind to take him on."

He shook his head. "I don't do 'kind' when it comes to business. I want that sort of initiative on my team."

She beamed him a grateful look before saying, "Wait here." She went to the reception desk, knelt, unlocked a drawer, and pulled out a ring of keys. Returning, she handed it to him with a gold one separated from the rest. "Here you go. There's no alarm up there."

He let his fingertips brush across her palm as he took the keys. She inhaled sharply at his deliberate touch.

"You'd better get back to Marta," he said. "Or I might be tempted to throw you over my shoulder and take you to your office anyway."

"Well, that would provide the salon with some really good gossip." Natalie flashed him a wicked look before she sashayed down the hall.

He stayed long enough to enjoy every last swing of her hips before she disappeared into the main room. Tonight was going to be real good.

Natalie slipped out of her lavender smock and dropped it in the laundry bin. “Good night, Bianca,” she called to the receptionist as the young woman left the now-quiet salon. Natalie rubbed a hand over the back of her neck and then jumped when two big hands came down on her shoulders and began to knead them. “How do you walk so quietly in cowboy boots?”

“Training at Quantico and practice.”

His strong fingers pressed against the knotted muscles in her shoulders, balancing on the precise edge between pleasure and pain. “Oh, God! That feels amazing. Did they teach you that at Quantico too?”

“Well, my firearms instructor always told me I had good hands.” His voice seemed to rumble up and down her spine in a delicious way. Then he leaned down to whisper right beside her ear, “I hear there are massage tables in the room next door.”

Heat shimmered through her, winding into a tight, pulsing point between her legs.

His whisper came again as he continued to massage her shoulders. “You could take all your clothes off and let me work on every muscle in your body.”

She moaned at the image he conjured up of her body naked on the table while he ran those powerful hands all over her bare skin. She could almost feel his fingers sliding between her thighs and stroking into the ache she felt growing low inside her.

“Those massage tables can’t hold two people who are . . . moving,” she said with regret.

“Well, depending on how you feel about it, the table would only have to hold one.” His voice was a warm rasp now.

Now she had a picture of him bending her over the end of the table and driving into her from behind, his hands gripping her hips while her breasts were pressed against the smooth vinyl of the tabletop. "I think I may come just from thinking about it," she said on a gasp.

He moved in closer so she could feel his erection against her bottom. His hands skimmed down from her shoulders to her breasts, his finger finding her hard nipples through the silk and lace of her clothes and circling them. His touch set off a shower of sparks that burned down into the desire pooling in her belly.

"Yes!" she said, letting her head fall back against his shoulder.

"Yes to what, sweetheart?" Now he moved his entire palm over each breast, the friction making her hips begin to pulse in rhythm with his hands.

"All of it." She wanted his hands on her and his cock inside her.

Before she knew what was happening, he'd scooped her up against his chest and was striding toward the treatment rooms. "Very Neanderthal," she said, looping one hand around the back of his neck. "I like it."

"I just want to get there quicker," he said, waiting as she reached out to turn the knob for Room 1 and push open the door.

The scent of lavender with a citrus note of bergamot lingered in the room from the last aromatherapy message. Tully sniffed. "Nice."

He shoved the door closed with his boot before he eased her down onto the pale blue sheet covering the massage table. He leaned over to kiss her, his mouth soft and firm at the same time. She curled one hand around the back of his head, his hair springy against her palm. With her other hand, she gripped the hard muscle of his shoulder.

His kiss was so distracting that it took her a few moments to realize that his fingers were busy with the buttons of her blouse. She smiled against his lips. "Are you really going to give me a massage?"

"A promise is a promise," he said. "It may be a very short one."

When he got to the last button, she sat up and shimmied out of her blouse before she unfastened her bra and peeled it off.

Tully's gaze fell to her now-bare breasts, his face taut with lust. She leaned back on her arms and arched her back to tempt him. He gave in with a groan, leaning down to suck on one nipple. The heat and moisture on her sensitized skin sent exquisite thrills racing through her body. When he switched to the other breast, she dropped her head back and moaned.

And then he slipped his hand between her thighs to press exactly where she wanted it, rubbing the fabric back and forth against her. To her shock, she exploded into orgasm after only moments, her head thrown back to cry out Tully's name.

As the tremors lessened, she eased down onto the table, opening her eyes to find Tully standing over her and looking down with a blaze of heat lighting his gray eyes. "Every time I think you can't get any hotter, you prove me wrong," he said as he stroked a hand over her bare shoulder and down her arm. When he reached her hand, he picked it up and set a kiss in her palm, his lips warm.

A tingle ran down her arm. "You generated the heat. I just soaked it up," she said, the orgasm still sending gentle ripples of pleasure through her.

"Let me know when you're ready for your massage." He kept her hand in his warm, strong grip.

"That wasn't it?"

"You don't know much about massages, do you?"

She smiled up at him with half-closed eyes. "I'm pretty sure that one was illegal in most states."

"Not half as illegal as what I'm planning now."

Her nerve-endings did a little dance. "Okay, I'm ready."

"Yes, ma'am." Tully stripped off her trousers, panties, and shoes, his heavy-lidded gaze skimming over her body like a torch. "I hate to say this, but roll over onto your stomach."

She obliged, putting her face in the cradle at the end of the table. She heard a sound that it took her a moment to place as a pump bottle being pressed. Then his hands were stroking down her back and buttocks with a lack of friction that meant he'd used the massage lotion to oil them. When he began to work on her shoulders, she moaned in bliss. The orgasm had relaxed her muscles enough so that he could loosen them fully. He worked over her arms and hands, then moved to her legs and feet. When he pushed his thumbs into her tired arches, she groaned in ecstasy.

"Sweetheart, I think this massage is over." His voice was husky and he skimmed his hands up her legs before wrapping them around her hips to slide her gently toward him.

Heat flashed through her like a brushfire. She put her palms on the table and helped him scoot her to the end so that her feet touched the floor. Arousal went liquid inside her as she heard his belt buckle clink, his zipper whine, and the sound of a condom envelope being ripped open.

He positioned his cock and then his hands held her hips while he thrust inside her in one smooth motion.

They both gasped out inarticulate cries of pleasure and he began to move. She couldn't do much except enjoy the feel of him filling her before he pulled almost all the way out and entered her again. His grip on her grew tighter as his rhythm increased. Her body skidded on the sheet, the friction stroking her peaked nipples. Her muscles began to tighten in anticipation, and then he reached around to find her clit with one hand.

Her climax ripped through her so hard that she arched up from the table, her back bowed, as she nearly shrieked at the intensity.

"Oh yeah, sweetheart," Tully panted, going still as her internal muscles clamped around him. "That feels so good. Make me come."

Which made her muscles contract again. And then he began to drive in and out of her in a frenzy, shouting her name as he pushed deep and pulsed inside her.

She lay still, savoring the feel of Tully still inside her, his thighs in their fine wool trousers pressed against hers, his breath gusting above her. He let go of her hips and braced his hands on either side of her. She sensed him shifting even before she felt the brush of his lips on her shoulder blade.

"I wish you could see how beautiful you look right now," he said against her skin.

She turned her head against the table to smile. "All you can see is my back."

"It's an amazing back—all curves and dips." His fingers feathered over her, triggering a delicious shiver. "Your skin looks like cream satin against the blue sheet."

"I didn't know you could be so poetic." Matt had preferred crudity during sex.

"Only when inspired." He shifted again and slipped out of her, leaving an ache of emptiness. It was dangerous to feel so connected to him during sex.

She shoved up from the table and looked around for her panties while he disposed of the condom. Before she could retrieve her clothes, Tully pulled her into his arms. All the expensive textures of his clothing grazed her naked skin, sending a sensual thrill skittering through her. "I feel like that painting of the naked woman picnicking with the fully dressed men."

"That painting is sexy as hell," Tully said.

"It was meant to be shocking." She leaned against him with a sigh. He was so solid, so strong. She could enjoy that for just a little while without compromising her promises to herself.

"One and the same, in this case," Tully said, clearly in no hurry to move either. He let out a long exhale, his breath ruffling her hair. "This is nice, Nat. This is real nice."

She tried to make herself move because it was *too* nice. But her muscles refused to obey her brain. Her body knew what it wanted.

They stood in an easy silence for several minutes before Tully exhaled again, this time with a note of regret. "Okay, sweetheart, let's go get some takeout. I've got a powerful craving for some barbecued ribs."

Half an hour later, she pulled into her driveway with Tully's Maserati right behind her. As usual, he told her to stay in the car until he'd done recon, so she entertained herself by watching the way his long stride ate up the expanse of lawn before he took her porch steps in a single leap. She lost sight of him when he walked farther onto the porch, so she pulled out her phone to check for stalker emails. So far today, there had been none. Maybe the psycho had gotten whatever nasty thrill he wanted and would leave her alone now.

When Tully knocked at her car window, she jumped before she unlocked the door. He swung it open and said, "We're leaving."

It was only then that she noticed the grim set of his mouth and the icy look in his eyes. "What is it?"

"He left something on your door that you don't want to see. You're coming to my place for the night."

Fear froze her as she tried to imagine what was on her door. "Is it a dead animal?" She would hate to be the cause of an innocent creature's death, even indirectly.

He shook his head. "Trust me, you don't need this image in your mind."

"Can you just tell me what it is? I think not knowing makes it worse."

He looked away for a moment as though debating before he pinned her with that hard gaze. "I'll tell you if you agree to leave."

Anger roiled through the fear. "I'll make that decision after I know what the stalker left for me."

He made a gesture of frustration. "It's the picture of you from the email, pinned to the door with a big ugly knife."

A strange sense of relief eased her tension. "That's bad but I can handle it."

"He threw blood all over your front door."

"You mean red paint?"

"No, I mean blood. You can buy it from a butcher." He took her hand. "Let's get you out of here. I'll have one of my people clean it up after they take photos and samples."

Maybe he was right that she shouldn't see what her door looked like. She might never be able to walk through it again with a quiet mind.

"Nat," he said, interlacing their fingers so that his hand enveloped hers. "This is a major escalation. You can't stay here tonight."

"I agree."

"Thank God! I thought you were going to argue with me." The tension in his jaw relaxed a fraction.

"I'm smart enough to know when you're right."

"That's one of the things I like about you," he said with a flash of a tight-lipped smile.

She huffed out a laugh and reached into her car for her purse and laptop bag. "Wait, why didn't Pam see something on the surveillance camera?" she asked as Tully took the laptop from her. "She had the video feed going to her cell phone."

"The UPS man had to be a fake," Tully said, his voice a growl. "He found a way to fool your front door camera. I should have replaced it with one of mine. They're a lot harder to mess with."

He held the door for her while she slid onto the luxurious leather seat of Tully's fancy sports car.

As Tully folded his big body into the driver's seat, another thought struck her. "He didn't want me to be home when he left his message, did he? That's why he cruised past the salon several times. To make sure my car was there in the parking lot."

Somehow it made her feel better that her stalker was avoiding her. She shuddered. Thank God she hadn't been home when the stalker splashed blood over her front door.

However, when she looked at Tully, the stern set of his profile wasn't reassuring. He backed out of the driveway and headed down the road before he said, "He's still hiding his identity." Then he bared his teeth in a smile that was downright feral. "But we've got the license plate number, thanks to Deion. We'll nail him with that."

"Do you think Dobs is doing this?" She couldn't picture the sobbing wreck of a man stabbing a knife in her door before splashing it with blood. But didn't the neighbors always say that the psychopath next door seemed like a nice person, just a little quiet?

"Yeah, I do," Tully said, his hands flexing on the leather-wrapped steering wheel. "Except he wouldn't do it himself. That's beneath him. He'd send his minions. That's who was cruising past the salon. Minions make mistakes because they've got less skin in the game."

"But why? He couldn't have known that I helped Regina." She was so careful, and Regina hadn't spoken to him since she packed her bag and left.

"My guess is that he had her watched. He's the type who would." Tully turned onto the highway, the car accelerating with a potent roar that Natalie would have enjoyed if she hadn't been so worried.

Natalie's stomach lurched at how close Regina had come to being caught by her abusive husband. "I'm so glad she's safe now."

"We have to keep her that way."

"What do you mean? As long as she's at Dawn and Leland's, she'll be fine, won't she?" Even Dobs—with all his wealth—couldn't drag his wife out of Leland's penthouse.

"The legal stuff may get complicated," Tully said. "You're meeting with Regina and the divorce lawyer tomorrow. See what he says."

Regina had asked Natalie to be there for support during the initial consultation. She'd said she wasn't sure her brain was functioning properly between her pregnancy and her fear.

Natalie understood. She'd gone through the divorce with only her lawyer to advise her. The woman had been smart and tough, but she had always told Natalie that the final decisions about what she wanted to fight for were up to her. Sometimes Natalie's emotions were so knotted up that she had no idea what the right answer was. So Natalie had cleared her schedule for the morning.

"And now I don't have to deal with Lincoln Tunnel traffic during rush hour," she said with a wry smile.

Tully threw her an approving glance. "That's right. Don't let the bastard get you down."

"But what if it isn't Dobs? What if it's some random stranger? Or someone I know who's doing this for an entirely different reason?" She would have two problems on her hands.

"I don't believe in coincidence." Tully's tone was hard. "I'll bet my favorite boots that the license plate will tie back to Van Houten somehow."

"How fast will you know?"

"I'm expecting the information any minute now. My guy is good."

"I guess there's nothing more we can do right now," Natalie said, letting herself relax into the cradling seat. "So I'll just look forward to satisfying my curiosity about where you live."

Tully glanced at her with an odd guardedness. "Why are you curious about that?"

"You've seen my place. Every square inch of it, in fact. I think it's only fair that I see yours." She ran her finger over the expensive burled wood of the dashboard. "This car tells me something about you. Your home will tell me even more."

"Don't you already know enough about me?" His tone was almost defensive.

"I know the fundamental things. You're a man of integrity and loyalty. You like the good guys to win and you fight to make it happen. You can be counted on."

"Don't stop now," he said in a bantering tone that meant he wanted her to stop. She could see his discomfort with her catalog of his virtues.

She threw him a wicked smile. "You're terrific in bed."

"As I hope to demonstrate later on," he said.

Her blood fizzed in her veins. She reached over and stroked her palm down the hard muscle of his thigh.

"No distracting the driver," he said after a sharp inhale.

"I'm just indicating my approval of your plans."

He covered her hand and gave it a squeeze before he grinned. "But first, we're getting ribs."

Chapter 15

All Tully had told her about his home was that he lived on the Upper West Side along the river. So Natalie was not prepared when he pulled into an actual driveway that led to an actual *house* in Manhattan. No, "house" was too modest a word. It was more of a mansion. He swung the car through a large iron gate that opened at his approach and then closed behind them as he parked in the paved courtyard.

Natalie leaned forward to gawk at the elaborate white marble–clad building that rose up for four stories. "Wow!" was all she could say.

Tully exited the car without a response, coming around to open Natalie's door before she'd recovered from the shock. "I'll grab the bags from the back," he said as she stood and stared.

Tully had insisted on stopping at a boutique to buy Natalie some clothes for her overnight stay. He said he had everything else she might need in his guest room. Not that she expected to sleep there.

"This wasn't where I pictured you living," she said, taking the insulated tote of ribs from him. She scanned the ornate carvings and green tile roof. There was even a fanciful little turret with swirling copper cornices.

Tully's lips slanted into a grimace. "It's a little over the top for my taste, but I don't like sharing walls with my neighbors, and I enjoy the view of the river."

He led her up the marble steps to the entrance, where he pressed his thumb against a black square and typed in a series of numbers on a keypad before he pushed open the massive oak door.

"This is the *back* door," Natalie said. "What does the front door look like?"

Tully looked puzzled. "Pretty much the same. Why?"

"Never mind." Natalie preceded him through the door into a hallway that made her gasp. The floor was marble, the walls were paneled in wood that ran up and across the ceiling in ornate corbels and carvings. The bronze-and-glass light fixtures hung on long chains.

She waited while Tully let his fingers dance over a high-tech panel to reset the alarm system.

They continued walking until they ended up in the main entrance. The vast space held a grand piano, a huge fireplace, and a carved staircase that featured leaded glass windows along its upward slope.

Natalie stood in the middle and slowly turned in a circle before she met Tully's gaze. "I can't believe you live here."

His eyes held a rueful glint. "Sometimes I can't either. Truth is I don't spend much time here. And virtually none on this floor. It's ridiculous."

"It's spectacular, but it's not you. I want a tour of the whole thing!"

Tully's grin held relief. "Glad to oblige . . . after we eat. The smell of those ribs has gotten me mighty hungry."

"Where do you eat?" Natalie spotted a long table with about twenty chairs around it through a square archway. "Not at the banquet table, I'm guessing."

"Nope, there's a small kitchen on the second floor where I have my meals." He made a face at the grand dining room. "The decorator said the room needed a table that size but I've never used it."

"What a shame! I was picturing you presiding over dinner with a bewigged footman behind every chair." She slid him a teasing glance.

"You think I could talk Leland into wearing his wig here?" Tully said, referring to the Regency ball Derek had staged for his proposal to Alice.

"He said it itched, so no."

Tully chuckled and gestured toward the stairs with his handful of bags.

"Let me carry some of those," Natalie said, reaching for the shopping bags.

"I'm good," Tully said, because of course he would.

"Fine. I will pretend like I'm Cinderella in my ball gown ascending the royal staircase." She put her hand on the gleaming wood bannister and, lifting her chin, walked slowly up the steps as though she were wearing a crown. The piano caught the corner of her eye. "Do you play that?"

"No, it came with the house. Too much trouble to move, I guess." He glanced down at it. "Maybe when I retire I'll take lessons."

He sounded serious and a little wistful. "You like music?"

She knew so little about him and yet she had given him her unquestioning trust. She needed to rein it in fast.

"I like to dance," he said with a wicked twinkle in his eye. "Especially the two-step."

The dance that had started this. Well, maybe taken it to the next level. "You're a man of surprises."

"Actually, I'm a pretty straightforward guy." But his answer sounded automatic, like he'd said it many times before to deflect . . . what?

They reached the top of the stairs and he directed her down a hallway that was slightly less intimidating. The door he indicated led into a beautiful updated kitchen with dark hickory cabinets, a white subway-tile backsplash, and leaded glass windows. A round oak table surrounded by four matching chairs stood on the herringbone brick floor. *This* was Tully.

Natalie plunked the tote on the granite-topped island while Tully set the clothing bags on the counter by the door. "Let's eat."

Natalie followed his directions about where to find dishes, flatware, and napkins while Tully unloaded the bag. The aromas of barbecue sauce, melted cheese, and jalapeño cornbread made her mouth water.

When they had settled at the table, Tully raised his beer bottle and touched the neck of hers with a clink. "I'm glad you're here. And that you understand."

"Understand what?"

He swept his hand around the room. "About the house. That it's not really who I am."

"And yet it is," she said. "It's solid, independent, and built to last."

He smiled but his eyes held genuine gratitude. "That's a compliment I'll take." He put down his beer and picked up a rib. "Now let's eat, woman, so I can take you to bed."

"Tour before sex," Natalie said, even as arousal slid through her body.

"Only if you're willing to take it naked."

Natalie woke up the next morning to sunlight painted across a strange and enormous bed with Tully's big heat-generating body pressed smack up against her. She blinked at the tray ceiling above her centered by a large bronze-and-etched-glass light fixture as memory returned. Tully's house . . . no, mansion. She lifted her head to check out the landscape of pale green treetops in the near view and the wide, brown Hudson River in the far before she let it fall back on the pillow.

Tully stirred and tightened the arm he had thrown over her waist. "You okay?" he mumbled into the pillow.

"Just confused."

"About what?" His voice was more focused now.

So many things, she thought. Why someone would stalk her. How Dobs had connected her with his wife. What her feelings for Tully were. "I couldn't remember where I was," she said.

"You're with me." He kissed her shoulder and settled back against her.

The simple truth of that punched her in the chest. It didn't matter where she was as long as she was with Tully. She didn't feel in danger when Tully was by her side. She didn't question that her stalker would be caught because Tully would do it. When he touched her or even just looked at her, her body responded. She'd entrusted him with the secret of how she assisted other women without a qualm.

She was with him in every way and that was not a good thing.

She twisted in his grasp to reach for her phone to check the time.

"If you keep squirming, things are going to get real interesting," he said in a husky voice.

It was only six thirty, but she needed to get away from him. "I can't sleep, so I'm going to shower."

"Why don't I join you?" he rumbled as he feathered a kiss on her temple.

Because she was afraid of what she was feeling. She turned her head to find him looking at her through half-open eyes. "You should get some more sleep," she said. "I'm just feeling antsy about Regina's meeting with the lawyer."

"Alastair is a good guy," Tully said. "He'll make sure Regina gets the best divorce possible."

He gave Natalie a sweet, lingering kiss on the mouth that nearly had her changing her mind about the solo shower, but he lifted his arm so she could slide to the edge of the bed. She sat there for a moment, thinking about how he had sensed her unwillingness so he hadn't tried to pressure her to make love.

Matt had never cared what mood she was in. If he had wanted to have sex, he would do everything in his power to make her give in to his demands.

For all his strength and authority, Tully never forced anything on her.

Natalie and Regina sat at a small conference table across from Alastair York, the divorce lawyer KRG's legal department had connected them with. The surprisingly young lawyer had auburn hair, a faintly British accent, and a gentle twinkle in his blue eyes. Natalie hoped he was tougher than he looked because Dobs Van Houten wasn't going to be a pushover.

On the other hand, Regina had visibly relaxed when Alastair shook her hand with a disarming smile and led them into the small, almost intimate meeting room. The younger woman had confessed her nervousness to Natalie and Tully on the drive to the law office, saying that she was intimidated by the prospect of having a high-powered, cut-throat New York City lawyer represent her.

"Coffee, tea, or something chilled?" Alastair asked in his charmingly clipped voice as he hovered over a credenza with various beverages arrayed on it. Natalie would have expected him to have an assistant to pour the drinks. After all, he was a partner in the fancy law firm.

Instead, he brought two steaming mugs of coffee and one of tea to the sleek glass-topped table before he sat in front of a closed laptop.

Folding his long, elegant hands on top of the computer, he said with a sad smile, "I'm very sorry you have to use my services. Divorce is always difficult. I know a little of your story but why don't you tell me in your own words why you are seeking to end your marriage?"

Regina straightened her shoulders and inhaled deeply. She was dressed in a blue-and-white-striped cotton blouse over navy trousers, an outfit Dawn had helped her choose. Natalie had styled Regina's dyed-brown hair into a loose bun at the nape of her neck to give her some confidence.

"My husband has hurt me on several occasions. I finally left when he threatened to throw me down the stairs. He also insulted and humiliated me verbally whenever we were alone."

Natalie had coached Regina to be concise and as unemotional as possible. As she'd learned from her own divorce, when you got right down to it, most of the negotiations were about the division of assets. Although this one had the complication of an unborn child.

Alastair looked sympathetic. "How long has this behavior been going on?"

"About six months." Regina reached for Natalie's hand. "I thought he was just stressed about us getting pregnant at first. He wanted it so badly and I kept getting my period. So I tried to smooth things over. I didn't want to admit that Dobs was abusive but . . ." She trailed off as her grip tightened. Natalie gave her hand a gentle squeeze. "But things escalated. He scared me."

"Are you still afraid that he would do you bodily harm?"

Regina nodded before she said in a near whisper, "Yes."

"Then our first order of business is to get a restraining order." Alastair flipped open the laptop. "I apologize for making you relive this unpleasantness, but can you tell me specifically what he did and said? I also need to know if anyone else witnessed any of the incidents."

"No, no one did. In public, he was loving and considerate, the way he had been before we got married and on our honeymoon. Every time we'd go out and he'd be so nice, I'd think—hope—that this was the real Dobs coming back." Tears stood in Regina's eyes and Natalie's heart twisted. "But we'd get home and he'd go back to being . . . horrible."

Regina's words dredged up ugly memories from Natalie's marriage. How Matt would smile and laugh and put his arm around her when they were out with friends. The moment they were alone, he would whip his arm away from her and put two feet of distance between them.

Then he would enumerate all the things she'd done wrong during their evening out.

The emotional whiplash kept her walking on eggshells as she tried to gauge Matt's mood and propitiate him.

"Did you ever have any visible injuries?" Alastair asked, his fingers still poised over the keyboard.

"Bruises," Regina said. "Natalie saw them on my arms. That's when she told me I could stay with her. But I still didn't think Dobs would really hurt me, so I didn't leave then."

"Sweetie, those were ugly bruises," Natalie said. "He'd already hurt you."

"I understand that now," Regina said, her eyes bleak. "Back then I was still making excuses for him. I feel so stupid."

Natalie understood. She'd believed it when Matt told her that their problems were her fault, that she needed to work harder to be a better wife. He didn't like it when she went out with her friends, so she'd curtailed her social life. He resented it when she was sick, so she went to bed only when she almost couldn't stand up any longer. He complained about the time she put in at the hair salon, but he liked the money she brought in. She took advantage of his ambivalence about her job to continue working.

The salon had saved her. There, she could feel good about herself because her clients felt good about themselves when she did their hair. She listened to their problems, sharing their burdens for just long enough to make their mood lighter when they left. Instead of Matt's voice droning in her ear that she was a failure, her boss and her customers told her what a great job she was doing.

But it almost hadn't been enough.

"Do you have any photographs of the bruises?" Alastair asked.

Regina surprised Natalie by nodding. "Not the first ones because I thought they were an accident. But after that, I took pictures just so I'd know I wasn't crazy." She looked down at the table. "He kept telling me that I was exaggerating and that he hadn't really hurt me. I knew he had put bruises on me, but he was so definite about not having done it that I started to think he was right."

"That was a very clever thing to do." Alastair's encouragement reminded Natalie of Tully offering the same support to Regina. "Now tell me as much as you can remember about each incident. Date, time of day, what happened, what your husband said to you, if you can remember."

Regina pulled her cell phone and a folded piece of legal paper from her purse. She passed the paper to Alastair. "That's a list of my best guess on the dates. I marked the ones I'm sure of because I have photos on my phone." She turned on her cell and handed it to Alastair. "This is my old phone. I saved it for the photos. You can keep it here."

He looked at the paper and then at the phone. Natalie saw anger flare in his blue eyes and she stopped worrying about how tough he would be in divorce court. "In your own words, tell me what happened."

Regina nodded and took a deep breath. "When Dobs told me he wanted to have a child right away, I was thrilled. That meant he really loved me, right? And I always wanted to have a big family. But when I didn't get pregnant right away, he said . . ." Regina stared into the coffee mug she had clutched in her hand before she continued in a barely audible voice. "He said that he'd only married me because I looked like a good breeder and now I was failing."

Natalie's hands balled into fists that she wanted to slam into Dobs Van Houten's snooty face.

Regina seemed to curl into herself. "He made me have sex whether I wanted to or not. When I tried to refuse, he grabbed my wrists or slapped me, so finally I just let him do what he wanted. I felt like a prostitute." Tears ran down Regina's cheeks. "But then he would give me jewelry and flowers and clothes. I thought that meant he loved me again."

"He was manipulating you," Natalie said. "Trying to make you believe that his behavior was loving and normal when it was abusive. It's called love bombing."

When she and Matt were dating, he had brought her gifts and told her how amazing she was, making her feel adored. It wasn't until after they were married that he began to undermine her with little jabs of criticism. By then, she was convinced he loved her, so she believed his harsh words, especially when he claimed his comments were meant to help her be even better than she already was.

"I never knew which Dobs he would be when he walked in the house," Regina said.

"He wanted you off-balance," Alastair said, nodding.

"The day I left him, I had been to the doctor because my period was late. I was pretty sure I was pregnant." She laid her hand over her belly. "But I didn't want to tell Dobs without being absolutely certain. He'd be furious if it turned out I wasn't."

She took a deep breath. "I hadn't told him I was going out because I didn't want him to know where I was. And I'd left my cell phone at home because he tracks me on it. It turned out he'd come looking for me to have sex and couldn't find me. So when I got home, he was in a rage. He was waiting for me at the top of the stairs. Before I could tell him the good news, he grabbed me and said he was going to throw me down the stairs because I was useless to him."

She had both hands on her abdomen as she choked on a sob. "I was pregnant and he was going to hurt my baby."

Natalie put her arm around Regina's shoulders. "So you protected your baby by leaving. That took great courage."

Regina shook her head. "I almost told Dobs then because I knew it would make him love me again. But then I thought about raising a child with him. What if the baby disappointed him? Would he throw our child down the stairs?"

"How did you get away from him?" Alastair asked.

She flushed. "I told him I wanted to have sex with him." She shuddered. "It was the hardest thing I've ever done in my life. As soon as we were finished, he went back to his office while I threw some clothes in my gym bag and told him I had a session with my personal trainer. I went to the gym and left my phone in my locker there before I drove to Natalie's house."

"I'm impressed by how you kept your wits about you in a highly stressful situation," Alastair said, pushing a box of tissues closer to her.

Regina took one and wiped her face. "It was like Dobs had cast some kind of evil spell over me. Once I broke it, my brain started to work again."

Natalie knew how hard it was to cut through those chains made of lies and humiliation. "You are amazing, sweetie," she said to the younger woman.

"I didn't want to get you in trouble by bringing the phone to your house," Regina said to her. "I was afraid Dobs could track it even if I turned it off."

Alastair typed a bit longer before closing the laptop. "I've sent all the information off to be set up in a formal complaint. I know a judge in New Jersey who will expedite it." He folded his hands on the computer again. "Now we need to talk about divorce."

"All I care about is getting custody of my baby," Regina said. "Dobs can keep his money."

Alastair nodded. "I understand, but this is going to be tricky. Your child has no rights until it is born, so neither of you can be granted custody at this point. However, your husband will easily be able to delay the divorce proceedings until the child is born. Then we'll have a tough custody battle on our hands."

"Not if it's a girl," Regina said. "Dobs only cares about carrying on the family name."

"Then let us hope you have a daughter," Alastair said.

Natalie heard the faint note of skepticism in the lawyer's voice and agreed with him. Dobs would want to punish his wife, so he would try to take the child she cared about away from her, whether it was a girl or a boy.

"In the meantime, let's discuss what I would recommend you ask for in the divorce settlement," the lawyer said.

Natalie gave Alastair kudos for subtle persuasion. Regina wanted to have nothing to do with Dobs Van Houten for the rest of her life. However, Alastair pointed out that she owed her unborn child a secure financial future, so they worked out a way to manage that without being tied to Dobs after the divorce.

After they rose from their seats at the conference table two hours later, Alastair walked them through the firm's lobby to the elevators. "I'll send the restraining order papers over for your signature as soon as they're ready," he said, shaking Regina's hand.

He turned to Natalie and grasped her hand in both of his. "I admire what you do very much. If another one of your guests should require legal assistance, please don't hesitate to call me."

"That's very kind of you," Natalie said, surprised by his offer.

The flash of anger lit his eyes again. "I find domestic abuse appalling. No one should be forced to live in that kind of situation."

Natalie rubbed her eyes and closed her laptop. The appointment with Regina's lawyer had been early in the morning, and on Thursdays the Mane Attraction was open late, so it had been a long day. She had stood up to tell Pam she was ready to leave when her bodyguard appeared in the doorway. "You have a visitor."

Pam stepped aside and Deion bounded into Natalie's office. With his dreads pulled back in a neat ponytail and his necktie loosened so his shirt collar stood slightly open, he looked like a fashion model. "My boss—who's a great lady like you—let me resign from the store without giving two weeks' notice, so I can start with KRG any time." He threw his arms around Natalie. "Thank you so much."

"I didn't do anything to earn your gratitude," she said, although it was nice to be hugged by Deion.

He let her go and stepped back. "You introduced me to Mr. Gibson. You told him I was a good guy despite my record." He gestured toward the ceiling. "You gave me a nice place to live so I could start over. You've done a shitload." He waved an apologetic hand. "Sorry, but it's true."

"You earned your good fortune," Natalie said with a smile.

Pam walked all the way into the office with her hand held out. "Welcome to KRG, Deion, and congrats on the job. It's good to have you on board."

"Hey, thanks!" Deion's face lit up as he shook his new colleague's hand. Then his beautiful face turned serious as he faced Natalie again. "You ever need any kind of help that I can give you, you better ask."

"I promise." Natalie was touched by the young man's earnest gratitude. It washed away some of the ugliness she still carried with her after hearing Regina's story that morning.

"Have you heard from the stalker today?" Deion asked.

"Not a peep," Natalie said. "Pam's been monitoring the surveillance feed, and Tully sent someone to check my house in person a couple of times."

Natalie had almost been able to forget about her stalker because she'd been so busy at the salon.

"Why don't you scope out the salon before Natalie gets here tomorrow morning?" Pam said to Deion. "That way we won't walk into anything nasty. Just be careful."

Deion's eyes lit up. "I'm on it. And no heroics—I promise. I know I have a lot to learn."

Two hours later, Pam pulled the big SUV into the courtyard behind Tully's house. His back door opened and warm, buttery light painted the edges of Tully's silhouette in the entrance before he jogged down the steps to open Natalie's car door.

She was so tired that she practically fell out of the high seat of the SUV into his strong, welcoming arms. "You okay?" he asked, brushing a kiss against her temple.

"I just want to stand here a minute," she said, her voice muffled because she had her face pressed into his warm chest, the clean, male smell of him filling her lungs.

His arms tightened slightly and he called a good night to Pam. Natalie heard the car pull away and then only the usual sounds of the nighttime city filtered into her awareness.

"What the hell happened today?" Tully asked, his voice worried, as she clung to him in the middle of the courtyard. "Pam said the stalker went silent."

"It was the meeting with Regina." She blew out a breath. "It brought back some unpleasant memories."

"Shit!" Tully said, then gentled his tone. "Sweetheart, let's get you inside."

She nodded against the fabric of his shirt before she loosened her grip from around his waist and stepped back. "Honestly, I'm fine. I just needed to feel . . . safe."

"You're always safe with me." He put his arm around her shoulders and guided her inside and down the hall to a cozy den. "I know you stopped to eat, but how about a drink? One of those Manhattans you like so much?"

The burn of rye whiskey might blot out some of the memories. "That sounds good. Have you got what you need to make one?" Manhattans required some uncommon ingredients.

"I laid them in today when I knew you were staying here." He gave her shoulders a gentle squeeze before he released her and walked to the built-in bar.

Her heart gave a little leap of pleasure because he'd remembered her favorite drink.

Pushing that feeling away, Natalie glanced around the room lined on two sides with book-filled oak shelves and furnished with matching overstuffed blue velvet sofas, a carved-wood coffee table, and a wine-and-navy Persian rug. The sofas invited her to kick off her shoes and curl her legs under her while she leaned against a throw pillow in the same wine color as the rug. She let her head fall back as she watched Tully through half-closed eyelids.

The standing lamp by the bar threw gold across his face, outlining the blade of his nose and sharp line of his jaw while keeping his eyes in shadow. The hair dusting his arms picked up glints of the light as he measured the liquor into a jigger and poured it into the cocktail mixer. He moved with precision and economy, just the way he did when he inspected her house for security flaws.

"You're very quiet," he said, with a quick glance her way. "Don't want to talk about it?"

"Actually, I think I do, but right now I'm enjoying your presence."

He flashed a grin as he swirled the cocktail shaker in circles. "A lot of folks run in the opposite direction."

"Only the folks who are doing something they shouldn't be. The rest of us wrap ourselves in the mantle of your strength."

"That sounds like something out of a Greek epic poem." Tully poured the amber liquid into two martini glasses and dropped in Luxardo cherries skewered on cocktail picks. "I always wanted to be a Homeric hero like Odysseus."

"You certainly could pose for a statue of one." Natalie smiled at him as he settled beside her on the couch.

He laughed and handed her a drink. "I'm not much for standing still." He touched the rim of his glass to hers. "To the end of a long day."

She took a sip, closing her eyes as the liquor slid down her throat like liquid flame, loosening her muscles before it even hit her stomach. "So your day was long too?"

"A lot of work stuff, projects I needed to catch up on." He snaked his free arm around her and shifted so his solid body pressed against hers from thigh to shoulder. "But I had this to look forward to, so it went by fast."

"You've been spending too much time on my problem," she said as guilt nipped at her.

"No, I spend too much time at brain-sucking meetings." He tipped the glass to his lips and swallowed, the muscles of his throat rippling under the skin dusted with five-o'clock shadow. "I have some bad news on the license plate Deion caught on video. It's stolen."

"They were driving around Cofferwood with stolen plates? Isn't that kind of risky?"

"Not if they behave themselves. It's a pro move for short-term surveillance. Costs money to acquire them but Van Houten has plenty of that."

"But now we can't prove it's him." Not even the effects of the Manhattan could fend off the tension that crawled through her.

"Not yet." Determination ran like steel through his voice. "You ready to tell me about the appointment with Alastair?"

Natalie took another swig of her Manhattan. "He's great. Do you know anything about his background? He seems to feel strongly about domestic abuse."

"Just that he's from England and came here to go to law school. Maybe the fact that he put an ocean between himself and his home tells you something right there."

Tully's perception still surprised her when it shouldn't. Being good with a gun was only part of his job. "You're a very smart man," she said.

"I'm going to get a swelled head tonight if you aren't careful." But there was an undertone of gratification in his voice.

"Dobs is even worse than I thought," Natalie said. "He forced sex on Regina because he wanted her to get pregnant so badly." And Regina had made excuses for him. "She only left him because she was worried that he would hurt the baby." It had taken a near tragedy to open Regina's eyes to the fact that Dobs wasn't the person she thought she had married.

Natalie understood that mindset only too well.

She felt the muscles in Tully's body tighten as a wave of fury rolled off him. "When I take him down, I'm going to take him down *hard*."

Natalie half turned to him. "Can you find a way to keep him from getting even visitation rights for his child?"

Tully stared straight ahead for a few seconds. "We have to tie him to stalking you. That will put him in jail, whereas domestic abuse is hard to prove. If we can demonstrate that he's a psychopath, we might get a judge to keep him away from his kid."

"Then we have to do it. Whatever it takes."

Tully turned to her, his eyes hard but his voice gentle. "Did your ex hurt you?"

"Not like that. It was more subtle." She would have left sooner if Matt had hit her. "I didn't understand that I was being abused until—well, for a long time."

"He struck me as the type who needs to be the center of his universe and will do anything to make sure everyone around him agrees."

"It took me years to figure that out, yet you nailed it in one meeting with him." She felt like an idiot all over again.

"Sweetheart, you loved him. That makes it hard to see a person clearly." Tully's voice was gruff with understanding.

"I was like Regina with Dobs. I thought he loved me, because he gave me extravagant gifts and took me to Broadway plays." She had been dazzled at first, then guilty that she wasn't more grateful.

"He had to substitute grand gestures to trick you into believing he cared about you." Tully looked thoughtful for a moment. "He was also showing off, proving how successful he was to the world."

Natalie laughed without humor. "He got angry if I didn't flaunt his gifts in front of our friends."

"What made you finally leave him?" Tully asked, his voice holding nothing but compassion.

Natalie stared at the dark-red cherries in her empty Manhattan glass. If she told him, he would think she was a coward. If she chose not to tell him, she would *feel* like a coward. Something about Tully compelled her to honesty. In fact, she *needed* to tell him.

She took a deep breath and lifted her gaze to the bookshelves across from her. "He insisted that I was wrong and a failure so many times that I believed him. I felt worthless." She looked back down at her glass. "I was visiting my mother and saw a bottle of sleeping pills on her bedside table. I picked it up and slipped it into my pocket to take home." She blew out a breath. "It seemed like just going to sleep forever would be better than the life I was living."

"Shit!" Tully hissed. Before she knew what was happening, he'd taken her martini glass away and pulled her against his chest, his arms wrapped around her like warm steel bands. "That bastard!"

Sobs welled up from deep inside her as she relived that moment of utter hopelessness when she stared into the black hole that was her future. Tully stroked her hair as her tears soaked the cotton of his shirt.

"Cry all you want," he murmured.

She wanted to burrow in so that all she could feel was Tully's heat and strength enveloping her. But she forced down the sobs and unclenched her fingers from the fabric she'd seized without knowing it. Giving a little push against his chest so he would release her, she brushed at the tears on her cheeks.

"I didn't expect to cry," she said with a crooked grimace of apology. "That was four years ago and I put the damn pill bottle back on the table about a half an hour later. Obviously."

"Because you are one hell of a strong woman." Tully swiped a cocktail napkin out of the stack on the table and handed it to her. "Even a scumbag like your ex couldn't keep you down."

His words sent a tendril of warmth spiraling into her heart. He didn't think she was a coward after all. "That's when I decided to get a divorce. I figured I couldn't feel any worse than I already did."

She blotted the moisture under her eyes and dared to look at him. His jaw was tight with anger but his eyes were luminous with concern—a potent combination.

"I hate that you had to reach that point," he said. "But it got you to the right decision."

"I feel sort of spineless that I didn't leave him sooner but . . ." She shrugged. "Divorce wasn't something I expected to happen to me."

But she never wanted to feel engulfed in that terrifying darkness again.

"You weren't spineless." He brushed back a damp strand of hair that had stuck to her cheek. "You were invested in the marriage."

"You have to know when to cut your losses." She had herself under control again, thank God. "How about another drink?"

"You sure?" Concern laced his voice. "They fool you because they go down smooth."

"When it comes to Manhattans, I could drink you under the table."

Tully's smile held disbelief but he picked up the two glasses before unfolding his body from the sofa. The cushion under her lifted noticeably as his weight came off it. She felt untethered and vulnerable without him anchoring her.

That's when she knew that he had been wrong about what he'd said when he'd walked her into the house. She wasn't safe with him at all.

Tully lay on his back in the big bed, one arm around the woman who pillowed her head on his chest. The silk of her hair brushed his chin and the curves of her breasts pressed against his skin with enthralling softness. She slept deeply, no doubt exhausted by the wringer of emotions she'd been through today.

He'd been stunned by her revelation that she'd considered suicide. The fact that her husband had done his best to destroy such an extraordinary woman sent anger surging through Tully's veins. Her *husband*, whom she had loved and trusted. Her *husband*, who was supposed to care for her instead of beating her down with his manipulative lies. He hoped Matt Stevens would one day give him an excuse to smash his fist into the man's face.

Natalie stirred and Tully eased the grip he'd tightened on her without realizing it.

He'd also been stunned—and moved—that she'd chosen to share her secret with him. She'd confessed that she'd never told anyone else; she was too ashamed of her weakness. Her trust soothed his anger into something warm and peaceful that spread through him like a gentle wave.

But that feeling worried him. Her serenity was hard-won. He didn't want to be the cause of any more hurt in her life. He had good reasons for choosing not to have a woman in his life full-time. His job still exposed him to some danger and sometimes he craved even more. Not to mention that he sure as shit wasn't handing down the defective family genes to a child. Alcoholism and addiction were diseases that ran in his family.

He'd allowed himself to start a relationship with her because Natalie swore she never wanted to marry again. Now he wondered, though. Stevens had hurt her badly, but she didn't hate all men. She had built herself a new life in the three years since her divorce was final. She might decide her new life should include the kind of husband she deserved. And Tully wasn't that man.

The hell of it was that he wanted to be.

Chapter 16

"You good with Regina staying at your place until we get Van Houten locked up?" Tully asked Leland as he sat down in one of the empty chairs in Mission Control. His partner's usual T-shirt and jeans caught the ever-present glow of the computer screens. "She feels comfortable with you and Dawn."

"I'm insulted you would even ask," Leland said, swiveling to face his colleague. "You're planning to get Van Houten locked up? How?"

"By proving he's a psychopathic stalker."

Leland lifted a quizzical eyebrow. "You haven't got anything to tie him to stalking Natalie."

"Yet." Tully drummed his fingers on the desk. "I saw the way Van Houten treats his staff. I'll get one of them to flip on him." He had surveillance on the security guards, so he would find the weak link. It would just take time.

"What's the latest from the stalker?"

"Nothing." Tully's fingers curled into a fist. "That's a problem."

"I'd think Natalie would be relieved."

"She is. I'm not." Tully frowned. "Stalkers don't stop without a reason. What's changed that would make Van Houten quit? He doesn't know that his wife is back in the area."

"Are you sure of that? Maybe one of his goons was watching Natalie's house when Regina showed up."

"I don't think so. He'd have come to the salon again if that were the case." Tully shook his head. "He's trying a different tack, and I don't like waiting to find out what it is."

"Does Natalie know you're worried?"

"Hell, no! She's been through enough these last couple of days." And in the years before. She didn't need to worry about something that might not happen.

Leland looked away and then back before clearing his throat. "I know this is none of my business, but you seem especially . . . protective of Natalie."

"And?" Tully put an edge in his voice to warn Leland off the subject.

But his partner was made of sterner stuff than that. "You remind me of someone." Leland tapped the arm of his chair as he pretended to think. "Oh yes—myself when Dawn was being threatened by a black market arms dealer."

"Yeah, you went a little crazy back then. Worked 24-7, as I recall. I'm not doing that." Although he was still catching up on the projects he'd put on the back burner to deal with Natalie's issue.

"Come off it, Tully." Leland's voice lost all its disarming southern drawl. "I saw how you looked at Natalie the night you brought Regina over. And you were at her house in the middle of the night. Don't try to convince me you were sleeping in the guest room."

"You're right. It's none of your business." Tully started to stand up.

"Sit down and listen to me." Leland could be surprisingly authoritative when he wanted to be.

Tully decided it was better to let his partner get whatever he wanted to say off his chest. So he leaned back in the chair and stretched out his legs to cross them at his booted ankles. "Go ahead." He kept his tone casual and unconcerned.

"Dawn's told me a little about Natalie's past with her ex-husband," Leland said in a carefully measured tone. "You are a good and honorable man. I know that you would not deliberately add to her bad experiences. However, you might not realize that she is fragile because she appears to be very strong."

"She *is* strong—stronger than you'd believe." Tully could take criticism of himself but he wasn't going to let anyone sell Natalie short.

Leland raised a hand in acknowledgment. "You've stated your intention never to marry with great conviction. I may disagree with your reasons but I respect your decision."

"Natalie has the same intention," Tully pointed out, keeping his temper in check.

"Dawn thinks that will change once Natalie has had time to heal." Leland shifted in his chair. "Neither she nor I wish to see Natalie drawn into a relationship that might cause her hurt."

Tully felt a punch of guilt since he'd had the same thought last night. "She knows who I am. She knows where I stand."

"What one knows and what one feels sometimes lead in different directions," Leland said.

"Tell me about it," Tully said before he could stop himself.

Leland didn't let the honesty slide by. "So you're in deeper than you want to admit."

"Shit, I don't know how deep I'm in. But I hear you, partner." He wanted to get out of there before Leland pushed him into making a decision he didn't want to face just yet. He stood up. "Right now my focus is on keeping Natalie safe and Regina protected from her psycho husband."

"There's more to safety than just the physical," Leland said.

"You've made your point." He turned on his boot heel and stalked out of the room. Leland was lucky that Tully had already been beating himself up. Otherwise he would have ripped a strip off his partner's hide for nosing in Tully's personal life.

Since he was now spoiling for a fight, he went back to his office to call that jackass of a client, Henry Earnshaw, and give him the bad news about how much his next meeting would cost.

~

Natalie fell into the familiar rhythm of combing and cutting, the metallic hiss of the scissor blades a comforting sound. Her client chatted about her daughter's upcoming graduation from medical school while Natalie made appropriate comments.

But beneath the surface serenity, she wrestled with how she'd come to depend on Tully so profoundly. She'd slipped into a relationship with an overpowering man again. What the hell was wrong with her?

Granted, Tully didn't buy her jewelry to impress her. His gifts were security bars and surveillance cameras. He sent a bodyguard and gave her favorite tenant a job. Tully's way was far more seductive and dangerous to her hard-won independence.

And he hadn't considered her a coward when she confessed to contemplating suicide. She'd expected him to look at her with pity at best and disgust at worst. Instead, he'd told her how strong she was.

She traded her scissors for a blow-dryer, the noise silencing her client's chatter. Her stalker seemed to have fallen silent as well. No twisted messages had arrived in any form for the last day and a half. Maybe Natalie could go back to her house and her life of solitude again. Then Tully wouldn't need to protect her.

They could see each other casually every now and then. Because the sex was great.

Natalie nodded to herself. Keep it about sex. Don't open the door to another man who could make her doubt herself.

A niggling little voice said Tully wasn't like Matt, but she used the hair dryer to drown it out.

As she tossed her client's lavender cape into the laundry bin, Pam strode over and said in a low voice, "Still no sign of the stalker, either here or at your house."

She sounded more worried than relieved. "Isn't that a good thing?" Natalie asked.

Pam pressed her lips together for a moment as if debating how much to share. "Stalkers don't stop for no reason. So why has he gone silent?"

Tully hadn't pointed that out, although he had pulled Pam aside for a short, intense conversation when she'd picked Natalie up at Tully's house that morning. But now that Natalie thought about it, the silence didn't make sense, especially if Dobs was her stalker. "Why do *you* think there have been no new messages?"

Pam just shook her head, but Natalie could see concern in the grim set of her jaw.

"You believe he's planning something worse, don't you?"

The other woman looked away and then back. "You can't predict what a psychopath will do. I'm telling you this so you stay careful."

"Luckily, I have you to make sure I do," Natalie said with a smile.

"I'm off tomorrow, so you'll have someone else. Just as good," Pam added.

A ping of disappointment hit Natalie in the chest. She'd come to trust Pam as much as Tully.

Before she could say anything more, Natalie's cell phone vibrated in her jacket pocket. Her next client was still being shampooed, so she slid the phone out to check the caller ID. *Tully.* She closed her eyes for a moment, trying to quell the happy dance her heart insisted on doing. When she answered, she kept her voice even. "Tully, I was thinking that it would be nice to sleep at my own house tonight since the stalker isn't bothering me now."

There was a brief pause before he said, "I was thinking that I'd like to take you out to dinner in the city tonight. Maybe at Cruz."

He had named one of the best restaurants in New York, where it was nearly impossible for a normal human being to get a reservation. "Is that a bribe to keep me from staying here in New Jersey? Because it's a very effective one."

"Not an intentional one, but if it works, I'm good with it." She could hear the smile in his voice before it turned serious. "The stalker has only missed one full day so far. That doesn't mean he's done."

A shiver of nerves ran through her, wiping out her false sense of security. But nothing could stop the hum of pleasure she felt at the prospect of sitting across an elegant table from Tully for an entire evening. And then going back to the big bed in his house. One more night couldn't hurt.

"Dinner sounds terrific," she said. "I'll be done here at six." She would get Gino to supervise readying the salon for the next day's business. "Then I'll need Pam to take me home to grab some clothes." She wasn't going to Cruz in her work outfit.

"Don't rush. I'll tell them to expect us when we get there," he said.

"Isn't the reservation for a specific time?"

"They know me." His tone of unconcern changed to warmth. "I'm glad you're coming."

When he disconnected, she stared at her phone for a second. Getting a table at Cruz was a miracle, but not having to choose a time was inconceivable. It was strange that a mere restaurant table brought home how different Tully's life was from hers. A mansion in Manhattan you could buy, if you had the money. A table at the city's hottest restaurant showed a level of influence that she couldn't imagine.

Yet another reason that Tully was the wrong man for her.

~

When Pam pulled into the courtyard behind Tully's house, his Maserati was already crouched low and sleek on the pavers. Once again the back door opened to show his silhouette against the interior light. When he stepped onto the porch, she saw that he wore a gray suit perfectly tailored to his broad shoulders and trim waist. She let her gaze travel down the knife-edge front pleat of his trousers to the polished black cowboy boots. She used to think those boots were strange footwear for a businessman, but now they seemed exactly right for Tully. He might be from Pennsylvania but he was a cowboy in spirit. Strong, honorable, protective, with an independent streak a mile wide.

He ran lightly down the steps and helped her out of the SUV, his grip radiating support and warmth.

When she stood firmly on the ground, he stepped back and gave an appreciative whistle as he scanned her outfit.

After Tully's call, she'd spent the rest of her workday mentally debating what to wear for such a special occasion. Since the restaurant was in Manhattan, where black was practically required attire, she had chosen a "little black dress." Originally purchased for a fancy business party with Matt, the dress had never been worn because they'd had a fight and he told her to stay home. It gave her a wicked pleasure to wear it for Tully now.

It was a simple silk faille sheath that outlined her curves in a tasteful but sexy way. The bodice of the dress was strapless, cut straight across, while her shoulders and arms were covered with a fine, sheer black netting embellished with small touches of lace at the shoulder and sleeves. The skirt had a subtle slit on one side, mostly so she could walk more easily. She'd paired it with high-heeled black satin pumps, cut low over her toes, and a small beaded evening bag. Sparkling rhinestone chandelier earrings swung beside her neck, while she'd slicked her short hair back in the illusion of a french twist.

"You look beyond beautiful," Tully said, his voice a low, husky rumble.

He bracketed his hands around her waist and pulled her in against him. Then he kissed her like he wanted to have sex with her right then and there.

Desire zinged through her to pulse between her legs, but two could play the game. She slipped her arms under his jacket to rake her manicured nails over the fine cotton of his shirt where it pulled taut over his back. Then she skimmed her hands down to cup his firm butt.

She caught his quiet groan in her mouth.

When he released her, she looked around to find that Pam's SUV was already gone. Had they been kissing that long, or had Pam preferred to give her boss some privacy?

He smiled down at her, a slanting, sexy smile. "The only thing better than looking at you in that dress across the dinner table will be slowly peeling it off you later tonight."

"But first you're going to peel off this very handsome suit." She pretended to straighten his patterned silk tie. "While I watch."

She heard his sharp inhale. "You play dirty, sweetheart."

"Never doubt it." She patted his tie. "Are those horseshoes?"

He glanced down at his chest. "Yeah. It was stupid expensive but I like the design. And Derek told me I needed to upgrade my ties."

"It's Hermès," she said, recognizing the distinctive look and feel of the fabric. "They started out making saddles, so it seems appropriate."

Tully grinned. "Not the kind of saddles I use." He offered her his arm. "May I escort you to my gasoline-powered steed?"

She slid her hand into the crook of his elbow, letting her palm rest on the soft wool that covered the solid steel of his arm. "Lead the way."

When they arrived in front of the skyscraper that housed Cruz, a valet helped her out of the car and onto the dark-blue carpet that covered the sidewalk. Tully passed over the key to the Maserati and joined her, interlacing his fingers with hers as a doorman sprang to swing open the huge glass-and-stainless door. They walked into a lobby that soared up several floors.

A young man dressed in a navy suit stood by the door. "Good evening, Mr. Gibson. Ma'am." He smiled at Natalie. "Welcome to Cruz."

The host escorted them through the entrance to the restaurant itself, the two-story space warm and almost rustic, with low stucco arches lining the dining room over which a wire-mesh sculpture hovered. But he continued through the large room into what looked like a rain forest. The walls appeared to be made of cascading vines and leaves woven through copper trellises dotted with votive candles, while the city lights and night sky glowed through a domed glass ceiling. He showed them to a table tucked in one corner, secluded by planters of bamboo. Even the chairs were upholstered in a fabric that resembled close-clipped grass.

Tully held the chair for Natalie, brushing his fingertips against her cheek before he sat down himself. A tingle of delight danced over her skin at his soft touch. She tried not to gawk like a tourist but she knew her eyes were wide with delight as she glanced around the verdant space.

"You like it," Tully said, satisfaction lacing his voice.

"I feel like I'm in an enchanted garden." She dropped her gaze to the table itself. The flatware was wrought in rubbed bronze to look like twigs, and the napkin's pale green fabric was a jacquard woven in a leaf pattern. "Every detail works together."

A server arrived and placed two Manhattans on their table.

"I hope you don't mind that I ordered these ahead of time," Tully said. "I figured you might like a drink fast."

She picked up her glass with genuine gratitude, lifting it in a toast. "To the very clever man sitting across from me."

His smile was pure sin. He held up his own glass. "To the even smarter woman across from me."

Her hand stopped midway to her mouth as she asked, "Why am I smarter?"

"Because you taught me to appreciate a Manhattan." Tully took a swallow and half closed his eyes as he said, "Good stuff."

She sipped the sweet burn of the cocktail, thinking how strangely endearing it was that big masculine Tully had adopted her favorite drink, even though some guys might consider it froufrou.

When the server presented them with their menus, Natalie saw a side of Tully she'd never been exposed to before. She didn't know why it surprised her that he could talk about gourmet food and fine wines with knowledge and authority. After all, he had to entertain CEO-level clients on a regular basis. But she found herself feeling a little out of her depth with the Tully who knew which vintage year was best in Catalonia. Not to mention that the server and the sommelier treated him with a cordial respect that indicated he knew what he was talking about.

Natalie decided to let Tully order the entire dinner since he was the expert. She reserved the right to choose her own dessert, though. "It's a very personal decision," she explained. "Not to mention the most important part of the meal."

Tully chuckled. "They make a mean chocolate soufflé but you have to order it now to get it ready on time."

"Done," Natalie said to the server.

When the menus had been whisked away, Natalie took another sip of her drink before she set it down. "Let's get the ugly topics out of the way first. Regina told me that the restraining order was served on Dobs today. He immediately tried to get in touch with her through the law firm, which doesn't bode well for him obeying the order."

Tully put his drink down with the air of a man who knew he was about to deliver bad news. "For someone like Dobs, a restraining order is like waving a red flag in front of a bull. Now that he knows Regina is somewhere in the area, he's going to do everything he can to find her." Tully's smile was cold. "Fortunately, Alastair and his associates can't be intimidated by Van Houten. How's Regina holding up?"

"I was working when she called, so I couldn't talk with her long. She sounds amazingly strong and determined. It helps that she has Dawn and Leland right there." That was what Natalie tried to provide for the women she helped: a safe place with someone to support them. "How far does he have to go before he can be thrown in jail?"

Tully grimaced. "Even though the restraining order prohibits him from contacting her via any means, he's more likely to get fined than jailed, especially for the first or second offense. She needs to document every attempt."

"She's good at documentation," Natalie said, remembering the photos of Regina's injuries.

"Her best strategy is to stay hidden from Van Houten until we nail him," Tully said.

"She can't impose on Dawn and Leland indefinitely," Natalie objected.

He lifted his eyebrows. "Why not? Their place is huge and they like her. It won't be for much longer anyway."

"Do you know something I don't?" Natalie said it with a half smile, but she didn't want Tully keeping secrets to protect her.

"I know Van Houten's type. Regina has struck at his pride. That makes him angry, and angry men do stupid things. I'll be ready when he does."

Natalie twisted the stem of her glass between her fingers. "Now for unpleasant topic number two. You and Pam both think my stalker isn't done with me, even though it's been nearly two days since I've heard from him. I don't want to keep jumping at shadows for the rest of my life."

Tully stretched his arm across the table to take her hand. "You won't have to, sweetheart, I promise." He rubbed his thumb across her knuckles. "Remember what I said about angry men doing stupid things."

"That's assuming Dobs is my stalker."

"He is," Tully said in a flat voice that carried utter conviction. "He fits the profile in every way." He held her gaze with his. "One thing I learned in the FBI was to trust my gut. Van Houten either knows or suspects that you helped Regina. That's what set him off."

"So how do we flush him out?" Natalie was tired of the constant tension of waiting for the other shoe to drop. Regina needed to have full custody of her baby when it was born, so Dobs had to be put away.

"You don't." Tully's face was like granite. "You do absolutely nothing that would incite him to go after you." She saw him make an effort to soften his expression. "Trust me, Nat. I will get him. Without endangering you."

If she'd had an idea of how to prod Dobs into a foolhardy action, she might have argued with Tully. However, the only methods she could think of involved exposing Regina and that was obviously not happening. "Okay, I'm done with unpleasant subjects. Do you have any?"

He shook his head. "All I want to do is enjoy a good meal with a spectacular woman."

Spectacular. That wasn't something she got called every day. Her smile deepened and she added a little heat to it before she extended her foot to run the side of her instep up Tully's calf.

His eyes lit with appreciation and lust. "Those are sexy shoes," he said. "I want to see you wearing those and nothing else."

Arousal flashed through her, making her skin warm and tighten. Holding his gaze over the rim of her Manhattan, she dipped her tongue down to scoop up the Luxardo cherry resting on the bottom. She held the dark-red fruit between her lips, biting down so she could suck the sweet juice out of it.

"If you don't want dinner to be takeout, you'd better stop doing that," Tully said, his voice turning hoarse.

She slowly drew the cherry into her mouth, chewed, and swallowed it. "I was only eating the garnish." But she felt very smug. Ruffling Tully was an accomplishment.

He just threw her a steamy look.

"So," she said. "Tell me about working at the FBI. What made you join?"

Surprise flitted across his face. "Why do you ask that?"

"Because it's not a job many people choose." She wanted to understand him better and tonight might be the last chance she had.

He shifted in his chair as though the question made him uncomfortable, a strange reaction from a man who seemed so sure of his place in life. "I studied engineering in college and got a job with the state." He grimaced. "It wasn't exactly exciting. I figured catching bad guys would be less boring than organizing orange traffic cones."

"You're an engineer?" She'd always assumed he'd majored in criminal justice or something similar.

"Yes, ma'am. I can build you whatever kind of bridge you desire. I guess you haven't read my bio on the KRG website." His mouth twisted into a wry smile.

"Why bother when I can go straight to the source?" It was odd that she hadn't done the most basic homework on Tully, since she was noted for being up to date on both celebrity and local news. However, it had seemed wrong to have her opinion of him molded by outside sources. "I didn't know the FBI hired engineers."

He shrugged. "It's useful when analyzing weak points terrorists might hit or analyzing building blueprints to set up raids. I also grew up handling firearms, so that was in my favor."

"You're from Pennsylvania, but that's about all I know."

"And that's about as much as you want to know." He looked relieved when the server appeared with their appetizer—a tapas platter loaded with exotic olives, various cheeses, and paper-thin slices of jamón serrano—along with a basket of assorted breads and herbed olive oils.

He really didn't want to talk about his childhood, so she let him focus on the delicious food arrayed in front of them. He suggested combinations of cheese and ham, explained what the flavorings in the olive oils were, and kept her glass filled with fruit-laden sangria.

"I won't be able to eat the main course," she protested after he'd nudged a wedge of tortilla de patatas toward her.

"We can always take it home," he said with a wicked glint in his eyes.

"Oh no! I'm not missing the chocolate soufflé, no matter how much liquor you ply me with."

He chuckled and leaned back in his chair before launching into an amusing story about one of his corporate clients, with names and identifying characteristics carefully redacted. She got the feeling he was doing this to forestall further questions about his past but she didn't mind. It was fascinating to glimpse the world he worked in, which included private jets, multiacre estates, priceless wine and art collections, and fleets of exotic cars. The whims of his clients were sometimes capricious—like the woman who wanted a bodyguard who could go riding cross-country with her—but Tully considered each one a new challenge.

However, the stories that made his face light up were the ones where he got to use his FBI training the most, planning antikidnapping tactics or setting up security on one of those giant estates.

He insisted that Natalie tell him about the salon, asking her questions about her staff and her customers, treating her as though her job was just as important as what his own clients did. She realized that this dinner was the first time they'd talked about their normal lives, although calling Tully's life normal was pushing it.

As she watched the play of expressions across his face, she knew she would never forget the way the corners of his dark-gray eyes crinkled when he smiled or how sharp and clean the line of his jaw was. She could almost feel the texture of his golden-brown hair as it caught the candlelight. The leisurely cadence of his deep voice stroked her like the notes of a steamy tango.

By the time the chocolate soufflé arrived, she just wanted to go back to his house. Until she dipped her spoon through the light crust to find the warm chocolate sauce the server had poured in at tableside. The heady scent of chocolate swirled around her like a delicious cloud and when the soufflé hit her taste buds, she nearly groaned in ecstasy.

"You know, you look almost exactly like that when you come." Tully's voice was a low rumble and Natalie realized she'd closed her eyes to savor the dessert.

She opened them as his words sent a ripple of desire through her. "This is one of those dishes that actually deserves the label 'better than sex.'" She filled her spoon and lifted it to her mouth again. This time she kept her eyes open to watch Tully's face.

His gaze was on her lips as she drew the spoon slowly out of them. Chocolate burst on her tongue again and she allowed herself a moan of pleasure.

"Is it really better?" he asked with mock offense. "Because you're almost convincing me it might be."

He hadn't ordered the soufflé, so she pushed her plate toward him. "See for yourself."

Picking up his coffee spoon, he took a bite, looking thoughtful for a moment before he shook his head and gave her a blistering smile. "Nope, you taste much better than the soufflé."

She squeezed her thighs together as arousal slid down into her belly. "How fast can you get the check?"

"You haven't finished your dessert." His eyes flared but he nudged the plate back toward her.

"I've always heard that after three bites, the taste becomes less satisfying anyway."

He leaned forward, his gaze locked on her. "It all depends on what you're tasting. Let's go." He stood.

"Don't you need to pay for dinner?" But she rose as well.

"They'll put it on my tab." He stepped close to her, his splayed hand resting right on the boundary between her waist and her bottom as he guided her between the tables.

He has a tab at Cruz.

It was strange how easily she'd ignored that he was a high level of rich. When he had come to her house in his jeans and cowboy boots, he seemed like a regular guy. Even his Maserati hadn't changed her impression. It wasn't until she saw his home—a mansion in the middle of the city!—that it began to impinge on her brain that this man lived in a way she didn't understand. Now he'd demonstrated how comfortable he was at an ultra-exclusive restaurant in Manhattan.

After tonight, she really needed to go back to her life in suburban New Jersey.

It took less than five minutes for the valet to retrieve Tully's car, helped by the fact that the young man had already gone to fetch it by the time they reached the front door. The host must have called ahead when he saw they had left their table.

Tully held the door for her, leaning down to brush a kiss on her cheekbone and say, "I wish I had used the limo tonight. I want to touch you right now."

The lace of Natalie's panties was already damp, so she decided to do something daring. After Tully folded his big frame into the driver's seat and pulled away from the curb, Natalie unlatched her seat belt and worked her hands up under her skirt. Hooking her fingers in the lace and lifting her butt to slip her panties down her thighs, she wriggled until she could get them down to her knees.

"I like where those are going," Tully said, glancing over at her as she bent to drag the wisp of fabric down to her ankles and over her heels.

"We both want you to touch me," she said, sliding her skirt halfway up her thighs and opening them as far as she could in the tight fabric before she fastened her seat belt again.

"Sweetheart, I'll be touching *and* tasting." He turned onto a narrower street. "Less traffic here in case I get distracted."

Natalie ran her hand up the inside of his thigh to find his cock half erect. "Will this distract you?" She stroked it lightly through the wool of his trousers.

He grabbed her hand and brought it to his lips before he moved it back to her side of the console. "Let me do the touching right now."

His palm skimmed up under her skirt until he found her opening and slipped his finger partway inside it. "Like wet silk," he rasped, stroking in and out a few times before he moved to her clit, his finger damp enough to slide easily against it.

"Oh, Tully!" she moaned as delicious sensation surged from that one point of contact to flood through her body, hardening her nipples and impelling her hips into his hand. "Yes, more!"

He shifted in his seat so he could slide his index finger inside her while his thumb pressed against her clit. She could feel the liquid heat coiling low in her belly and she cupped her own breasts, running her thumbs over their sensitized tips so the cloth of her dress and the lace of her bra dragged across them.

"God, Nat, you are so hot!" Tully's rumble of a voice sent more flames licking through her.

"You *make* me hot," she gasped, pushing harder against his hand. "More!"

He shifted again to thrust another finger inside her while still working her clit. The city lights strobed through the dark interior of the car as he drove her closer and closer to her climax, adding their rhythm to his. When every nerve in her body teetered on the edge, she closed her eyes and waited in that perfect moment of anticipation. And then she convulsed, arching up from the seat against the restraint of her seat belt and gasping out his name.

"Keep coming for me, baby," Tully said, finding the spot inside her that triggered another cataclysm. "That's it."

The rush of pleasure blotted out everything except where his fingers worked their magic, wringing more from her until she collapsed back onto the leather seat, unlocking the grip of her thighs from around his wrist.

He kept his fingers motionless within her as tiny shocks continued to pulse through her. She let her head fall back against the seat. "Tully," was all she could manage as her body went lax with satiation.

When he eased out of her, she made a small sound of regret at the absence and turned her head to watch as he sucked his fingers into his mouth.

He made a humming sound before he wrapped his hand around the steering wheel and gave her a slow, sexy smile. "Now *that* was better than any soufflé."

"And you didn't hit any taxis."

"I'm a trained professional when it comes to driving."

"I guess the other part you just have a natural talent for." She injected a purr into her voice.

"If you say so, sweetheart." But his grin was satisfied.

Another part of him wasn't. She could see his erection tenting his trousers. But his house wasn't far, so she relaxed in the cradle of the sports car's luxurious seat while her body still shivered with delicious aftereffects.

"Are you driving faster than normal?" she asked after a minute.

"Maybe." He dodged around a lumbering delivery truck. "The sooner we get home, the sooner I can strip that pretty dress off of you so I can see your even prettier body."

His words sent a blast of heat through her.

"Do you think the piano would hold me? I've always wanted to have sex on a grand piano."

The Maserati accelerated. "As long as it lasts until we're done, I don't care if it collapses afterward," Tully said.

Natalie relished the skill with which he maneuvered the car through the crowded streets, his hands firm on the leather-covered steering wheel, his long legs flexing as he braked, shifted, and accelerated. After he roared into the courtyard, he was out of the car so fast the rumble of the engine had barely died.

Her door swung open and his hand was there, palm open, offering strength and support as she stepped onto the pavers with her sky-high heels. "I'd kiss you right here except we'd never make it to the piano," he said, slamming the door and hustling her up the steps to the back door.

Once they were inside, he ushered her to the glossy black piano standing on the ornately inlaid wood floor of the grand entrance. He bent his head to take her mouth in a long, searing kiss. As his tongue teased hers, she felt the zipper of her dress glide downward, releasing the embrace of the fabric so cool air whispered over her heated skin.

He pulled his lips away from hers and peeled the top of the dress off her shoulders, pulling it inexorably downward to expose her black lace bra and the fact that she hadn't bothered to don her panties again in the car. He hissed in a breath as he pulled the dress down to the top of her thighs. "I didn't realize . . ."

"It seemed like a waste of effort," she said.

He smiled in a way that said he agreed with her. Then the dress was a pool of black on the floor and he reached around to unhook her bra, tossing it away. For a brief moment, he cupped his hands under her breasts, rubbing his thumbs over her already-tight nipples.

"I'd like to suggest a variation on your idea," he said, his gaze on his hands. "Let's use the piano bench."

She glanced at the seat with its black leather-upholstered top.

"I'll sit and you kneel over me," he said.

"Deal." She imagined what it would feel like to have him thrusting upward into her and her inner muscles contracted in anticipation.

He took her hand and led her to the bench, pushing it back slightly before he seated himself facing the piano and positioned her so her behind just touched the keyboard. He pulled a condom out of his pocket and put it on the keyboard next to her.

"You said you wanted to watch me undress," he said, shrugging out of his jacket and letting it drop to the floor behind him.

She laughed deep in her throat. "Keep going." She hitched her bare bottom against the keyboard, sending a crash of discordant notes echoing through the big open space.

Tully's gaze skimmed over her. "Now that's a picture I'd like to hang on my wall. You, naked, on a piano keyboard."

She arched her back, posing for him. "Like this?"

"Hell, yeah!" He ripped his tie from around his neck with a hiss of silk on cotton. "I want to suck on those beautiful breasts."

Then he was yanking at the buttons of his shirt so hard that one popped off and rolled away. The shirt went the way of his jacket and Natalie gave an admiring gasp of her own. The chiseled muscles of his shoulders and chest were painted with the golden light from the huge bronze chandelier. His gray eyes blazed with a flame that came entirely from within.

Crossing his ankle over his knee, he dragged off one of the glossy black cowboy boots and his sock and tossed both aside before he did the same for the other foot. He stood to jerk open his belt buckle and unzip his trousers, stripping them and his briefs down in one swift motion before he kicked them away.

Natalie scanned from his bare feet up the curved muscles of his calves to his powerful, ridged thighs. When she came to his erection, she could almost feel the hard length of it inside her already. Her inner muscles clenched again.

He sat on the bench. "Come here." He wrapped his hands around her hips and brought her in close, opening his thighs so she could stand between them. And then he fastened his mouth on one of her nipples while he rolled the other one between his fingers.

She dug her fingers into his shoulders and held on for dear life as electric sensation streaked from her breasts to her belly and back again. When he shifted his lips to the other breast, she pushed into him with mindless want.

Just as her knees were about to buckle, he pulled back. "I need to be inside you now," he panted, grabbing the condom.

Natalie took it from him. "My turn," she said, before putting the edge of the envelope between her teeth so she could run her fingers over the hard, velvet length of him.

He allowed it for a few seconds before he said through gritted teeth, "You need to get that condom on right now."

She smiled with a sense of power as she stroked it down over his erection. As soon as she finished, he crooked his hand behind one of her knees to guide it onto the bench beside his hip. Then he wrapped his hands around her waist and lifted her without apparent effort so she could kneel over his lap, his cock brushing her clit so that she gasped at the zing it sent along her nerve endings.

He positioned himself between her thighs. "You ready, baby?" he asked.

"Go!" she commanded.

He brought her down as he rocked his hips, driving deep inside her in one hard thrust. It was powerful and thrilling to be filled so abruptly.

"Oh yeah!" His grip on her tightened. He lifted her so that he nearly slid out of her and then moved her downward again.

She could feel the slight dig of her high heels against her buttocks, adding to the sensual assault. And then he sucked one of her nipples into his mouth while she was impaled on his cock. That sent her over the edge into a shriek of an orgasm that slammed through her without warning.

Her body bowed back in a paroxysm of brain-bending release. But she knew Tully would keep her from falling. As her muscles contracted around his cock, he pulled hard on her nipple as he released it, sending a shower of sparks through her.

He held her while she came down from her climax, his grip sure. When she sagged onto his shoulder, he ran his hand down her back and up it again so that tingles shimmered over her skin.

He was still hard and deep inside her, which kept her arousal smoldering despite the orgasm. After a few moments, she lifted her head. "Time for you now, cowboy."

"I'm in no rush." He pulled her in so her breasts were crushed against his bare chest while he kissed her with slow intensity.

Desire seeped through her again. She pulled her mouth away to surge upward and drop down so his cock stroked in and out of her.

"Oh, sweetheart," he said, his eyes half-closed as he braced his hands on the bench and leaned slightly backward to give her a better angle. "You are so perfect."

Holding his shoulders for balance, she started out in an unhurried rhythm, savoring the slide of him within her, watching the way his face tightened with pleasure. Then he began to raise his hips to meet her as she came down, driving even deeper. His shoulder muscles bunched under her hands as he lifted his hips higher and faster until she held herself still and let him find his own speed as he thrust.

With a final lunge that nearly lifted her off the bench, he threw back his head and shouted, "Oh, hell, yes!" as he pulsed inside her.

He subsided onto the bench, wrapping his arms around her so tightly that it was hard to take a full breath. "Natalie," he murmured against her temple. "My amazing Nat."

He claimed her as his with a rumble of satisfaction in his voice and she liked it too much. But she stayed melded together with him until he softened and slid out of her.

He pressed a tender kiss on her mouth and smiled into her eyes. "Let's see if we can make it to the bed now."

Natalie stood on wobbly legs, deciding to kick off her heels for safety's sake. Tully disposed of his condom while Natalie gathered up their clothes. Tully grabbed his boots and took the armful from her before he put his free arm around her waist to steer them up the stairs.

"I feel strange walking up this grand staircase stark naked," she said. "It's meant for ladies wearing ball gowns."

"Are you kidding me? There's nothing I'd like more than to watch you walk down these stairs just the way you are. Of course, you might not make it all the way to the bottom before I joined you."

"How about if I wore a tiara and nothing else?"

He chuckled and swept her down the hall and into his bedroom, dropping their clothes on a chair. Natalie watched appreciatively as he walked to the bed, his corded muscles flexing as he turned down the quilt. "I want an armful of warm woman right now," he said, gesturing to the inviting sheets.

"That's the disadvantage of grand pianos," she said as she slipped into bed. "No comfortable place to relax afterward."

He climbed in beside her, making the mattress dip as he rolled over and hauled her in against him. "Hey, now I won't feel guilty that I don't play. I've found an even better use for the piano." He nuzzled against her shoulder, rubbing the scruff of his chin over her skin.

"Mmm, that feels good. Like a loofah." She squirmed in his arms to give him access to more of her back.

"A what?"

"A scratchy sponge. It exfoliates your skin."

"So you're hinting that I should rub my chin over your back?" His voice was amused.

"Only if you want to make me purr."

"Oh, I definitely want to hear that." He grazed his soft whiskers over her shoulder blade and toward her spine. She rewarded him by humming in the back of her throat.

He rubbed a little longer before he kissed her shoulder and settled on the pillow.

Natalie drifted in a pleasant state of satiation, warmth, and contentment with the press of Tully's body against hers. She didn't need to feel guilty, because this was just the aftermath of great sex.

"Now I *really* don't understand why you're not married," she murmured. She felt the flinch in his muscles and smiled. "You need to stop jumping every time I say that word. You know you're safe from me."

"Like I said, I'm not cut out for marriage." It was one of his stock answers, meant to deflect serious conversation.

Suddenly, she wanted to know the real reason. She twisted in his arms so she was facing him, so close that she could see the bands of silver and gray in his eyes. "That's garbage. You have every quality that makes a great husband. So what has kept some smart woman from snapping you up?"

He smiled an easy, meaningless smile. "Maybe the right woman hasn't tried."

"I'm sure a lot of women have tried. After all, you're rich, successful, and great in bed." Her tone was wry.

"Thank you, ma'am." His tone matched hers.

"So why?" She prodded him in his shoulder with her index finger.

He rolled onto his back. But he kept one arm around her so she was still against his side. "Hell, Nat, all kinds of reasons. You know that marriage is complicated."

She remained silent, waiting.

He blew out a long breath. "You're a tough interrogator."

He slid his arm away from her and hitched himself into a sitting position, stuffing a pillow behind him against the headboard. Natalie sat up as well, wrapping the sheet over her breasts and curling her legs under her.

Tully gave her a straight look. "When I was in the FBI, I liked the risky assignments. I saw how many of my fellow agents ended up divorced because their wives couldn't hack that. As for being a dad, I was likely to end up injured or worse. It wouldn't have been responsible parenting."

"You aren't in the FBI anymore."

"I can't sneak anything past you, can I?" He smiled crookedly before his mouth settled into a grim line. "Okay, sweetheart, here it is. I come from a family of addicts. My mother and father were alcoholics. My father played the ponies with the rent money. My brother belongs to Gamblers Anonymous . . . when he's not at the casino. My sister"—his eyes held deep sorrow—"overdosed on drugs two years ago despite several stints in rehab."

"But *you're* not an addict."

"Don't kid yourself. I told you I'm an adrenaline junkie and I was dead serious. I can't live without the rush that comes of running into a bad situation with a gun in my hand."

"You don't do that now, though."

"Not often." He sighed. "I miss it."

"But that's not the same as drinking or gambling or drugs."

He looked away. "Addiction is in the genes. I'm not passing my crappy DNA on to some poor innocent kid." He turned back to meet her gaze. "Marriage means children, and I will *never* have kids of my own."

"You could adopt."

He shook his head. "It doesn't matter how much you discuss not having children before you go into a relationship. Women change their minds. I'm not going to change mine."

It broke her heart that he would deprive himself of love because of some misguided idea that every woman wanted her own baby. "You know, some woman might think having you as a husband would be worth not having a child."

The angles of his face softened and he looked vulnerable. "She'd be making a bad bargain."

How could he think that? "You should let her decide that."

"I did. Once." The softness disappeared. "She came to her senses and backed out."

Someone had hurt him deeply. "I didn't think you would give up so easily."

He laughed, although it was with an edge. "You gotta know when to fold a bad hand. I think it might be the one useful thing I learned from my pa. Other than how *not* to be as a husband and father."

"He treated you badly, didn't he?"

"He thought I was a worthless piece of shit, as he often told me." His lips curled into a sneer. "Maybe I owe him for that because it lit a fire under me to prove that I wasn't."

So that was why he believed he was a bad bargain. "Well, you certainly proved it beyond a shadow of a doubt."

"Who did I prove it to?" He shook his head, unhappiness clouding his eyes. She wanted to put her arms around him, to comfort him, but he reached out and hooked his finger in the sheet where it stretched over her cleavage. "Didn't you say something about me being good in bed?"

"I might have." He wanted to banish all those ugly memories by losing himself in sex.

"Let me prove it." He tugged at the sheet so she released her hold on it.

And then he tipped her onto her back before stretching himself out over her.

~

After he'd driven her nearly out of her mind by exploring every inch of her body before he came inside her, they lay spooned together again. Tully's breathing settled into the steady rhythm of sleep. The arm he had draped over her waist went lax and heavy.

She couldn't relax because his words kept running through her mind. She could accept his determination not to have children. Natalie suspected that the parental dynamic had more to do with his siblings' addictions than any genetics, but alcoholism did run in families.

But he wouldn't even consider adoption because he believed he wouldn't be enough as a husband. Natalie wanted to punch whatever woman had convinced him of that. He must have really loved her. And her rejection meshed so perfectly with his father's opinion of him that Tully would have felt he deserved it. Anger roiled inside her.

How ironic that *she* wanted to protect *him*. Now that she'd glimpsed that deep insecurity within him, it made her want him more, not less. Because she could pour her love into all those dark, ugly corners and make him understand how very worthy he was.

She pulled her thoughts up short, nearly gasping out loud. Yes, she'd used the word "love." About Tully.

Her heart pinched as she shoved the idea away. She could not be in love with him. She didn't want to be. He didn't want her to be.

Her life was perfect the way it was, the way she'd so painstakingly rebuilt it. Her new house set up just for her, her growing business, her trusted friends, her helping hand for women who needed it. Tully would explode all that without meaning to.

She wasn't going to change herself for a man again, not even for Tully.

She needed to end this now. Before she got pulled in any deeper.

Chapter 17

"I want to go back to my house today," Natalie said as they ate the Mexican omelet Tully had whipped up for breakfast. In his blue button-down shirt with its sleeves rolled up to his elbows, he looked even more delicious than the food. "There's been nothing from the stalker for more than forty-eight hours."

Tully put down his fork. "That just means that he's going to come at you from a different direction." He shook his head. "You're staying here until we catch him."

"I need to be home." She could see him winding up to say no again, so she added, "I want to go back to my normal life." She needed to put distance between the two of them.

"Sweetheart, your life won't be normal until your stalker is in police custody." His tone was patient but unyielding. "You're safer here."

"I'll have the bodyguard with me at all times. You said she's just as good as Pam."

"Fine." She saw a flare of annoyance in his eyes. "I have to go to the office today but I'll come to your place tonight."

Natalie looked down at her plate, her throat tight with the tears she was holding back. "I would prefer you didn't," she said in a low voice. She forced herself to lift her gaze to meet his. "I need a little space."

"What the hell, Nat?" He scraped one hand over his hair in frustration. "You're being *stalked*. This isn't a good time to need space." He drew in a deep breath and softened his tone. "I'm trying to protect you."

"I know." She was trying to protect both of them.

"Is this about something I said last night?" he asked. "You wanted honesty."

She couldn't tell him that she'd seen how vulnerable they both were, so she lied. "I'm just feeling overwhelmed."

He reached across the table to lay his large hand over hers. "So let me take care of you."

His words hit her like a splash of ice water. That was how Matt had lured her in. But being taken care of had come with too high a price. She couldn't fall into that trap again.

"Let your bodyguard handle it," she said. "Just like you would a client."

He winced as though she'd hit him. "You know you're far more to me than a client. What I said last night doesn't mean I don't care about you." He squeezed her hand gently, his gray eyes locked on her. "I can't lose you, Nat. It would rip my guts out."

She saw the truth of that in his face. Her heart twisted painfully as she understood that she was going to hurt him. She didn't want to be one of those women who made him feel bad about himself. So better to do this now, stalker be damned.

"That's why I think it's time for me to go back to my life in New Jersey"—she waved her hand in the direction of the river—"while you stay here in Manhattan."

Tully pulled his hand away from hers. His jaw was tight with anger, but she saw the confusion in his eyes. "So you're saying you don't want to see me anymore?"

"Of course I want to see you. We have close friends in common, so it's inevitable anyway. I just think it's a bad idea to continue sleeping with you."

Pain glazed his eyes and twisted his mouth. She wanted to tell him she was doing this for his own good.

"Why?" he asked.

She folded her hands on the table and did her best to project an air of serene certainty. "If we go on much longer, things will get messy."

"That's not an answer." He folded his arms across his chest, the muscles in his forearms flexing as he curled his fingers into fists. "But you're right. Since it's going to end, better to keep it neat."

"I'm sorry," she said with genuine regret.

"Shit, so am I." He shook his head. "I knew this would happen. I just . . ." He stared toward the window. "Just not so soon." When he turned back to her, he'd shuttered all emotion except for a wistful smile that barely curled his lips. "It was real good while it lasted."

"Better than good," Natalie agreed.

Tully's cell phone pinged and he glanced down at where it lay on the table. "Jenya's here. She's your bodyguard for the weekend." He tapped his index finger on the table a couple of times. "Look, Jenya's excellent, but I'd feel better if I took the night shift at your house. I'll sleep in the guest room."

Every cell in her body yearned to say yes, to keep him with her just a little longer. She gave him a level gaze. "There's no way you'd sleep in the guest room. And I'm not suggesting that it would be your fault."

For a moment, they simply looked at each other, the air around them charged with the truth of that.

He shoved his half-eaten omelet away and stood. "Right. Jenya stays."

Natalie rose too, feeling awkward about how to say goodbye. "Thank you," she started.

He waved off her gratitude as he came around the table. He leaned down to kiss her briefly on the lips. "We're okay, Nat? No hard feelings on either side. That's keeping it neat."

His mouth was so warm and firm. She wanted to grab his shirt and yank him back for a longer farewell kiss. "We're okay," she agreed, lifting her hand to press her palm against his cheek for a mere second. It would have to be enough.

She pivoted toward the kitchen door, somehow managing to get through it without releasing the sob trying to climb out of her throat. Worse, Tully was right behind her in the hallway. She could feel his presence even though, as usual, he walked as silently as a cat.

"I'll introduce you to Jenya and then you can be on your way. Back to your normal life," he repeated with a slight edge.

She nodded because she couldn't trust herself to speak, grabbing her bag and heading for the back door. She waited until he'd disarmed the alarm before she reached for the knob, their hands colliding as he also extended his arm to open it. The unexpected contact wrenched a strangled sound from her, but Tully either didn't hear it or chose to ignore it. He opened the door for her to pass through.

A tall woman with huge dark eyes and lustrous black hair pulled back in a ponytail stood by the now-familiar black SUV. She wore a white silk blouse and navy trousers.

"Natalie, Jenya here will be taking care of you," Tully said as they walked down the steps. "Jenya, slight change of plans. You'll be staying with Natalie in New Jersey the entire weekend."

A flicker of surprise crossed Jenya's face before she smiled and came forward with her hand outstretched. "A pleasure, Natalie."

"Same here," Natalie said, forcing an answering smile. Maybe it was better to have a buffer when she parted from Tully.

He opened the car door for her and offered his hand to help her climb into the high vehicle. One more painful reminder of how perfect it felt to be touched by him. And then she was in the seat and the door closed firmly between them. Tully lifted a hand in farewell as Jenya pulled the car onto the quiet cross street.

Natalie kept her gaze resolutely forward even as she felt every fiber of her heart and body being ripped away from the man she'd stupidly fallen in love with.

As the SUV rolled out of the courtyard, Tully let his hand fall and trudged up the steps to his house. Walking into the grand entrance hall, he stopped and stared at the piano, images of Natalie spinning through his brain. He walked over to it and ran the back of his fingers up the keyboard in a ripple of sound that echoed off the walls and ceiling.

That was how he felt: empty enough for echoes of her to ricochet around inside him.

He pressed his fingers on a random set of keys, a discordant jangle, as anger seethed inside him.

What the hell had he done to spook her? She wouldn't be frightened away by his revelations about his family. She didn't judge people that way.

She was firm on the fact that she didn't want to get married again, so his stance on that subject wouldn't have bothered her.

He slammed his hand down on the keyboard once more. What had made her run?

Because that was what she had done.

He tried to hold on to it but the anger drained away, leaving that hollowness again.

He sank onto the piano stool and put his elbows on the keys in another clash of sound before he dropped his head into his hands.

He'd gone into this with his eyes open. He'd been attracted to Natalie since he'd met her at one of Derek and Alice's parties. When they'd had to spend so much time together during the run-up to the wedding, the attraction had flared hotter and he'd seen the reflection of it in her eyes. So he'd acted on it, figuring they were both going into the relationship with the same expectations.

Natalie had stayed true to hers. He wasn't so sure he had.

There was always some fallout when two people split up, but it had never before made him feel like his life had turned gray.

So maybe he'd gotten in deeper than he thought. Maybe that was what Natalie had sensed last night. And she didn't want that from him, so she'd ended it.

Or maybe she didn't want him because he had so little to offer. She was a smart woman.

But he felt like shit.

~

Natalie was grateful that it was Saturday and therefore the salon was hopping, although the howl of blow-dryers gave her a headache. Gino made her eat lunch at about two o'clock because he said she looked pale. Little did he know that it had nothing to do with physical hunger.

She had just finished a blowout when Deion appeared beside her chair. She'd noticed the sudden drop in chatter and now she knew why. When she glanced around, most of the customers, as well as her female stylists, were either openly or surreptitiously eyeing him in his well-cut suit. Deion, however, was frowning and oblivious.

"Nat, I need to talk to you in private," he said in a low voice.

"Give me about three minutes, and I'll meet you in my office." She needed to check her client's bangs for length now that they were dry.

When she got to her office, Deion was pacing the small space in front of her desk. "You look like you're dressed for work at the mall. I thought your boss let you go without the two weeks' notice," she said, sinking into her chair as the depression of Tully's absence swamped her.

"Someone called in sick, so I did her a favor and filled in." Deion sat down but exuded a coiled tension that made him seem ready to spring up again at any moment. "I just got back from the store and was unlocking the back door when a woman came up to me. Her name is Sarah Lacey and she says she's a customer here."

The name was familiar but Natalie couldn't put a face to it. "What does she want?"

"To use your guest room to hide from her husband."

Natalie sat up in her chair. "Tonight?"

"Yes. She has a bag with her and she looks scared shitless."

"Where is she?" Natalie couldn't believe this was happening right now. She had never felt less able to be someone else's pillar of strength. And her stalker was watching her house.

"She's in the kitchen," Deion said. "But before you start with her, you need to make sure that she's really a client."

"Why would she lie about that?" But Natalie flipped open the laptop to query her client database.

"Because of the timing. Maybe your stalker sent her."

Natalie glanced up at Deion's stern expression. "Wow, you've already gotten in the security mindset. But it seems a little farfetched."

He shook his head and shifted his gaze to her laptop.

Natalie typed in the woman's name. "Sarah is one of Gino's clients. She's been coming here for about two years."

"I want Gino to see her in order to confirm she's really who she says she is."

Natalie was touched and a little impressed. Deion was taking this seriously. "I'll get him and meet you in the kitchen."

"Jenya should join us too."

"You know Jenya?" When Natalie had left her chair to come to her office, Jenya had checked in on where she was going.

"She vetted me before she let me come to your office," Deion said. "She's good."

As Natalie and Deion walked into the spa room, Jenya got up from the sofa and joined them, a frown on her face. "I think we should find Sarah Lacey somewhere else to stay."

Natalie was tempted but she couldn't do that to a woman in need. "It's not just a room. It's support from someone who's been there."

Jenya and Deion both looked unconvinced. She waved them down the hallway and detoured through the salon to find Gino.

"What's this about?" Gino asked as she led him toward the kitchen.

"Sarah Lacey is your client, right?"

"Yeah, since a couple of years ago. Why?"

"She's here." Natalie lowered her voice to a murmur. "She wants to stay in my guest room. I just want you to confirm it's her."

"Not good timing with the stalker around." Gino kept his voice low as they passed the reception desk. Halfway down the hall, he came to an abrupt halt. "Shit, could this have something to do with your stalker?"

"So now you're jumping on the bandwagon? Jenya and Deion are worried about the same thing." Natalie just didn't see how Dobs Van Houten could persuade one of the Mane Attraction's clients to pretend she needed Natalie's help. What would he gain by it, even if he did?

"You can't be too careful." He squared his shoulders, shifting into the role of protective male. "Let's see what's going on here."

She didn't need Tully now, did she? She had plenty of people to protect her. The thought didn't cheer her up.

They walked through the kitchen door to find Deion, Jenya, and a young woman seated at the long table where the staff ate. Sarah Lacey's hair was brown with subtle blonde streaks, cut to just above her shoulders. Natalie gave Gino kudos for his good work.

The woman had wide blue eyes in a fine-boned face and wore a pink polo shirt, gold shell earrings, and a diamond engagement ring and matching wedding band that seemed too big for her delicate hand. Deion was right: she looked nervous to the point of terror, her pink lipstick half-eaten off her tightly pressed-together lips, her gaze jerking toward Natalie and Gino in panic.

"Sarah, so good to see you." Gino flashed his flirtatious smile. "When Natalie told me you were here, I had to say hello. How's the brightening shampoo working for you? Good?"

Sarah looked confused. "The shampoo? Oh . . . it's fine, I guess. Yes, it's great." She nodded emphatically. "I love it. Thank you."

"Great! Just wanted to check in." Gino turned so his broad back was to the table. He nodded to Natalie and gave a thumbs-up close to his chest to indicate Sarah was the real deal.

Natalie gave him a nod in return. "Thanks for checking on Sarah, Gino. I know you have a client waiting."

Gino hesitated, his glance traveling between Deion and Jenya before he nodded and walked out the door.

Natalie took a seat beside the frightened woman. "Sarah, I understand you need my help."

Tears leaked from Sarah's eyes. "Oh, God, yes! Yes, I do!"

"Deion, could you grab that tissue box from the counter?" Natalie asked before she took Sarah's shaking hands in hers. "Tell me what's wrong."

Sarah looked down at their joined hands and said in a low voice, "I need to stay with you. My husband is awful to me. I want to get a divorce, but I'm afraid to be in the house with him."

Natalie gave Sarah's hands a comforting squeeze. "Of course. Do you have children?"

Sarah's head lifted as though she'd been hit by an electric shock. "Why do you ask?"

"Because I want to make sure they're safe too."

"Oh." A sob shuddered through Sarah. "I have a daughter—Sophia—but Harry would never hurt her. He adores her."

"Even if you leave him? He might be angry about that." Natalie kept her tone gentle.

Sarah shook her head and repeated in a quavering voice, "Harry would never hurt Sophia. He would be so upset if something happened to her." She drew in a breath. "I know you think it's wrong that I didn't bring her with me, but he would come after me if I did. I was too afraid . . ." A fresh spate of tears ran down her cheeks.

Natalie didn't push it. However, she was still surprised that Sarah would leave her daughter behind.

"Please!" Sarah begged. "I need to stay with you. I'm so scared." She broke down and cried full out, her slim body shaking.

Natalie looked at Jenya and Deion. How could they not believe that this woman was in genuine distress?

She turned back to Sarah. "Of course you can come. I have one more appointment and then we'll take you there. For now you can sit in my office, where it's quiet and private."

Sarah leaped up from her chair. "Yes! I'll never be able to thank you enough." She grabbed her big tote bag from the chair and clutched it against her chest as though it held her most precious belongings. Maybe it did.

"I'd like to take a look in your bag," Jenya said to Sarah in a strange echo of Natalie's thoughts.

Sarah shrank back and stared at the bodyguard like a deer in headlights. "What?! Why?"

Natalie started to object, but Jenya gave her a warning look before she held out her hand to Sarah. "Because I'm in charge of Natalie's safety."

Confusion clouded Sarah's face. "It's just my wallet, my toiletries, and some photos I didn't want to leave behind."

Jenya's hand remained outstretched. Natalie held her breath, wondering if Jenya was right, until Sarah unlocked her grip on the tote and handed it over.

"Jenya's job is security," Natalie said soothingly as the bodyguard practically turned the bag inside out on the kitchen table. "She's very careful." It sounded ridiculous, she knew, but Sarah nodded, even though her gaze was riveted on Jenya.

The bodyguard put everything back in the bag and returned it to Sarah. "Thanks."

Once again Sarah cradled it to her chest. As the little group made its way toward Natalie's office, Sarah cast nervous glances at Jenya and Deion. When Natalie had settled her in one of the chairs in front of her desk, Sarah leaned in and whispered, "Are both of them coming to your house with us?"

"Just Jenya. She's staying with me right now." Natalie didn't want to add to Sarah's fears by telling her about the stalker. "Don't worry. I have room for both of you."

Although Jenya would have to sleep on the sofa bed. She didn't want to put Sarah on the ground floor near big glass doors. That would probably make her even more anxious.

"Oh." Sarah subsided into the chair, her bag still held tight against her like a child's teddy bear.

"Do you want something to drink?" Natalie asked, kneeling in front of her.

"No, I just want to go," the other woman said, her mascara streaked down her cheeks. Natalie reached over to her desk and grabbed more tissues to hand to Sarah.

Natalie stood. "I'll finish up as quickly as I can."

When she came out of her office, Jenya and Deion were huddled together in the hallway, talking in low voices. They stopped when they saw her.

"Let's go somewhere private," Natalie said. She led the way to the treatment room where she and Tully had made creative use of the massage table. The memory sent a flash of heat followed by a wave of sadness through her. She turned her back to the table. "I know what you're going to say, but how can I turn her away? No one could cry that much if she wasn't truly upset and terrified. Was there anything suspicious in her bag?"

"It had exactly what she said in it," Jenya said. "But that doesn't mean she's not a problem. What if your stalker decides to escalate while Sarah is staying with you? Then she's in danger too. And her presence might even be used as leverage against you."

"You mean he would threaten her to get to me somehow?"

"Something like that," Jenya said. "I can get her to a safe house that we use for KRG clients."

Natalie understood that Jenya—and now Deion—had to expect the worst in every situation. That was their job. Her job was to help a fellow human being through a tough time. She wasn't going to let the stalker prevent her from supporting Sarah Lacey when the terrified woman needed it most.

"It's a generous offer, but my sanctuary is about more than a place to stay. It's about support and sympathy. Your safe house doesn't offer those."

"I can take you there too," Jenya said.

Natalie shook her head. "The stalker hasn't bothered me in almost three days. I want to sleep in my own bed." She needed to wrap herself in the familiarity of her own home to help her get through the regret and misery of her breakup with Tully. Focusing on Sarah would keep those thoughts at bay too. "Besides, you'll be there to protect both of us, if necessary. Not to mention all the surveillance cameras."

"I figured." Deion shrugged at Jenya.

The bodyguard's mouth tightened. "Tully won't be happy about this."

The sound of his name plunged a dagger of pain into Natalie's body. She swallowed a gasp of shock. Thank God she'd broken it off with him now. If she'd let it continue any longer, she wouldn't have survived the ending.

Jenya opened the door of the treatment room and waved Natalie out without further argument.

Two hours later, the big black SUV pulled into Natalie's driveway and Jenya jumped out to do reconnaissance. Sarah started to open her door, but Natalie turned in her seat and forced a smile. "We need to wait. Jenya likes to make sure everything is safe, even at my house. Being a security pro, she's a little paranoid, so I humor her."

"Oh, okay." Sarah settled back against the seat, but her eyes were stretched open with fear again and she hugged her bag closer.

"To be honest, I've had some trouble with vandalism recently," Natalie said, deciding to embellish her thin story.

"Vandals? Out here?" Sarah looked around at the widely spaced houses on the quiet lane.

"Probably just kids who'd been drinking," Natalie said with a wry grimace.

"Oh." Sarah swallowed noticeably.

"You're going to be okay." Natalie reached over the seat to brush the back of Sarah's hand where it held the leather tote. The woman flinched, so Natalie drew back her hand. It looked like Sarah's husband had been physically abusive, given how jumpy she was. Anger coursed through Natalie's veins. "I promise he won't hurt you ever again."

Sarah looked more frightened, not less. "Oh, God, I hope you're right."

Jenya knocked on Natalie's window and Sarah jumped.

"We can get out now," Natalie said as she unlocked her door.

Once they were inside the front door, Jenya did her interior sweep while Natalie waited with Sarah. All was normal in the house, so they headed for the big open living area.

Natalie took out the ingredients for a Manhattan and offered her guests one. Jenya refused since she was on duty but Sarah accepted. Natalie set out cheese and crackers on the coffee table before she mixed the drinks. When she brought Sarah hers, the woman took a large gulp and choked on the strong alcohol. Natalie sipped hers, closing her eyes as the liquor burned smoothly down her throat and sent a warm ripple of relaxation through her.

Then she remembered Tully making her a Manhattan at his house. All the warmth drained away to leave a ball of ice in her chest.

"I'd like to cook dinner for you tonight," Sarah said abruptly. "I'm a really good cook and it's something I can do to thank you."

"Sweetie, you don't have to thank me." Natalie was touched. "I'm helping you because I want to."

"I was a chef before I got married. If you let me just look at what you have in your fridge and pantry, I'll figure out something to make," Sarah insisted.

She might have to be a chef again, depending on her divorce settlement.

Jenya scarfed down a cheese-laden cracker as she passed by while doing another sweep through the house. "Sounds like a great offer to me. I haven't had a home-cooked meal in two weeks."

"Where did you work before, Sarah?" Natalie asked. Maybe if the woman talked about a time before her marriage, she would forget her terror.

"Do you remember Myrtle and Pepper's in Summit? I was the pastry chef," Sarah said, her voice steadier.

"Dessert!" Jenya called from the front hallway. "Now we're talking!"

The bodyguard didn't have an ounce of spare flesh on her, so Natalie was surprised she liked sweets. "I probably have the ingredients for a cake," Natalie said.

"Great!" Sarah put down her drink and jumped up. "Why don't I get started so it will be ready for after dinner?"

She seemed relieved to have something constructive to do, so Natalie gave her a tour of the kitchen. She understood the need to think about anything other than the pain of a failed marriage.

While Sarah bustled around in the kitchen, looking less tense, Natalie and Jenya finished off the cheese and crackers. Just as Natalie took the last sip of her Manhattan, her cell phone vibrated with a text.

It was from Tully.

Just checking in. Everything okay there?

Had Jenya told him about Sarah? She must have. He was her boss. But Natalie tried to formulate a way to convey information without saying it outright.

She typed: No new developments. All quiet. Thank you for the check-in.

I'd like to come out tomorrow to see the lay of the land, if that's all right with you.

Every fiber of her body sparked at the thought of seeing him tomorrow. Which meant that it was a bad idea. However, more was at stake here than her emotional issues.

Sure. What time?

Does noon work?

Sounds good. She took a deep breath and added: Will you join us for lunch?

There was a noticeable pause before his answer came back. What had he been thinking during those seconds?

Thanks but I need to get back.

Tomorrow was Sunday but it was possible that he needed to catch up on work. He'd admitted that he had projects he'd neglected to work on her problem. Or he didn't want to spend more time than necessary with her. She couldn't blame him.

She put her phone down on her thigh and closed her eyes as the jumbled emotions whirling inside her triggered the urge to cry. After taking a deep breath, she got control of herself and opened her eyes again.

"Are you all right?" Jenya was watching her with concern.

"I've been fighting a headache all day," Natalie said truthfully. She gestured to her phone and spoke in a low voice. "Tully's coming by at noon tomorrow."

Jenya nodded and answered equally softly. "He wants to check out your guest. He tried to make it today, but he was tied up with a client."

The tears threatened again, but Natalie swallowed hard and fixed herself another Manhattan.

Sarah was, in fact, a very good cook. She whipped up a delicious chicken dish with the random ingredients Natalie had on hand. But the cake was the masterpiece: a confection of moist, dense chocolate and rich ganache with a touch of coffee flavor. Sarah insisted that even Jenya have a small glass of port with the cake; she claimed that was the perfect complement to her dessert.

When they had practically licked their plates clean, Natalie and Jenya both leaned back in their chairs with satisfied sighs. Sarah beamed, her culinary success wiping the haunted look from her face.

"You really need to open a bakery," Jenya said. "You'd make a killing."

Natalie was feeling drowsy from the combination of food, alcohol, and drama. "Maybe you could provide pastries for my salon's coffee bar. My customers would love them." She had to stifle a yawn.

For a moment Sarah's thin face lit up and then it looked as though someone had turned the light out. She dropped her gaze to her plate, where she'd left half her slice of cake uneaten. "Maybe once I'm through my divorce."

Natalie glanced at her watch. It was only nine o'clock but her body was telling her it was midnight. That's what major emotional upheaval did to you. However, she needed to stay awake in case Sarah was ready to talk.

Jenya stretched and yawned before she stood up. "You two ladies sit and relax. I'll do a quick security circuit and then take care of the dishes."

When Natalie started to object to the latter, Jenya pinned her with her gaze and gave a tiny shake of her head. So she thought Sarah might talk more freely if Jenya wasn't nearby.

With an effort, Natalie sat up. "Sarah, tell me how I can help you. Do you want to talk about why you left?"

Sarah continued to stare down at her plate. "I'm not ready," she said in a barely audible voice. "Can I just go to my room and sleep tonight? I'm so tired. I'll be able to face it all tomorrow."

"Of course." Making the decision to seek Natalie's help had clearly exhausted all the young woman's inner resources. "I'll show you to your room."

Sarah nearly bolted up from her chair and grabbed her tote bag from the sectional.

Natalie stood with a slight wobble. The Manhattans must have hit her harder than usual. She started toward the stairs but had to brace herself against a wall as her head spun. "I'm sorry. I'm a little dizzy," she said.

"Why don't you just tell me where my room is," Sarah said. "I can find it myself."

"No, I'll be fine in a second." She waited until a wave of nausea had subsided before she straightened. "Okay, let's go."

She got to the foot of the staircase and looked up. The stairs looked so steep and her legs felt so shaky. She turned and sat down on the bottom step. "I don't know what's wrong with me."

"I'll get you a glass of water," Sarah offered.

"Thank you." Another wave of nausea hit and Natalie had to inhale hard to prevent herself from throwing up. Too much rich food.

There was a loud crash of something hitting the tile floor in the kitchen, and she heard Jenya's voice as though through a fog. Several curse words. Something about Sarah being an evil bitch.

Then Natalie slid down off the step and curled up on the rug in her foyer, her eyelids so heavy she couldn't stop them from closing.

Chapter 18

Tully tossed the new Julian Best novel onto the coffee table and picked up the television remote. Usually he ripped right through the super spy's adventures but in this one, Julian found his soul mate, and reading about their love affair rubbed salt in Tully's new wounds.

It wasn't football season but Tully had found a video of Luke Archer and the New York Empire's last Super Bowl victory. As far as Tully was concerned, Archer was the greatest quarterback in football history and that was one nail-biter of a game. He had to admire a guy who retired when he was still on top.

Guilt nagged at Tully as he watched Archer coolly nail a precision thirty-yard pass. He should have gone to check on Natalie's new houseguest in person instead of relying on Jenya and Deion's reports. But the thought of seeing Natalie without being able to touch her had slashed at his chest like a bowie knife. So he'd stayed at the office late, working on a security plan for a Silicon Valley CEO's new mansion in the Hamptons.

He hit fast-forward to take him to the fourth quarter of the game, when the Empire were down by thirteen points and staged a stunning comeback, starting when Archer ran the ball himself. Just as the quarterback figured out he had no other options, Tully's phone vibrated.

He took a swig of beer before he checked the caller ID and frowned. It was Alastair York. What the hell would he be calling about so late on a Saturday night?

"Gibson. What's up?" he said.

"I've received a phone call from Dobs Van Houten." Alastair's accented voice was tight with tension. "He says he needs to speak with his wife immediately. It's of the utmost importance."

"It's midnight on Saturday. How the hell did he get through to you?" Tully was already sorting through possible reasons why Van Houten wanted to communicate with Regina at such an odd hour. None of them were good.

"The firm has a twenty-four-hour answering service. They judged the call urgent enough to route through to me."

"What did you tell him?"

"That he wasn't legally allowed to communicate with her as per the restraining order." Alastair paused a moment. "He became insistent, saying that she would be extremely upset if she found out I had blocked his call. He also threatened to file various legal charges against me." Alastair's tone became sardonic. "He must have some legal counsel of his own to have come up with a couple of the more obscure ones."

"So he wouldn't give you a reason?" Van Houten had to have known Alastair wouldn't just hand the phone to Regina.

"He told me that it was between Regina and him. He suggested that I tell Regina to contact him so she could make up her own mind about how important it was. I don't think he's accustomed to meeting with resistance when he wants something."

"You got that right. The restraining order forbids him from communicating with his wife in any way, correct?" That would be one charge they could lodge against Van Houten, but it wasn't enough by itself to win a custody battle, particularly if Regina herself chose to call him.

"That is correct. This can be construed as an attempt to communicate with her since he is threatening me. I have it recorded, by the way."

"Good man." Tully wasn't surprised. Alastair knew his legal stuff. "How did you leave it?"

"That I would consider his proposal and get back to him." There was a note of black humor in Alastair's voice as he said, "The response was, er, explosive, so I hung up. And called you."

Tully understood Alastair's desire to cut the call short but an enraged Van Houten was a dangerous animal.

Which meant Tully needed to warn Jenya to be extra-vigilant. In fact, he would send another trained guard over to Natalie's house, just to be safe.

"Call him back and stall him for a while. Push to get a reason for the contact. I need to check in with a couple of people before we proceed. And thanks for calling me right away."

"You know more about this situation than I do," Alastair said.

And it gave Tully something to think about other than how he'd scared Natalie away.

He hit speed dial for Jenya's cell, knowing his call would trigger a specific ringtone that she would answer no matter what the time.

Except his call went to her voice mail. He texted her a terse message to call him ASAP and he waited exactly sixty seconds. No response, so he redialed. Voice mail again.

"Shit!" He dialed Natalie's number. "Pick up, Nat, pick up!"

Voice mail.

He bolted for his home office, where he could track the location of the phones. His fingers flew over the keyboard as he launched the program and keyed in the numbers. The software quickly traced both devices to Natalie's address.

"So why aren't they answering?" He started to pull up his staff members' home addresses when he remembered Deion. He found the young man's number on his cell phone.

"Thank God!" he said when Deion answered, sounding sleepy but coherent. "How fast can you get to Natalie's house? Jenya isn't answering her cell phone."

"I'm dressing now." Deion's voice was wide-awake. "On my way in three minutes."

"Wait! You approach with extreme caution. No heroics. Just scope out the situation and report back to me. Got it?"

"Yes, sir."

Tully felt the surge of adrenaline that came with doing his job. For once, he didn't welcome it, because he was positive that Natalie was somehow involved with Van Houten's midnight phone call. Which meant that Regina was going to have to talk to her husband.

He texted Alastair: Call me ASAP.

Leaving his cell phone free, he used his computer to call Leland, his lips curling into a grim smile at the thought of waking up his partner yet again.

"This is getting to be a bad habit of yours," Leland said, his voice thick with sleep.

"I knew you'd whine." He explained the situation. "I hate to do this to Regina, but we need to know what Van Houten wants."

"Agreed. I'll get Dawn to wake her. I'll load the listening software on Regina's phone and you can tie in from there."

"And bounce her cell signal around so Van Houten can't trace it back to your place. I don't want you and Dawn in the crosshairs."

"I appreciate that," Leland said.

Tully's cell vibrated with Alastair's name in the ID. "Gotta go." He swiped in the call. "Any more information?"

"No, just a great deal of verbal abuse," Alastair said. "I'm not sure why he thinks that will change my mind."

"He's not rational. I'm concerned that Natalie has gotten caught up in this, because neither my bodyguard nor Natalie is answering her phone. So I'm afraid Regina will have to speak with Van Houten."

"Bloody hell!" Alastair exclaimed. "I hate to subject her to that."

"I do too, but we need to know what he's up to. We'll tap her phone but Van Houten doesn't know that."

"If I can be of any assistance, call me, no matter what the hour," Alastair said.

Tully heard the anxiety lurking beneath the British reserve. "I'll update you as soon as I can."

He set up the phone-tap software on his computer in anticipation of linking to Regina's phone. Then he took his cell phone to his bedroom to strip out of his office casual clothes before he pulled on black combat pants, a black long-sleeved shirt, and low tactical boots. After donning a bulletproof vest, he opened the gun safe in the back of the closet and took out his favorite big Glock and a shoulder holster that fit over the vest. For good measure he strapped a sheathed tactical knife to his left forearm. He collected ammunition for the gun, as well as his lock-pick set, and secured the safe.

As he loaded and holstered the Glock, he kept glancing at the cell phone sitting on his dresser, willing it to ring with news from Deion that Natalie and Jenya were safely asleep in Natalie's house. The longer it took for Deion to call, the less likely that scenario became.

Tully grabbed a black knit cap and headed back to the computer room, tensing when his cell finally rang with Deion's ID.

"Natalie and Sarah Lacey are gone. Jenya's unconscious," Deion reported tersely.

"Unconscious how? A blow to the head or drugs?" Fury seared through his veins.

"I don't see any lumps or bruising and there's no evidence of a fight, so I think it must be drugs."

"Sarah Lacey had to be part of this," Tully muttered, guilt ripping at him with steel claws. He should have checked up on the woman instead of feeling sorry for himself like a teenager who'd been dumped by his girlfriend. "Get Jenya to the nearest hospital. Keep me posted on her condition."

"Yes, sir. Once I do that, I want to help you find Natalie."

Tully liked the determination in the young man's voice. "It's a good thought but you're still not trained. Stay with Jenya."

"But I shouldn't have let Natalie take Sarah Lacey home with her. I *knew* that." Deion's voice was racked with guilt.

It was nothing compared with the claws of regret tearing at Tully's chest. "No, Deion, that's on me. You did everything you could. Now let me get Natalie back."

"Right. Get that motherfucker." Deion did not apologize for his language this time.

Tully went to his office to find Regina's phone linked to the computer program. He called Leland. "Let me talk with Regina."

"What's happening?" Regina sounded distraught when she came on the phone. "Why is Dobs trying to reach me now?"

"That's what you're going to find out for us," Tully said, injecting calm and reassurance into his voice. "I want you to imagine that you're sitting in a hotel room. No one is with you. Your divorce lawyer has just called to say the husband you hate and fear urgently needs to talk with you. Are you with me?"

"I think . . . yes." She sounded shaky but determined.

"You debate whether to do it. But you need to know what he wants, or you won't be able to sleep tonight. So you call him." He wanted her to react in ways consistent with his imagined scenario. "Remember, you are alone in a hotel room. No one is there to coach you or help you."

"I know what that's like." He heard the shiver of fear in her voice.

"Good. Whatever your husband says, I want you to imagine that's the situation you're in and answer him accordingly. It's important." Van Houten needed to believe that he had his wife at his mercy. It would make him less careful.

"Yes, I can do that." There was some confidence now.

"May I speak with Leland again?" When his partner got on the phone, Tully asked, "Is she going to be able to handle this?"

"I believe so," Leland said.

"Okay, I need you and Dawn to take her to her bedroom, close the door, and leave her there alone while she makes the call."

"I'd feel better if Dawn was with her."

Tully knew this would be hard for Leland to stomach. "I don't want any coaching. She has to sound natural . . . and scared."

Leland uttered a curse. "Understood. I'll be listening with you, though."

"Okay, set it up. I don't want to make Van Houten stew in his own anger any longer."

Tully put on a headset and stared at the computer screen, forcing himself to sit still when he wanted to leap out of his chair and race off in search of Natalie. Waiting had always been part of his job and he had trained himself to use that time to think. He had to see this as a standard client-kidnapping scenario so he could view all the angles with his usual cool precision. But visions of Natalie being touched in any way by Van Houten made red flare through his brain.

The electronic ringtone of a phone pinged through the headset and Tully focused.

"Regina, my dear." Van Houten's clenched-jaw, upper-crust voice grated on Tully's eardrums.

"You're not supposed to contact me." She sounded confused and upset. Perfect, in fact. "My lawyer said I shouldn't call you at all."

"Your lawyer is an asshole." Anger sharpened his tone. "But you made the right decision to override him."

"I couldn't go back to sleep after he told me." Her voice quavered. "Why are you calling in the middle of the night?"

"Because I miss you, darling. I want you to come home." He oozed insincere concern.

"You could have waited until tomorrow to tell me." Now she sounded just a touch annoyed. That would provoke him.

"I thought you might need some additional persuasion, so I've arranged for that." No more concern, all hard edge.

"There's *nothing* you could do to persuade me." She spit out the words like bullets.

"You had help from a nosy bitch named Natalie Hart. Remember her? Well, I have her now, and if you don't come home, some very bad things will happen to her."

"What?" Regina's shriek was genuine and ear splitting. "You can't do that. You can't hurt her. I'll call the police."

"No police or she dies right now." His voice was a whipcrack.

Tully felt his lips drawing back from his teeth as he snarled like a wolf. He was going to kill Van Houten with his bare hands and enjoy every second of it. And that was just for *threatening* Natalie.

"Okay, okay, no police." Regina was conciliatory, trying to calm him down as though she'd had to do it many times before. "What do you want me to do?"

"I told you. I want you to come home to me. You are my wife. You're carrying my child. You belong with me." His tone turned cold. "I was deeply offended that I had to learn of your pregnancy from Dr. Rowland. Thank God he's an old family friend and felt I should know. Why didn't you tell me yourself?"

"I-I was scared." Her voice was barely a whisper. "You hurt me."

"I'll never do it again. You're too important to me. I love you." All phrases spoken without any conviction.

"But you're going to hurt Natalie."

"Only if you force me to. Come home to me, and Natalie goes back to her nice little house without ever knowing she was here." He began with a coaxing tone, but his next words were pure sharpened knives. "If you make the wrong choice, Natalie will disappear forever, buried where no one will find her. And her death will be very, very painful." The last was said with relish.

Tully's anger was swamped by a wave of cold terror because he could hear in Van Houten's voice that the man *wanted* to kill Natalie. Even if Regina gave in to his demand to return, Natalie would still be in danger.

Once again he held on to his control and remained in the desk chair, one part of his brain considering and discarding options while the other part listened to the conversation.

An anguished sob came from Regina, one that sounded entirely genuine. "All right." Her voice cracked. "I'll come. But I don't have any way to get there. I'm at a hotel." Regina was sticking to Tully's imaginary scenario like a champ.

"I'll send a car for you. Just tell me where you are."

"My lawyer said I shouldn't tell you that." She paused. "I know, I'll take a taxi. You can pay for it when I get there." There was a slight edge of pleasure in her voice at the expense for her husband.

"Why can't you just . . . that's fine." Tully could hear Van Houten tamping down his anger at her defiance. "The taxi can drop you at the gate. The guards will pay for it and give you a ride to the house."

That screwed up Tully's plan to be the taxi driver.

"Please, don't hurt Natalie," Regina begged.

"As long as you cooperate, I won't." With audible effort, he softened his tone. "I'm so glad you're coming home, darling."

"I'll be there as soon as I can get the taxi." Regina's voice was almost strangled.

Van Houten disconnected first.

Tully called Regina. "You did great. You had me convinced you were alone in a hotel room."

"Do I have to take a taxi to his house?" she asked, fear vibrating through the phone.

"I'm really sorry to put you through this, but yes, you will. Don't worry. I'll be following the whole time. You just won't see me."

He heard Dawn's voice in the background. "Regina, are you okay?"

"Excuse me," Regina said to Tully before her voice became muffled. "Yes, I'm fine. This is Tully on the phone."

"Is Leland there?" Tully asked. "Could I speak with him?"

"Sure."

"What are we going to do to get Natalie back?" Leland asked.

"You're going to take Regina to the hotel nearest you, which is the Lennox. Go inside the lobby with Regina and stay low-key in a corner until I get there. Then get her a cab. I'll follow until the cab gets close to Van Houten's estate."

"I'm coming with you," Leland said. "I'll stay in the car and act as communications coordinator and backup."

Tully considered the pros and cons of Leland's presence. Number one, it would be hard to convince his partner not to come. Number two, he could be useful with his computer magic.

"Okay. Bring your souped-up laptop so you can monitor through my vest camera." Tully was already heading for the garage. "I'm leaving now. We'll talk further on the way to New Jersey."

The Manhattan streets were never empty, but traffic was light, so Tully made it to the Lennox in ten minutes, partly because he focused all his pent-up energy on dodging slow-moving vehicles and blasting through yellow lights.

When he pulled up in front of the canopied entrance, a standard yellow New York City taxi idled by the curb. That meant they wouldn't have to wait. Tully parked by a fire hydrant and strode into the lobby, where Regina, Dawn, and Leland stood in a tense group. Tully noticed that the only person dressed in normal clothing was Regina, who wore jeans and a blue-and-white-striped blouse with running shoes. She clutched the same damn Gucci bag that had almost gotten her caught by her husband's goon, and her dyed-brown hair tumbled over her shoulders.

Dawn and Leland both wore head-to-toe black.

Thank God it was New York City so no one looked twice at a group of black-clad people. They were just making a fashion statement.

"I'm coming too," Dawn said, holding up her hand to forestall Tully's objections. "Natalie's one of my best friends. I'll stay in the car with Leland."

"I don't have time to argue," Tully said. "But you and Leland better stay put. You know how I feel about civilians in the cross fire." The truth was Dawn could handle herself when it came to a crisis. She'd proved that a few months before.

Tully turned to Regina. The young woman's face was as white as a sheet but she gave him a shaky nod. "I hoped I'd never have to set foot in that house of horrors again," she said. "But Natalie helped me when I needed it most."

"You are a brave woman," Tully said with real admiration before he nodded toward Dawn and Leland. "And you're not alone."

"Knowing that is the only thing that's keeping me together," Regina admitted. "At least me being scared half to death is exactly what Dobs is expecting." She tried for a wry smile that went crooked.

"When I came in, there was a cab already at the curb. Do you have cash?" Tully asked, his hand going toward his wallet. "You may have to pay him up front to go to New Jersey."

"Leland gave me plenty," Regina said. She straightened her spine and took a deep breath. "Okay, I'm going now."

Looking like she was headed for a firing squad, she marched out the front door of the hotel. Tully trailed her, keeping out of sight of the taxi driver, just in case the man was more observant than most cabbies.

Regina had a long conversation with the driver, undoubtedly discussing how much she would tip for the lengthy ride. For a moment, Tully was afraid the driver would refuse, but then Regina climbed in.

"Let's go." Tully waved Dawn and Leland through the door. "I've got the cab's medallion and license numbers."

"I put the tracking software on Regina's phone so we can follow out of sight." Leland hefted his computer case. "Don't worry. It would take someone as good as me to find the software." He smiled.

They climbed into Tully's big SUV, Leland riding shotgun.

"Before you open up your computer, I want you to get my backup gun out of the safe," Tully said. He pressed his thumb to the biometric lock and the top clicked open. "Keep it in the car with you. I don't expect you to need it but better to be prepared."

Dawn gave a choke of disquiet from the back seat. "Shouldn't you call in some real backup? Like the police or the FBI? Leland and I are not exactly commandos."

"You and Leland are not even supposed to be here," Tully said. "I'm just worried about *your* safety."

"You mean we're not supposed to burst through the door with guns blazing?" Leland asked as he loaded the gun with practiced smoothness. Tully had insisted that both his partners learn gun skills when KRG got successful enough to attract international attention.

"If you do, I may shoot you myself," Tully said.

Dawn gave a crack of laughter. "Good to know your position on the subject."

Tully remembered Van Houten's voice with a cold shudder. "I'm serious. Van Houten will kill Natalie in a second if he thinks Regina has double-crossed him. Because he wants Regina back, he's decided to shift all the blame for Regina's flight to Natalie. So his hatred is targeted entirely at her now."

"Shit!" Dawn said.

Tully had stronger words for it but he just drove, keeping the taxi in sight until Leland had the tracking program up and running. In the city it was easy to keep vehicles between his car and the cab. Once they got through the tunnel, it would be more difficult to hide, so he was glad to have Leland's tech wizardry.

Until it gave him too much time to think. Sheer terror flooded through him like a frigid tide as he realized something. "He knows he can't get away with this. He's going to leave the country."

"I had that same thought," Leland said quietly. "I've been working on hacking into his confidential financial information."

"Why is it bad that he's leaving the country?" Dawn asked.

"There will be no legal consequences for his actions here," Tully said.

"Oh." She was silent a moment. "Oh, I see."

The tension in the car ratcheted up to a whole new level. Tully tried not to picture Natalie's blonde hair matted with blood or her blue eyes staring but empty of life. He'd been to too many crime scenes, which allowed him to vividly imagine what she would look like in death.

"Shit!" he said, his hands clamped so tight around the wheel that even with the leather padding it dug into his palms.

"Easy," Leland said, his fingers flying across the keyboard even as he spoke. "We'll get her out of this. I have total confidence in you."

"We broke up this morning," Tully said. "I was sulking instead of doing my job to protect her. This is on me."

"You had a bodyguard with her," Leland pointed out.

"I should have gone to meet the woman she took in, Sarah Lacey. Get her vibe in person."

"What do you think you would have found out?" Dawn asked from the back seat.

"That she was a phony, a plant."

"How?" Dawn prodded.

"I trust my instincts."

"I'm not sure you could have convinced Natalie not to take her in unless you had some kind of proof," Dawn said. "She's pretty protective of her abused wives."

"Jenya wanted to take her to a safe house but Natalie refused," Tully admitted. "That reminds me . . . I need to call Deion."

He called through the car's voice function. Deion picked up and said, "Jenya is going to be fine. She was drugged with a fairly heavy dose of rohypnol. The hospital is monitoring her overnight but they aren't concerned about her recovery."

"That's good news." Tully loosened his grip on the wheel slightly. "Stay there until she wakes up. Although I should warn you, she'll be pissed as hell that someone got the drop on her," Tully said as he imagined Jenya's reaction.

"That's a relief," Dawn said after Tully disconnected.

Now that Jenya wasn't in danger, Tully shifted to anger. "She got a heavy dose. She could have died. Another strike against Van Houten."

"Are you really keeping track?" Leland asked.

"Oh yeah, and he has a hell of a lot to answer for."

Minutes passed with only sporadic bursts of keyboarding from Leland. "I'm into his brokerage account," he said.

"What have you got?" Tully asked.

Leland whistled. "Van Houten has taken a lot of money out of the stock market in the last few days and then transferred it out."

"Probably offshore," Tully said and banged his fist against the wheel. "I'm going to nail that son of a bitch so he never sees another dime of his family fortune. Derek and Alastair can make sure it all goes to Regina and the baby."

The cab took the exit ramp off the highway.

"Okay, it's almost showtime," Tully said. "You'll see on my vest cam when I get inside the mansion. I'll let you know when I want you to get hold of the police chief in Cofferwood. He knows Natalie and me, so he'll make things happen."

"How are you going to get in if the taxi is being stopped at the gate?" Leland asked.

Tully smiled with a razor edge. "Van Houten is providing my transportation."

"I'm not sure I follow," Leland said.

"You will when you see where we're stopping."

They followed the taxi's route through the winding roads of rural New Jersey. The only streetlights were at major intersections, so most of the drive was lit by the moon, the headlights, and the glow of Leland's laptop screen.

Tully slowed to make sure he didn't miss the turn and then spotted the gateposts, pulling in between them and stopping almost immediately. "Here's where I get off. You go ahead to the estate, but park out of sight."

Leland peered out the window. "Where the hell are we?"

"At the stables." Tully pulled the black cap on. "Van Houten raises Thoroughbreds, so I can get there fast."

"You're not going to try to jump a horse over the gate!" Dawn said, sounding alarmed.

"No. I know a place where the border hedge is thin and low. The horse can brush its way through, even if it's a lousy jumper." Tully grinned. "No one expects a man on horseback, so the guards will figure it's a deer or something."

"Good, because you need to be in one piece to rescue Natalie," Dawn said, her voice both shaky and stern. "I'm counting on you."

Tully turned to meet Dawn's gaze. "She's as important to me as she is to you. Maybe more so."

Leland was still unconvinced. "You're going to ride a horse in the dark past armed guards?"

"Think of me as the cavalry." Tully swung out of the SUV and jogged up the road toward the barns.

In fact, his plan was risky, but he couldn't figure out any other way to cover the distance from the perimeter of the estate to the house fast enough to protect both Regina and Natalie. He didn't mention to Leland that he intended to take several horses to create confusion among the guards. He hoped like hell none of the Thoroughbreds got spooked and injured themselves.

As he veered right toward the barn that housed the tack room and the less valuable horses, he thanked his lucky stars that Van Houten had offered him the tour of the stables . . . and that he'd taken the man up on it. Some whims paid off.

He slid his lock-pick set from one of his pockets and made short work of the outside door into the tack room. As he walked into the dark space, the smell of saddle soap, fresh hay, and warm horses brought a welcome, if false, sensation of comfort, an illusion left over from his adolescent years, when Farmer Hollinger's barn had been his refuge. He shoved that aside and flicked on the lights since there were no windows in the room. Collecting one saddle and bridle along with two lead lines, he flicked off the light and opened the door into the stable's central corridor.

The head groom had pointed out a couple of their hunter-jumpers to him, so he headed for those stalls. Several horses put their glossy heads over their stall doors, following him with dark, liquid eyes.

"Sorry, fellows, no horse treats tonight," Tully said. "This is strictly business."

He found the horse he'd had in mind, a big bay gelding named Samson. Tully didn't ride light, so he needed a good-sized mount. Stroking Samson's nose, he hooked a lead line on him and led him out into the corridor. Tacking him up at high speed, he tested the security of the girth. Guessing his neighbors would also be hunter-jumpers, he snapped the extra lead lines on their halters and brought them with him. Unhitching Samson, he slid open the big barn door just enough to get his equine entourage outside.

He swung onto Samson's back, holding his mount's reins in his right hand and the other horses' lead lines in his left. Horses were herd animals, so they should follow Samson without too much coaxing on Tully's part.

He hoped.

He turned the big Thoroughbred's head toward the gravel road that led between the pastures to Van Houten's house and urged him to a brisk trot.

"Leland, are you seeing a horse's head and some fields in the cam?" Leland had his side of the mic muted for Tully's protection, so the vest vibrated on Tully's shoulder in two short bursts, the signal for yes. "Good. Make sure it's recording once I get onto the estate." Another double vibration of agreement.

For the few minutes it took to get close to the estate's perimeter, Tully allowed himself to revel in the feeling of his body and the horse's being in perfect sync, moving through the moonlight as one swift, powerful creature. He vowed to get out riding more often.

Tully veered off the road along the pasture's fence line, the two other horses obediently trotting along behind him. When he reached the vulnerable spot in Van Houten's hedge, he dismounted and unhooked the lead lines from the two extra horses.

"Okay, fellows, I need you to provide a little distraction for me." Holding firmly to Samson's reins, he smacked one of the horses on the butt. "Now get out of here." He flapped his arms and the horse shied away, taking off at a canter. Tully smacked the other one, who followed his buddy.

He leaped back on Samson and took him up to the hedge to show him it was there. Then he trotted back several yards and dug his heels into the horse's flanks. "Let's go, buddy."

The Thoroughbred sailed over the hedge with about a foot to spare. "You are a champ," Tully said, bending to lie almost along Samson's neck and patting his shoulder. Exhilaration surged through him as he guided Samson through the manicured scattering of trees and shrubs at a ground-eating canter.

It took only a couple of minutes before he heard shouting. The loose horses must have been spotted, which meant he probably had been too. Hopefully, no one would shoot at one of Van Houten's expensive Thoroughbreds.

He urged Samson into a gallop as the trees grew sparser and the mansion came into view. A voice rose from his left. "Hey, stop now! Stop or I'll shoot!" The guard must be able to see a rider on the horse.

Tully hugged Samson's neck more tightly and kept going, heading for an overgrown clump of rhododendrons near the side of the house.

"Stop!" Anger edged the voice, and then two gunshots sounded.

Samson shied sideways but Tully was prepared for a reaction, so he managed to stay on with an iron grip of his legs. He turned the frightened horse's head back in the right direction when another shot rang out that he swore he could hear whistle past him. He cursed under his breath. He'd feel like hell if Samson got hurt.

But a different voice yelled, "Don't shoot the horse, you idiot! It's worth a fortune and the boss will take it out of your pay."

Tully had started to smile when a hulking shape on the back lawn caught his eye.

A spasm of fear walloped him when he realized it was a helicopter. If Van Houten got in the air with Regina and Natalie, it would be almost impossible to stop him.

Tully wrenched Samson to a stop behind the bushes. While he stripped off the saddle and bridle to keep the horse from getting tangled in the tack, he spoke softly into the vest mic. "Leland, there's a helicopter sitting on the back lawn. That moves up our timetable. Get the police chief on the phone and tell him to use local air traffic control to stop that chopper from getting off the ground." A double vibration came in response.

Tully turned Samson toward the front of the house and smacked the horse on the rear. By this time, Samson's inborn taste for speed had taken over his equine brain, so he shot off like a rocket. Catching him would keep the guards busy for a while.

The helicopter meant Tully had no time for stealth or subtlety. He raced to the mansion, shimmied up a few feet of sturdy copper drain spout to reach a dark first-floor window, and used the hilt of his knife to smash the leaded glass. He was surprised when no alarms went off as he unlatched the window, swung it open, and hauled himself into what turned out to be a library, with fully loaded bookcases rising up two floors. Given all the activity at the house, Van Houten must have decided not to risk setting off an alarm and drawing the police.

Another shudder of fear ran through him at the further evidence that Regina's husband was in a rush. He needed to find Natalie before Van Houten decided he didn't need her anymore.

Chapter 19

Natalie awakened to pain and confusion as Dobs Van Houten's blurred face hovered over her.

"Let's just make sure you stay awake." He backhanded her across the face so the pain exploded again. She tasted salt and metal as blood flowed from her cheek where he'd slammed it against her teeth.

She cried out and brought her hands up to shield her face, baffled to find them stuck together so she looked more like she was praying than defending herself.

Dobs's face disappeared. "Get her on her feet," his voice said as she stared up at an unfamiliar ceiling with ornate plaster ornamentation.

A scary-looking man in a dark suit loomed over her and grabbed her shoulders to jerk her into a sitting position. "Stand up," he commanded.

She tried but her knees felt like rubber and she couldn't separate her hands for balance. She staggered and sat back down hard on the sofa she'd been lying on. "I can't," she whimpered, fighting the fog wrapped around her brain.

Where was she? And how did she get here?

"You! Help Vince get her moving," Dobs said. "My wife wants to make sure this bitch is all right. Untie her hands too. Don't want to upset Mrs. Van Houten. She's carrying my child." Pride oozed from his words.

Regina was here? This had to be Dobs's house . . . mansion. Why would Regina come here?

The scary man named Vince yanked at her wrists so they came apart, and she realized that they'd been tied together with the nylon rope Vince tossed on the floor. He took her elbow and jerked her to her feet, setting off a wave of nausea that she swallowed hard to quell.

"Take her other arm. I don't want her falling down. Mrs. Van Houten might not like that," he growled at his assistant.

With a large, frightening man on each side of her, Natalie staggered forward through a large formal living room toward a set of double doors, one of which stood open.

She pushed the tendrils of fog out of her brain, trying to think coherently while her cheek throbbed from Dobs's slap. She'd been at her house. Now she was here, feeling woozy. Probably drugged but that didn't matter. What was important was that Regina was here. Synapses fired in her brain, and hope fluttered to life.

Leland must know Regina was here, so Tully would know Regina was here. She just had to keep Dobs from doing whatever he was planning to do until help arrived. Because she knew in her bones that Tully would come.

Stall.

"I feel sick," she said, letting her weight sag against her captors. "I think I'm going to throw up."

Vince cursed. "The boss won't like her puking on his fancy carpet. Let's get her to the bathroom."

They lifted her so that her feet barely touched the ground and hustled her out the door and partway down a hall, where they thrust her into a powder room.

"Spew fast," Vince said, backing out but leaving the door open. "The boss don't like to wait."

Natalie lowered herself to her knees in front of the toilet and made herself gag. That was enough to kick the nausea into gear and she retched with dry heaves a couple of times before something came up.

"Where the fuck is she?" Dobs's angry shout jabbed at her eardrums.

"Puking up her guts," Vince said.

"Get her out as soon as she's done," Dobs grumbled.

Her stomach spasmed a few more times, emptying its contents and burning her throat and the cut inside her mouth with bile. She added as many fake dry heaves as she thought she could get away with before she flushed the toilet and dragged herself upright by holding on to the marble sink.

"You done?" Vince started back into the bathroom.

"Please let me rinse my mouth," Natalie begged, wiping her lips with the back of her hand.

Dobs's goon wrinkled his nose at the smell. "Do it quick."

She turned on the cold water and cupped her hands under it, bringing handfuls to her mouth to swish and spit out. Then she splashed the chilly water on her face, hoping it would sharpen her mind even more. Yanking the elegant hand towel embroidered with a swirling *VH* from the towel ring, she blotted her face gently, although she still hissed with pain when she touched her swollen cheek. She dropped the monogrammed linen on the floor and stepped on it.

Vince grabbed her arm and spun her around. "Move."

Her knees felt stronger now that her stomach was empty, but she decided it would be a good idea to continue to wobble on her feet. That brought the other guard over. Was that good or bad?

As they passed through a large entrance hall—although not as grand as Tully's—she noticed a set of matching suitcases piled by a doorway. Dobs was leaving. Taking Regina somewhere she couldn't escape from?

A tremor of nerves ran through her as she slowly connected the dots. He must have used Natalie as leverage to get his wife to come here. Once he had Regina, would he need Natalie anymore? Would he just let her go, or would he want to eliminate witnesses? She glanced at the man walking beside her. He was a witness, but Dobs paid him. Did that mean Vince would keep quiet if Dobs committed murder?

Could Regina have snuck out of Dawn and Leland's apartment without them knowing? No, she couldn't—wouldn't—have done that. Help was on the way. Natalie had to believe that.

She genuinely stumbled over the edge of a patterned runner in the long hallway they were walking her down. Vince's grip tightened painfully and she whimpered.

They marched her through another doorway into a room with a huge wooden desk and chairs upholstered in black leather. Regina was huddled in one oversize chair, looking pale and frightened, while Dobs paced in front of the desk. At the sight of Natalie, Regina jumped up. "Are you okay?" she asked, coming forward with concern darkening her eyes.

"Other than being drugged and kidnapped by your psycho husband, I'm fine," Natalie said. She was trying to provoke Dobs. If she could make him mad, make him pay attention to her, it would slow down his exit. She hoped.

She ignored Regina, who came to a startled halt.

"You sent me all those stupid emails and notes, didn't you?" she prodded as Dobs rounded on her, his face flushed with anger. "Did you honestly think those ridiculous quotations about beauty would scare me?"

The flush darkened and mottled. "They did scare you. You hired a guard and that asshole consultant."

"No, my friends sent the guard and the consultant. I thought it was an overreaction." Natalie started to shake off her two unwanted guards but decided that her knees still weren't reliable enough. "And you really overdid the melodrama by throwing blood on my door." She rolled her eyes. "Where did you get that idea? Some adolescent Halloween prank? I laughed when I saw it."

"What is she talking about, Dobs?" Regina asked, an expression of horror on her face. "What blood?"

Natalie hadn't told her about the stalking. Regina had had enough to worry about.

Dobs walked over to put his arm around his wife and lead her back to the chair, gently pushing her down into it. "It was just a little warning. Because she had interfered in our marriage."

"That's right," Natalie said. "I saw the bruises on her arms and told her she didn't have to stay with an abusive psychopath like you. I told her I would help her get away from you."

Just when she thought she'd really riled him, the anger seemed to drain away. His eyes became blank and unreadable and his fists relaxed. "I love my wife. I would never hurt her," he said. "You tried to come between us by telling her lies. I needed to punish you."

Regina looked terrified now and Natalie willed her not to say anything. She didn't want Dobs to focus his insanity on his wife.

"Well, it didn't stop me, did it?" Natalie said. "Because I took in your lying little accomplice, just like I took in your wife. You were counting on me doing that, so you must have known you hadn't scared me, you moron."

Dobs stroked his hand over Regina's dyed hair. "My dear, I need to talk with Natalie alone. Go with Vince and Arlo to the helicopter. I'll be right there."

Helicopter? So Dobs was leaving by air. And soon. She needed to find a way to delay him.

When the two men released Natalie, she staggered slightly before finding her balance. As the goons escorted Regina out of the room, the young woman threw an anguished glance toward Natalie, who steadfastly ignored it. She had to keep Dobs talking.

Natalie went on the offensive. "How did you get Sarah Lacey to drug me?"

Dobs closed the door and turned the key in the lock. "I borrowed her daughter for a day."

Natalie felt like he'd hit her again. Now she understood why Sarah's terror had been so genuine. "You kidnapped a *child*?! You don't deserve to be a father."

"Shut up, you stupid bitch!" He swiveled toward Natalie, his face lit with an ugly anticipation.

Natalie put a large chair between herself and Dobs as cold fingers of fear walked down her spine.

Where the hell was Tully?

Dobs walked over to his desk. "You're a hairdresser. I believe you are right-handed." He surveyed the vast desktop with its array of expensive accessories before he picked up a fist-size chunk of greenish-yellow crystals embedded in a white mineral base. "Brazilianite." He brought the rock up to his eye level and turned it back and forth so the faceted crystals glittered in the light. "Rare gemstone quality. It will do nicely to crush the delicate bones of your hand. And these points will penetrate the skin to draw blood."

He put the rock back on the desk before he pivoted toward Natalie. "I enjoy blood. The color is so vivid."

Natalie involuntarily tucked her right hand behind her back.

He came toward her, moving faster than she expected. She dodged behind the desk, but the sudden movement kicked up the drug-induced vertigo again. Dobs's lips drew back in something between a snarl and a smile. "If you think I'm going to play ring-around-the-rosy with you, you're wrong." And then he vaulted onto the desk, looming over her with a triumphant sneer. She shrank back against the bookcase as she tried to decide whether to dash right or left.

"It doesn't matter which way you go," Dobs said. "Pick one so we can get this done."

Natalie grabbed the wheeled desk chair, a heavy wood-and-leather piece, using it as a shield as she scooted sideways to the left. When Dobs committed in that direction, she gave the chair a hard shove to keep it going and bolted right, hoping Dobs would jump onto the chair and fall. Unfortunately, he managed to stop his momentum before he hit the edge of the desk, leaping onto the Persian rug to land only a few feet from where Natalie braced herself behind another chair.

His agility surprised her but maybe it was fueled by his insanity. She hoped his knees hurt like hell in the morning.

Feeling like a cornered rat, she tried to dart sideways as he closed in on her sheltering chair, but he managed to grab a handful of her blouse and yanked her back against him, wrapping his free hand around her throat and squeezing.

She clawed at his wrist, but between the drug and the lack of oxygen, she didn't have much strength.

"Van Houten, let her go now!" Tully's voice cracked like a whip, sending relief and joy rushing through her like a shot of adrenaline.

She twisted in Dobs's hold, expecting it to loosen, but instead her captor squeezed harder and spun toward the office door. Although Natalie's vision was beginning to blur, she saw Tully, dressed in black like some sort of ninja, advancing into the room, his gray eyes blazing with fury. He pointed a huge handgun toward her and Dobs.

"If you're trying to give me a legitimate reason to shoot you, Dobs, you're doing a good job," Tully said, moving smoothly into the center of the room, the black hole at the end of his gun never wavering. "And believe me, I'm looking for one. Let her go now!"

Dobs dragged her toward the desk, keeping her body between him and Tully's big gun. She pictured the chunk of rock resting on the leather top and reached out, her fingers scrabbling over the doodads arranged there until she felt the sharp crystalline points. She grabbed it and slammed the Brazilianite into Dobs's thigh as hard as she could, hoping the shock of pain would be enough to loosen his hold on her so she could get out of Tully's way.

Dobs shrieked but he kept squeezing harder while he called her horrible names. She tried to put an apology in her eyes as she looked at Tully, who stood like an ebony statue.

Then she jerked as a loud bang cut through the cursing and the black haze beginning to fog her eyes. As Dobs's grip went slack, she gulped in a lungful of delicious air and reached again for the desk to hold herself up.

"You shot me," Dobs said in a tone of disbelief.

"Move and I'll shoot you again, except this time I'll aim for a more essential body part." Tully's voice was closer. Natalie lifted her head to see him pulling something out of his back pocket with his left hand while his right held the pistol steady.

"Nat, are you okay?" he asked, his voice tight.

She opened her mouth but nothing came out. She nodded as she worked some saliva into her mouth. "Yes," she croaked.

"Would you tie Van Houten's hands behind his back with these?" He held up something that looked like large zip ties.

"You can't tie me up. I'm bleeding," Van Houten whined.

Natalie pushed off the desk and started toward Tully. He shook his head. "I'll toss them to you."

"Okay." She held out her hands, not entirely sure she would be able to catch anything at this point, but Tully threw them right into her palms so all she had to do was close her fingers around them.

Natalie turned to find Dobs slouched in a chair, his hand pressed to his upper arm with blood seeping through his fingers, his shirt-sleeve stained red. His eyes were wide and his mouth slack as though he couldn't believe what was happening. Still, she found herself reluctant to get near him again.

"Stand up, Van Houten!" Tully barked. "Step away from the chair and put your hands behind your back."

Dobs stayed in the chair. "I'll bleed to death, you fucking asshole," he said.

"We should be so lucky," Tully ground out, his gun never wavering. "Get up!"

"I'll stand up after she calls an ambulance." Dobs jerked his head toward Natalie.

Natalie looked at Tully and flinched. His lips were drawn back from his teeth in a snarl like a wolf's. "You have one more chance to do as I say, or I will pistol-whip you unconscious without a qualm." His voice made granite seem soft.

Dobs stared at Tully for a few seconds before he clambered to his feet. "I'm going to sue you for assault with a deadly weapon."

"Your hands behind your back," Tully said. "And if you make a single movement that even *hints* at threatening Natalie, I will shoot you in the other arm."

Dobs slowly bent his arms behind his back. Natalie grimaced as she wound the restraint around his bloodstained wrists. Then she cringed away from him, sliding behind the desk.

"Good job, Nat," Tully said. "Okay, Van Houten, back in the chair."

Dobs sat down gingerly, his face screwed up in pain as he jarred his injured arm. "If you're going to make me sit down, at least tie my hands in front of me."

"Shut up!" Tully snapped. "Nat, you should sit down too. You look pale." Tully's voice had a hitch of anguish in it.

"Are we waiting for someone?" Natalie asked, sitting down in the desk chair when Tully still didn't move.

"Backup's on the way," Tully said tersely.

Dobs stared at Tully, hatred blazing in his pale eyes as the red stain on his shirtsleeve grew.

"Shouldn't we put pressure on his wound?" Natalie couldn't stop herself from asking, even though she didn't want to go near him.

"He won't die of it, which is a damn shame," Tully said.

Natalie began to tremble now that she had no reason to hold herself together. Tears pooled in her eyes and rolled down her cheeks uncontrolled. She brushed them away with the back of her hands, but Tully saw them and his mouth twisted. "Nat, it's okay. I just need to make sure the outside guards are under control before we walk out of here. But we *will* walk out of here. I promise you that."

"Tully." Leland's voice sounded like it was coming from Tully's vest. "The police are here. They're rounding up the outer guards. I'm on my way to you with Chief Borland."

"You coming in the front?"

"Yup, right now," Leland said.

"Take a right under the grand staircase. Down the hall, third door on the left," Tully directed.

Natalie heard the thuds of running footsteps before Leland and the police chief burst through the door, both with guns drawn.

Tully lowered his pistol as though it weighed a ton. "Van Houten's got a flesh wound in the arm. His hands are tied. I'm taking Natalie out of here."

"I have to get your state—" the chief began.

Tully held up his hand. "Leland's got it all on video. I need to take care of Nat. Then we'll talk."

The police chief and Leland both turned toward Natalie, who still couldn't stop the tears running down her cheeks. "Right," Chief Borland said. "I'll handle things here."

Tully holstered his gun and came around the desk to kneel in front of Natalie's chair. "Are you hurt anywhere but your face?" he asked gently but urgently.

"No, I already threw up everything in my stomach," she said, not mentioning that it felt like a mule had kicked her in the abdomen.

He closed his eyes for a brief moment and whispered, "Thank God!" Then he stood and scooped her up out of the chair, holding her against his warm, solid chest. She wrapped her arms around his neck and buried her face against the softness of his shirt, breathing in the strength and decency that was so distinctively his.

She felt him turn sideways to get through the door and then he was striding along somewhere, far enough away that the voices faded behind them.

"Oh, God, Nat! I'm so sorry," he said over her head, his voice breaking on the last word. "It's my fault that you had to go through this."

That made her lift her gaze, but she couldn't see enough of his face to understand his emotions. "What are you talking about? It's Dobs Van Houten's fault that I had to go through this."

"If I hadn't been sulk—" He cut off the rest. "I didn't do my job."

He pivoted sideways again and walked into a room lit only by the moonlight streaming in through the windows. It seemed to be a library with books lining the walls all the way to the high ceiling. Tully strode to an overstuffed sofa and laid her gently on it. "Let me get the lights," he said.

He flicked on a switch, bringing to life a huge brass chandelier that threw a golden glow over the spines of the books, picking up glints of gilt lettering on the leather. But Natalie only wanted to watch Tully as he strode toward her across the jewel-toned Persian rug, his face set in an anguished mask of guilt. Stripping out of his black bulletproof vest, he tossed it into a nearby chair.

She sat up and curled her legs under her as he eased onto the couch beside her. He touched her cheek with fingertips as light as butterfly wings. "Did Dobs do this?"

Natalie had almost forgotten the slap that Dobs had administered, the throbbing in her cheek minor compared to everything else that had happened. "That's how he woke me up. Does it look bad?"

Tully shook his head. "It's just red and swollen but I know what that kind of injury means. He hit you. Hard."

She didn't tell him about the cut inside her mouth. That would only add to his guilt. "At least I got to hit him back with the rock. Thank you for shooting him. I hope he's in a lot of pain."

Tully made a sound like a strangled groan. "When I saw him with his filthy hands around your neck, I nearly aimed for his head. I might have done it except I didn't want you to have to see the mess it would make."

"He'll suffer more in prison," Natalie said, wishing Tully would put his arms around her. "He *will* go to prison, won't he?"

"Oh yeah. We've got a boatload of witnesses as well as video." Conviction rang in his voice.

"Oh, God, is Regina all right?" Natalie felt terrible that she hadn't asked about her first.

"She's fine. I took out her two guards after they left the office and stashed her in the kitchen. Dobs wasn't going to hurt her since she's carrying his child. He transferred all his hatred to you." Tully was practically vibrating with restrained rage.

"Could—could you put your arms around me, please?" Natalie flat-out begged as Dobs's contorted face rose up in her mind's eye.

He tilted his head to gaze at the floor as though debating something. Then he shifted on the sofa so their thighs touched and put one arm around her shoulders in a gesture so tentative she couldn't believe it was Tully.

The careful touch was better than nothing, so she snuggled up against his side, tucking her head against his neck.

"Oh, hell!" he muttered and wrapped both arms around her to pull her onto his lap while she felt his lips against her hair. "I was terrified of what might happen to you, Nat. I could barely think through my strategy because fear kept distracting me. I've never had that problem before."

It felt so good to be enclosed in the steely circle of his arms, protected from the world. "I knew you'd come."

That's how she'd had the courage to provoke Dobs, to look into his mad eyes and keep defying him.

"I let you down."

Natalie pulled away to look at him, seeing the guilt dragging at his eyes and mouth. "Why do you keep saying that? You saved me and Regina."

He shook his head. "I should have checked out Sarah Lacey in person. My intuition would have told me she was faking it. Instead, I . . ." He stopped.

"*I'm* the one who should have figured out Sarah Lacey was lying," Natalie said. "Every time I tried to start a conversation about her husband, she got vague and avoided the subject. Most women can't wait to tell me what their husbands have done. It's a relief to have someone who believes them and understands." Natalie hissed in a breath as she remembered Dobs's confession. "She was genuinely terrified because Dobs kidnapped her daughter. You have to make sure the little girl is all right!"

"Shit!" Tully said and grabbed his vest, toggling a switch. "Leland, Van Houten took Sarah Lacey's little girl as leverage on the mother. Make sure you find her."

When Leland's confirmation came through, Tully hit the switch again and tossed the vest aside.

"Relax, sweetheart," Tully said, stroking her hair in a way that made her lean into his hand. "The police will follow up on Sarah Lacey's involvement right away."

The sudden worry that had stiffened her shoulders drained away and she sagged against him once more, his arms tightening around her.

They sat that way in silence for several seconds before Tully spoke. "I've been thinking about what you said this morning. And what I felt tonight when I knew Van Houten had you."

Natalie tensed, a strange anticipation licking through her as she waited for his next words.

He spoke again. "Maybe we both went into our relationship thinking it was one of those wedding hookups that wouldn't last for long. Maybe that's even why we started it. But it changed—well, *I* changed."

He shifted as though uncomfortable but he kept his arms around her. "The reason I didn't come check out Sarah Lacey was because I was afraid to see you. I was hurting way more than I should have been. I didn't have the courage to face you when I knew it would rip my heart out."

Natalie hadn't thought his pain would make her happy, but little sparks of joy danced through her. She wanted to lift her head to see his face as he talked but she was afraid he would stop if she moved.

"Somehow you've gotten past all the crap I've been telling myself for years." His chest pushed at her cheek as he took a deep breath. "I think we should give this a real shot. Hell, what I'm trying to find the courage to say is that I love you, Nat. I bone-deep, head-spinning, gut-wrenching love you. I don't want to let you go. Ever. Again."

Natalie waited for doubt or dismay or reluctance to smother the happiness fluttering in her chest. She'd been so afraid of Tully and his big, protective personality crushing her hard-won independence. But she'd gotten it backward. She had faced Dobs because she trusted Tully to be there when she needed him. In fact, she could always trust him to use his strength to support her, not stomp on her. That's who Tully was.

"Nat?" His prod was soft and tentative. "I understand if this is the wrong time. You don't have to answer me now but I just needed to . . ."

She lifted her head and leaned back in his arms to smile into his worried face. "We're both stressed, exhausted, and feeling the aftereffects of adrenaline overload."

His eyes clouded with resignation. "Yeah, that's what I figured. Bad idea."

"*Good* idea," she contradicted. "All our barriers are down. We've got nothing but honesty to offer each other."

"I've been as honest as I know how," he said, but hope lit the strained angles of his face.

"My turn then," she said. "I was afraid of you."

Horror twisted his expression. "Nat, I would *never* hurt—"

She laid her palm over his lips. "Let me finish. You're so larger than life, so insanely protective, so overwhelming. I thought you would smother me back into my old role of nodding and smiling and forgetting who I was."

He looked shocked. "Why would I want you to be anything but what you are? That's why I love you."

"Matt said he loved me but what he really loved was winding me into a pretzel that would suit his needs. I was afraid that would happen again. Neither of us would have meant it to, but I didn't trust myself to stand up to someone as powerful as you are."

"But you're the strongest person I know," Tully said. "You got yourself out of a bad situation and made a whole new life for yourself."

"A new life *alone*. It was so much easier that way." She cupped his cheek with one hand. "Then you strode in with your cowboy boots and made alone look not so good. But I fought it, fought you. I used what you told me about yourself on Friday night as an excuse to run. I told myself I was doing it because you'd shown me how vulnerable you were and I didn't want to hurt you. But I was lying."

"What were you lying about?" Tully asked, his gaze as intense as a laser beam.

"I didn't want to admit that I'm in love with you." She smiled as she said the words out loud. It felt amazing.

"Can you say that again?"

"I love you." She slid one hand around his neck, trying to pull him down for a kiss.

But he stayed rock still, closing his eyes for a long moment. "That sounds so good." Then he opened them, and his face softened with relief. "I've never been so scared in my life as I was just now, waiting to hear what you would say. Because if you'd said no, I would have had a hell of a time figuring out how to change your mind."

"I have no doubt you would have come up with a plan," Natalie said. "Are you going to kiss me or not?"

He frowned as his gaze skimmed over her face. "I'll kiss you after we've gotten some ice on your cheek. I don't want to hurt you."

But she saw the heat in his eyes. "There's nothing wrong with my lips." She gave a little tug on the back of his neck.

"You make a valid point," he said and lowered his mouth to hers. What began as an achingly gentle touch grew avid when Natalie traced his lips with her tongue. He threaded his fingers into her hair and pulled her head back so he could press searing kisses against her throat and collarbone. He ran his mouth back up to her ear and spoke beside it so his breath tickled her skin. "If I wasn't worried that Leland and Chief Borland were going to walk through that door at any minute, I would peel your clothes off one piece at a time and make love to you right here on this couch."

"Maybe if we skipped the striptease, we could manage it," Natalie said, hunger coiling in her belly.

He huffed out a laugh. "You are my soul mate, but I was thinking about that nice big bathtub of yours. We could scrub the stink of this place off each other real slow with lots of slippery soap. Then I'd float you up over my lap and we could do an encore of the piano bench."

Natalie's inner muscles rippled at the memory of Tully thrusting up inside her. "I know exactly which part of you I'm going to wash first."

Epilogue

Ten months later

The pastor sprinkled water over little Kirk Olson's head, making the baby's mouth open in a perfect circle of surprise. Regina smiled proudly when her son didn't burst into wails of complaint. Natalie was the one who had to blink back tears as the pastor pronounced a blessing on the beaming mother and her white-gowned baby.

She looked at the circle of people around the baptismal font and more tears welled up. Everyone here had pitched in to help Regina and her baby. Alastair had done battle with Dobs Van Houten's army of lawyers to win Regina sole custody of Kirk and bar Dobs from ever approaching his son without Regina's permission. It seemed unlikely that Dobs would get out of prison for several decades anyway, despite the reams of paperwork his lawyers continued to generate. Tully had made sure the case against Dobs was airtight.

Derek had set up a special sort of trust for the substantial settlement Regina had received in the divorce. He'd fixed it so she could draw on the income for Kirk's benefit but never have to touch what she called the dirty money.

Dawn and Leland had opened their home to Regina until she'd felt comfortable living on her own. Alice, Dawn, and Natalie had thrown a baby shower for the first-time mother at Natalie's house.

It truly took a village.

After the ceremony was over, everyone strolled to the back of the church to congratulate Regina and wait for the limousines Tully had arranged to take them to the restaurant for a celebratory dinner.

"That is one good baby," Tully said as they stood in a circle. "Not a peep out of him, even when he got wet."

"He's pretty calm," Regina said modestly before she turned to Natalie. "Since you're the godmother, would you hold him for a minute? I need to talk with the pastor about something."

"Of course." Natalie cradled the wide-eyed baby in her arms, smiling down at him. Regina had temporarily moved into the apartment over the salon once Deion found a place in the city, so Natalie often stopped by after work to play with Kirk and give Regina a break. Natalie had been honored beyond words when Regina asked her to be the little boy's godmother.

She glanced up to find Tully watching her with a wide grin. He looked magnificent in his charcoal-gray suit, white shirt, and red tie . . . and tooled leather boots, of course. He'd taken special care dressing for the baptism, which she'd found so sweet. Of course, she couldn't wait to peel all that custom tailoring off him later to uncover his gorgeous muscles.

"You're a natural," he said, giving her a secret, warm look.

"As you pointed out, he's an easy baby." She swayed back and forth when Kirk started to fuss and he settled down again.

"I love the simplicity of this church," Tully said, his gaze scanning the space. "What do you think of it?"

Natalie looked around at the white-painted walls and soaring wooden arches. The focal point was the wall of stone that rose behind the altar, decorated with a large but plain wooden cross. Since the location had been Regina's choice, Natalie hadn't focused on the church itself, just the pastor and the ceremony. "It's very peaceful. Why?"

"Just curious." Tully seemed strangely keyed up.

Maybe it was because they'd made a life-changing decision two days before. Natalie had been curled up against Tully on the sectional in her living area, drinking a Manhattan and watching the fire flickering in the gas fireplace when he had said, "What would you think of adopting? I know it's a big decision but I've been thinking that maybe—"

Natalie's heart had nearly exploded with joy at the thought of being a parent with Tully. She'd been hoping he would come around to the idea sooner rather than later, but she hadn't wanted to push him. "Yes! Let's do it!"

"Really? No reservations?" His face lit with happiness, but then his expression turned serious again. "If we want to adopt, we should probably get married. I know neither of us planned on that but I'm kind of old-fashioned about starting a family."

"You're kidding, right?" At that point, Natalie had put her glass down so fast the alcohol sloshed all over the table. She climbed onto his lap so she could look him right in the eyes. "If I'm going to be the mother of your children, you had better marry me."

Then she had shown him in every way she could how much she wanted to be his wife.

Tully had asked her not to tell anyone about their engagement until he'd gotten her a ring to make it official. Which meant it was still their secret.

Natalie smiled inwardly as she hugged the knowledge to herself.

Regina rejoined the group. "Here, I'll take Kirk again," she said.

"I'm in no rush to let go of him," Natalie said, loving the feel of the small body in her arms. She and Tully had decided not to adopt an infant because there were so many older foster children who needed permanent homes, but Natalie still enjoyed holding a baby.

"Oh, I think you might want to have your hands free." Regina grinned as Natalie passed the baby carefully back to her.

"Why would I need my—?" Natalie started to ask when Tully took her hand and turned her toward him. He looked nervous, which was not an expression she was accustomed to on his face.

Then he dropped down onto one knee, moving with his usual panther-like smoothness.

Someone gasped before silence fell, the atmosphere charged with anticipation.

Natalie stared down at Tully, her startled brain focusing on odd details like the little lines at the corners of his eyes, the blond glints in his hair, and the bold slash of his jaw.

"Nat, I want to do this right," he said, wrapping his big hands around hers. "Because I never thought I'd do it at all."

She forgot to breathe as she waited.

He scanned around their audience and nodded. "In front of these people, who are our best and closest friends, I want to declare that I love you with everything in me and that I cannot imagine living without you."

Natalie opened her mouth, but he shook his head to stop her.

"I've got more to say because you deserve more. That first part was all about how *I* feel and what *I* want. The next part is about you because that's more important." Tully's face was solemn. "I promise that I will put you first and always consider your needs before my own. I swear that I will never knowingly hurt you. If I hurt you without meaning to, I will do everything in my power to fix it. Because love is about putting yourself in someone else's boots and making sure they are comfortable for that person to walk in."

His grip on her hands tightened and he gazed at her with such love and hope in his eyes that tears clogged her throat. "Nat, will you marry me? Right here and right now in this church?"

She nodded several times, even as she absorbed the surprise of the second part of his proposal. Tully was always a man of action. "Yes! Yes, I will! Right here and right now."

Applause and cheers broke out, but Natalie couldn't take her eyes off Tully's radiant face. An answering joy sparkled through her.

He grinned and released her hands to reach into his jacket pocket, pulling out a black velvet box. He flipped it open with one thumb and pulled out a ring that glittered in the afternoon sunlight. Taking her left hand in his, he slid the ring on so that she could see it was set with a deep blue sapphire flanked by two diamonds.

"To match your eyes," he said before he patted his other pocket. "And I have wedding bands."

"You thought of everything," she said, smiling down at him through her tears. "But that doesn't surprise me."

"Do you like it?" he asked.

"It's perfect, but I would have been happy with a plastic ring from a bubblegum machine if it was from you."

"I know, but I wouldn't be." Surging to his feet, he cradled her face tenderly between his hands and brought his lips down to hers in a kiss that held love and passion and excitement. She wrapped her arms around his neck and poured all her joy into her response. She was aware that people around her were talking, but all she could hear was the way her heart beat in perfect synchronization with Tully's.

Then Tully lifted his head and brushed away the tears that had run down her cheeks with gentle strokes of his thumb. "Our friends are going to think you're unhappy about marrying me," he teased.

"I can't believe we're doing this right now." The thrill of it fizzed through her veins like champagne.

Uncertainty flickered across his face. "Is it too soon?"

"No! It's exactly the right time!" She stood on her toes to press another kiss on his mouth. "I can't wait to be your wife."

Dawn was the first one to hug Natalie. "Thank goodness you two came to your senses! I knew you were meant to be married."

Alice joined the hug. "I'm so happy for you and Tully. You both deserve this."

Regina gave Natalie a peck on the cheek since she was holding Kirk. "That was so romantic."

"You were in on this, weren't you?" Natalie asked with a smile.

"I was just the liaison to Pastor John," Regina said. "I'd talked with him about you and Tully so much that he said he felt like he knew you already. So he felt comfortable with the idea of marrying you in his church." Her smile faded into a worried look. "This is okay, isn't it? Tully said you didn't want a big fancy wedding."

"I had one of those before and it didn't end well. I can't think of a better way to have a wedding than this," Natalie said with a reassuring smile.

Derek joined the group, bending down to hug Natalie warmly. "Tully's a lucky guy, but I want to point out that you've gotten yourself a very fine man too. Take good care of him."

Natalie nodded, tears welling up at the depth of Derek's friendship for his partner. "I understand that I'll have to answer to you and Leland if I don't."

"We may have to appoint Tully our new efficiency expert," Leland said as Derek stepped aside. "Proposing in a church was a stroke of genius." He leaned in to kiss Natalie and shake Tully's hand. "I wish you both great happiness."

Natalie looked up at her fiancé to find a twinkle in his eyes as he said, "The planning for Alice and Derek's wedding convinced me to streamline things."

"Hey!" Alice poked Tully in the arm even as she laughed. "If it wasn't for our wedding, you wouldn't be engaged to my maid of honor."

"She's got you there," Derek said, his arm going around his wife in a way that made Natalie's heart squeeze.

"I like to think we would have found our way to each other eventually," Natalie said, smiling at Tully. "We do have friends in common."

Tully grinned at Leland and Dawn. "If you want me to plan your wedding, let me know. I'll get it done in twenty-four hours."

Dawn gave him one of her "don't mess with me" looks and Leland laughed. "I'm a more patient man than you are." He looked at Dawn in a way that made Natalie sigh and press herself tighter against Tully's big, hot body.

A babble of new voices drifted in from the church foyer, and Regina looked toward the big entrance door. "Oh, good! They're here!"

Natalie pivoted to see her entire staff from the Mane Attraction pour in. Her heart nearly burst as Gino waved a bouquet of cream-colored roses over his head like a flag. "The flowers have arrived!" he announced.

Natalie glanced at Tully to find him watching for her reaction. She stood on tiptoe to give him a kiss of delight before they were engulfed by more well-wishers.

They had brought bouquets for Alice and Dawn as the maids of honor, as well as boutonnieres for the groom and his two best men. Gino arranged a headband of silk roses on Natalie's hair and stepped back. "Yes! You are a beautiful bride." He gave her a smacking kiss on each cheek.

There was a chorus of appreciative murmurs from the women when Deion walked in, looking like a model out of a high-fashion magazine in a slim-cut blue suit. "I'm so glad you came," Natalie said, feeling like the day couldn't get any better.

Deion wrapped her in a bear hug. "If anyone deserves happiness, it's you. Tully's a good man. But if he ever makes you cry, he knows he'll have to answer to me even if he is my boss."

Natalie laughed and hugged him back.

Alice and Dawn swooped down on her and carried her off to the bride's room. "Not because you need any help looking gorgeous," Alice said as she closed the door in the small antechamber, "but because we want you to ourselves for five minutes. Besides, I take credit for this wonderful news since it all started at my wedding. Of course, then I missed all the excitement while I was off on my honeymoon."

"Trust me, I would have liked to miss all the excitement," Natalie said. Although it had given her Tully, so she couldn't regret it . . . since they'd both survived.

Alice looked hesitant as she said, "I thought you and Tully were both against marriage. For your own very good reasons," she hastened to add.

Natalie started to explain about their plan to adopt, but she realized that wasn't the real reason they were getting married. "I couldn't imagine myself ever trusting a man in my life again. But you know Tully. He would literally die for me." She smiled. "Which is wonderful in some ways and terrifying in others."

"I hear you." Dawn shuddered.

"But I would do the same for him," Natalie said. "So that's why I want to marry him."

"Well, there's no need to explain why Tully changed his mind," Alice said. "He knows how lucky he is that you love him."

"Don't make her cry. You'll ruin her makeup. Not that I disagree," Dawn said, handing Alice's bouquet to her. "Let's see how we look as a bridal party."

They stood in front of the floor-length mirror the church had hung for last-minute dress adjustments. The flowers looked perfect against the medium-blue raw-silk sheath Natalie wore. She'd added nude high-heeled pumps and a pearl necklace since she was going to be in church. The floral headband gave just the right bridal touch to the look.

Alice wore a lavender dress with a fitted bodice and full skirt, while Dawn was in a burgundy A-line that showed off her toned arms.

"You know what I love about this?" Natalie said, her eyes misty. "We all look like who we are. Dawn, you look strong and fierce. Alice, you look smart and romantic."

"And you look like Grace Kelly," Alice said. "Elegant and beautiful as always."

"You'd think we planned it," Dawn agreed. She pulled her phone out of her purse. "We need to record this historic moment!"

A knock sounded on the door before it opened and Gino leaned in. "Showtime!" After he'd been pressed into taking the photo, they all proceeded to the back of the church.

The organ was playing a soaring classical piece as Alice began her walk down the aisle, followed by Dawn about ten steps later.

Natalie looked past them at the three men standing so straight and tall at the altar—very different people who had been brought together by recognizing each other's brilliance. From that they had forged a deep friendship that had carried them here. A bright happiness glowed on their faces as the women they loved walked toward them. As Tully's gaze met hers, Natalie knew she would carry this memory with her forever.

When she stepped through the doorway, Gino joined her. "I've been deputized to give you away," he said, offering her his arm. "Except you'd better not leave the salon, or we'll all be pissed at Tully."

Natalie laughed as the music changed and the guests stood and turned.

It was not the wedding march. It was the country-western song she and Tully had danced to at Alice and Derek's wedding.

She looked up the aisle to see Tully looking pleased with himself. "Do you know how to do the two-step?" she asked Gino in a murmur.

"I am a dancing machine," he said.

"Then let's make this a memorable entrance." Natalie shifted her bouquet to one hand so she and Gino could intertwine their arms at waist level in the side-by-side position. "One, two, three, go!"

So she two-stepped down the aisle in country time to meet her groom at the foot of the altar, with all the guests bobbing in rhythm as she passed. When Gino relinquished her hands, Tully took the free one and twirled her twice around before he bent her into a dip, his gray eyes alight with adoration and mischief as he gazed at her from a few inches away. "You are my kind of woman."

His arms supported her with a tensile strength that made her feel safe and secure. When he stole a quick kiss, his warm lips made her feel loved.

As he effortlessly lifted her back onto her feet, steadying her with care, she looked into his eyes and said, "I'll never dance with anyone but you for the rest of my life."

Author's Note

This book was begun in a very normal way in January 2020. It was completed in May 2020 during the COVID-19 pandemic, which was not normal at all. Since writing a novel is about sitting in front of a computer alone—conjuring up imaginary characters and seeing what they do—being under lockdown would not appear to interfere with my work. Yet I—and many of my fellow writers—have struggled to tap into our creativity during this strange and frightening time.

Deep down, novelists must be control freaks. We shape our material so it has a beginning, middle, and end; a crescendo to the big finish; a conclusion where loose ends are tied up. Reality isn't like that but we have a compulsion to make it so in our stories. Which is perhaps why the time of coronavirus is destructive to our creativity. It's impossible to shape a narrative of our world because there is so much uncertainty, so much anxiety, so many unanswered questions and endings that we can't make sense of. So much sadness and tragedy that we can't turn into a big finish, no matter how hard we try.

Yet the human spirit continues to show its resilience and caring in the thousands of stories about neighbors helping each other, as well as helping total strangers; about celebrities using their media platforms to raise millions of dollars to help laid-off workers; about the incredible bravery of medical professionals and first responders on the front lines;

about the cashiers, delivery people, and other essential workers doing their jobs in masks and gloves so we can continue to live our lives.

I'm all choked up as I type this because these selfless stories are what make me a romance writer: I have a soul-deep belief in the ultimate goodness of the vast majority of people around me. These uplifting stories are about love. Not romantic love, of course—although there is some of that in the Zoom weddings—but love of one's fellow human beings.

So when I struggled to find the words for this book, I reminded myself that I was writing about love and, therefore, hope. Because falling in love is an act of hope, and we all need to hold on to that comfort as we stumble into the strange and uncertain future.

Acknowledgments

With all the worrisome events going on in the outside world, I am so lucky to have a network of folks who share their experience, expertise, and support with me through thick and thin. They have held out a helping hand and been a steadying presence no matter what else was happening around us, and I thank them from the bottom of my heart. There would be no book without all these amazing people:

Maria Gomez, my marvelous acquiring editor, who brings such passion and professionalism to her work and who is my treasured anchor and friend at Montlake.

Jane Dystel and Miriam Goderich, my brilliant agents, who always have my back, always give excellent advice (most of which I take), and whom I admire immensely.

The entire superb Montlake Romance team, who care so much about the quality of my books, who are always finding new and better ways to support my work, and who are an absolute pleasure to work with.

Andrea Hurst, my beloved and admired developmental editor, who is a consummate professional with an unerring eye for how to make a book better. It's been a privilege and a delight to work with her on every novel I've published with Montlake Romance.

Rachel Norfleet and Claire Caterer, my eagle-eyed copyeditor and proofreader, who make sure my typos, screwy timeline, mixed-up facts, and word repetitions all get caught and fixed before my readers ever see them. Bless you for your care and conscientiousness!

Eileen Carey, my fantastic cover artist, who always finds a way to capture the essence of my story with a great visual that grabs the eye and hooks the reader. I bow down to her talent.

Coleen Hart, the owner of Velvet Salon in Lyndhurst, New Jersey, who shared her invaluable insight into what it's like to run a salon, giving me the benefit of all her experience and knowledge. In fact, kudos and thanks to the folks at Velvet Salon—Coleen, Barbara Ryan, Susan Smedberg, and Mary Zaremba—who have helped with *two* books in the Consultants series (and they keep my hair looking terrific). All errors are entirely my own.

Bonnie Jerbasi, Esq., of Montclair, New Jersey, who generously put her legal expertise at my disposal, guiding me through the intricacies of restraining orders and the custody issues of an unborn child in a divorce. If there are mistakes, they are all mine.

Miriam Allenson, Lisa Verge Higgins, and Jennifer Wilck, my wonderful critique group and magnificent friends, who teach me about writing and life at every meeting and without whose support I couldn't survive.

Sally MacKenzie, my best conference buddy and cheerleader, who keeps me sane and on track with her enthusiasm, concern, and humor when I'm feeling under pressure . . . and at other times too.

The New Jersey Romance Writers, my tribe, my home chapter, who have been there for me through all the ups and downs of my career with unflagging friendship and endless help. Not to mention Jersey Romance Writing Month, which got me through nearly half this book. 30K Write Away!

Rebecca, Loukas, and now Emily (by marriage), my spectacular children, who have grown into extraordinary adults whom I adore spending time with, whether in person or via technology. Love you guys so much!

My marvelous readers, who complete my stories by buying them and reading them and telling me they were worth all the struggle of writing them. You are the final key piece in the process, the element that brings my words to life. Thank you so much for all you do to make my writer's heart sing.

About the Author

Photo © 2015 Lisa Kollberg

Nancy Herkness is the award-winning author of the Consultants, Second Glances, Wager of Hearts, and Whisper Horse series and other contemporary romance novels. A two-time nominee for the Romance Writers of America's RITA Award, she has received many other honors for her work, including the Book Buyers Best Top Pick, the Booksellers' Best Award, and the National Excellence in Romance Fiction Award.

Nancy graduated from Princeton University, where she majored in English. In addition to completing her academic work in literature, she was accepted into Princeton's creative writing program, and her senior thesis was a volume of original poetry.

After graduating, Nancy followed a varied career path. Once her children were in school, she published her first romance, *A Bridge to Love*. A native of West Virginia, Nancy now lives in suburban New Jersey with two tabby cats. For more information visit www.nancyherkness.com.